The Colour of Evening Light

by Jeremy Fraser

First published in 2013
by Ardachy Publishing
Vale Lane
Tattingstone
Ipswich
Suffolk, IP9 2PA

ISBN: 978-0-9926045-0-9

Cover picture: detail from 'Winter Evening, Camber Sands', oil, 1999, by kind permission of Fred Cuming RA.

Printed and bound by
Book Printing UK , Woodston, Peterborough.

The Colour of Evening Light

Part One

He had been living for a few days in an inn at the edge of the airfield tucked under the Downs. You could see the sea from there, beyond Dover. Most of the town and the old port crouched at the foot of the cliffs and lay hidden from the inn by a hump in the land. From the airfield you could watch the sea shift in changing bands of colour when clouds drifted over the sun, and sometimes, at dawn, mist wrapped the world in a veil.

It was a happy time for him, and in the evenings after flying he made friends with a bar maid at the inn. She teased him a little but promised to let him kiss her properly if he would take her up in the 'plane. He completed his flying training swooping with her over the inn and following the line of the cliffs where the sea washed the chalk like milk.

On his twenty-first birthday, he sat in his new Royal Aircraft Factory B.E.2 with the engine ticking over as the squadron lined up on the grass for take off to France. His head throbbed from the party in the inn the previous night, and the cold damp of his flying helmet pressed like old flannel against his forehead.

From the open air cockpit, he suffered the crescendo from the squadron's engines as they roared low over the grass and swept out over the great void of the beach and the English channel below. Sweating, he gripped his stick, and forced himself to concentrate on formation flying. Of the twelve starters that morning, one ditched in the sea after engine failure, to be rescued by a fisherman, and one crashed on landing, maiming the pilot. His papers certified that Second Lieutenant Hugh Baird had notched up seven hours solo flying.

Young men recover quickly and, the following morning, Baird flew at five thousand feet above Belgium, elated, pleased as punch with his new aeroplane. Flying was damned good fun.

He heard the observer shout a muffled warning into his voice tube. The man waved a gloved hand, gesticulating with a finger over the side of the front cockpit. Baird peered below, and saw ant-like figures crawling in a column of troops on the way to the French border. They had struck gold.

The fuel gauge indicated petrol for another thirty minutes. Baird banked the machine and set a new course to follow the convoy of horses, guns, and infantry. In the distance, sunlight glinted on the Mons canal, and smoke drifted across coal fields, intermittently obscuring the advancing German army. He gained height, seeking the sanctuary of broken cloud cover as a precaution against rifle fire.

He glanced at his fuel gauge again, and decided it was safe to fly on for another five minutes. Precious extra time in the air would give them vital information about the enemy's position, and earn the gratitude of the staff at General French's headquarters. Blue morning light flooded across France, warm summer air swirled through the cockpit, and God was in His heaven, even if not on the ground below.

Without warning, the engine missed a few beats before recovering. Baird looked at his instruments. He tapped the petrol gauge. Everything seemed to be in order. Perhaps a bit of dirt in the carburettor, he thought, but it might be wise to get the engine checked. He shouted to the observer that he was turning back, and headed south for the airfield. He checked the map, holding it on his knees, and took the 'plane down to fifteen hundred feet, following the river towards Cambrai.

They were nearly home when the engine died. In the infinity of space, the only sound came from the singing of the wind over the 'plane's wings. Baird sat petrified, his heart thumping. 'Maintain speed to avoid a stall' the instructor had taught him. Rigid with fear, he eased his stick forward, lowering the nose to keep the 'plane in a glide. He craned over the side of the fuselage, desperate for height as they came to a village, and saw the observer twist round in his seat. The man's goggled eyes stared back in terror.

He went over the village and a railway line at three hundred feet, frantically trying to calculate speed and distance. There were people running in the street, waving. A man picked up a little girl wearing a pink dress, and held her in one arm. Baird thought he could make it to the far side of the village, but the undercarriage hit the top of a barn and the 'plane fell, fragile as an autumn leaf, nose first into a stone wall. With a bang like a car crash, the B.E.2 disintegrated. The observer was catapulted into the wall, his head crushed against the stonework, and Baird lay hunched in the twisted wreckage of his cockpit, blood pouring from windscreen glass embedded in his face. In the silence, his body relaxed gently into death, and the British Expeditionary Force remained oblivious to the location of the enemy.

**** ****

Captain John Pearson, newly commissioned in the Royal Army Medical Corps and innocent of events further up the line, found himself in the crowded compartment of a troop train moving slowly across northern France. He gazed out of the window at a landscape of timber-framed farmhouses, orchards with grazing cattle, corn fields bustling with men and horses at harvest, and slag heaps from coal mines. He studied his reflection in the window, wondering how long it might take him to get used to the strange young soldier looking back from the glass.

Even with all the windows open, the place felt like an oven. Specks of soot from the engine blew in amongst the occupants, landing on uniforms regardless of rank. Pearson took off his hat and placed it with his leather gloves on his case in the luggage rack. He sat back, and drifted in and out of sleep, his thoughts wandering to the house in Hampshire; his mother, tall, calm, and imperturbable, and the old general grumbling over a newspaper. Freddy, his twelve year old brother, would be playing hide and seek in the shrubbery or climbing the copper beech tree at the bottom of the garden.

Pearson was in a war, and he didn't know if he should be frightened or exhilarated. Sore feet and blisters, he had told his mother. He knew, of course, that it wouldn't be like that. As a qualified doctor, wounded men would depend on him if the battalion had to fight. What about bullet wounds, he wondered? An arm hanging off, loose from the shoulder? Arteries, severed by shrapnel, pumping blood? An eye halfway down a cheek? A man, belief suspended by shock, gazing into the hole that had been his belly? "Help me, Doctor. Can you sew me up?"

The train jolted over points, waking him. He might have to deal with all of that. That's what the training was for at Millbank, practising on the victims of traffic accidents. He looked out of the window and saw the tail of an aeroplane sticking up into the air. The nose of the 'plane had concertinaed into a wall, and a small group of men lifted wreckage off the wings. Two bodies lay side by side on the ground.

"Poor buggers," said the man sitting opposite Pearson. "Must have just come down."

"What d'you think happened?"

"God knows." The 'plane's tail disappeared down the line.

"I haven't been up in an aeroplane," said Pearson.

"Nor me," said the man opposite. "Can't say I fancy it. A motor car's all right. The thing just stops if it breaks down. In a 'plane you're....." he shook his head and shaped a descending spiral with his hand.

The train slowed, clanking over uneven tracks as they came into a station. An enamel sign with white lettering on a blue background read BAZUEL. The airmen would have died

8

quickly, Pearson thought, in a crash like that. He felt a sharp sorrow for the two men, strangely mixed with relief that he hadn't been given the task of dealing with mangled crash victims on his first day in France. A nice clean bullet wound, he thought, would be the thing to start with. A neat job with stitches, and the man cheerful. "Thanks, sir. Arm's as good as new." Relief on the faces in the mess that night, and a quiet voice from the corner: "Pearson's all right."

With a great hiss of steam, the train came to a halt. Pearson collected his case and climbed down onto the platform. It was like the first day at a new school. He seemed to be the only person amongst hundreds of others milling along the platform who didn't know the way. It was a scene of carnival, but he was the outsider, a solitary figure amongst a sea of alien faces. Watson, his batman, came to find him in the crowd. An escapee from the Southampton docks, Watson looked cheerful, strong and wiry, with red apples in his cheeks.

"I'll get a cart, sir," Watson said. "And load up your stores."

"You'll need some help."

"I'll dig out some orderlies. And a mule."

"How old are you, Watson?"

"Thirty-eight, sir. Twenty years in the army."

"Six months for me. I'm afraid it's not much."

"You'll be all right, sir. I'm here to look after you."

Pearson adjusted his hat. "How did you choose me, or was it pot luck?"

Watson grinned. "It was the colonel's idea, sir."

"I must remember to thank him."

Pearson watched the troops marching off up the road, singing cheerfully, to their camp, while his stores were loaded. Watson fussed around him, taking charge, preventing him from lifting heavy boxes. The mule flicked long ears to keep away flies.

"Captain Pearson?" A junior subaltern, who looked as if he had just left school, saluted. "I'm to show you to your storeroom, sir. There's an outbuilding at the back. Will you come this way, please?"

Pearson followed, and looked in the shed. A window, festooned with cobwebs, let in plenty of light, and the place seemed dry enough. He brushed away the cobwebs with his cane, and thanked the boy. "How did you know it was me?" he said.

"You're on my list, sir. RAMC. You're the only one."

Watson and one of the muleteers stacked stores on shelves in the shed. The boy-soldier pulled a piece of paper from his pocket, and gave it to Pearson. "Your billet, sir. It's at the far end of the village street. On the right, a tall house with white shutters." He consulted a notebook. "Major Mansell is in with you. It's the schoolteacher's house. A Mr. Alazard. Perhaps you'll settle in while we set up the mess?"

"Thank you. That all sounds fine. What's your name, by the way?"

"Smith-Fenton, sir."

"First posting?"

"Yes, sir."

"Well, that makes two of us." He smiled at the boy, and turned to his batman. "Come on, Watson. We'd better go and find the schoolmaster."

They walked down the village street, followed by the mule with the rest of the luggage. Dust rose from the crushed stone and gravel of the road, and the mule padded along on soft feet. There was a smell of drains.

At the end of the street Pearson found the house with white shutters. The wooden doors of an arched gateway stood open, inviting, leading to a sunlit courtyard and the entrance to the house. He left the others in the roadway and walked into the courtyard. On one side there were two stables, one empty with its door open, and from the other, a pony's head looked out at him. A trap stood in an open cart lodge alongside. He crossed to a flight of stone steps which led up to the house, and paused, looking around trying not to appear intrusive. In a corner of the yard, some hens scratched in the dust, and at the far end, an open gate in a rose hedge led to an orchard of apple trees.

"Hallo?" he said. It sounded awfully English. He cleared his throat and tried again in French: "Is there anyone here?"

A black and white dog came bounding from the orchard, barking with excitement, and a girl's voice:

"Jacques, shhhh."

She came through the gate in the roses, a tall girl in her early twenties, with long dark hair tied back and held with a ribbon. She wore a white blouse over a printed cotton skirt, and carried a flat wicker basket of eggs. Her arms and legs were bare and suntanned and Pearson thought she was the most beautiful thing he had ever seen. He took off his hat and held it in his left hand, with his cane. He wished he didn't wear spectacles.

"Bonsoir, Mam'selle," he said, holding out his hand to her. "I am very sorry to disturb you."

"You do not disturb me at all, Monsieur. We are expecting you all day." She smiled at him, dark brown eyes in an oval face.

"My name is Pearson," he said.

"And I am Agnès," the girl told him. "My father will return soon. He has a meeting in the village."

You have a lovely way of speaking English, he thought. And you are so beautiful that it's a pity there's another officer coming. He wondered what Mansell would be like.

"Your English is very good," he said.

"I learn from my father, who is the schoolteacher." She looked towards the road where the mule was trying to reach some roses on the wall. "Bring in the others, with your luggages. Monsieur Smith-Fenton says you are the Capitaine-doctor. My father will be very content with this. He has a

11

brother who is also a doctor. There will be much to talk about."

The muleteer led his animal in a wide circle round the courtyard and stopped by the steps. The dog ran behind, sniffing at the cart's wheels. Watson took off his hat and stood, twiddling it in his fingers. Pearson was surprised to see that he was almost completely bald.

"I will show you the rooms," said Agnès.

She picked up the eggs and ran up to the first floor. They entered the living area of the house into a large kitchen, comfortably furnished with chairs and a farmhouse table. A wood burning range stood in the fireplace and beside it, under a window, a stone sink with a pump alongside to draw water from the well.

"It is necessary to go up to the two attics," she explained. "I will show you. Be careful. The stairs are difficult."

They were narrow, too, Pearson found, as his shoulders brushed the sides of the stair well. But the attics had a simple charm, with heavy country beds and fruit wood wardrobes.

"You can choose as you are the first to come," she told Pearson.

"This is a lovely room," he said, standing aside to let her enter.

"I am afraid it is always hot up here in fine weather." She opened the window and threw back the shutters. A rickety table stood in the corner with a mirror and a china bowl and jug. Under it, lay a chamber pot. A rug covered bare wooden boards beside the bed.

"The maid will bring you water and see to everything there," said Agnès, pointing to the table.

"I hope we are not turning you out of these rooms," said Pearson.

She shook her head. "Since my mother died we are only using the rooms near the kitchen. It is more convenient in that way." She stood in the doorway. "You are most welcome here with us, you know. You must come and go as you wish. The house is always open for you." She turned to Watson as he laid Pearson's case on the bed. "Now, Private, if you will follow me I will show you how to find the loft. My father has put some camp beds for you."

Pearson leaned on the window sill and looked out into the courtyard, breathing in the grassy smell of rural France. He watched Agnès walk across the yard with a fluid movement and a slight swing of her hips. He hoped that Watson would be comfortable in his loft.

He heard a horse's hooves grating on the gravel, and watched a man with short grey hair ride into the yard and lead his horse into the stable. Pearson unpacked a few of his belongings, leaving the rest for Watson to attend to later, and went down to meet the teacher. He found him in the stable, attending to the horse.

"Monsieur Alazard?"

"Michel Alazard. Bonsoir, Monsieur." A horseman's handshake, firm and strong, and piercingly black eyes.

"My name is Pearson."

Alazard led him out into the courtyard, and shot the bolt on the lower half of the stable door. He brushed stalks of hay from his cotton jacket. "This war is going to hurt us," he said. "I am very afraid for France, but perhaps with the help of you British we will be able to stop the Germans. You know we are already fighting in Alsace, to recover what is ours?"

"Yes, I..."

"But I don't believe that will stop them from coming at us through Belgium. To attack a neutral country like that is despicable. Despicable." He laughed, throwing back his head, showing white teeth with a flash of gold. "I am sorry. I forget my manners. You are very welcome in my country and in my house. We have not much information about what is happening but perhaps you will tell us if there is some news we should know." He looked at Pearson's cap badge. "RAMC. You are the doctor?"

"Yes."

"An aeroplane crashed here today. I expect you will have heard."

"Yes. We saw it from the train."

"Two British pilots. Both killed, I'm afraid. My brother is a doctor, too. In the hospital at Le Cateau. It's not far from the *lycée* where I teach."

As the summer day drew to a close, Pearson re-arranged some of the clothes that Watson had unpacked, and put his mother's photograph on the table beside one of Freddy. There was no sign of the other officer, and the house was silent. He went down from his room, stepping quietly, not wishing to intrude. But in the kitchen, Agnès smiled at him and Alazard welcomed him with a bottle and some glasses. An oil lamp burned on the table.

"An apéritif, Monsieur?"

"Thank you."

Alazard filled the glasses with amber liquid. "Vin de noix," he said. "It's made from walnuts." He raised his glass. "To us all, to France, and may God help us."

They drank the sweet, fragrant wine, and Pearson said: "I should be most interested to meet your brother, and see his work at the hospital. As we are in reserve here, I hope to have some spare time."

"Of course. If you let me know when you would like to go, I can talk with him." He looked at his daughter. "Perhaps Agnès will take you in the trap. She knows the hospital well and works there as a nurse sometimes when they are busy. It will make a pleasant day for you."

"I shall look forward to it." He smiled at Agnès, thinking how pretty she was.

"You have your own home in England?" said Alazard.

"With my parents."

"The doctor has no wife to care for him?" The dark eyes teased him.

Pearson laughed, brushing back his hair. "No. No wife."

"Ah," said Alazard. "There is plenty of time perhaps for that."

Pearson walked back into the village in the half-light. Many of the shutters that had been closed earlier, were now open, and he could see into dimly lit rooms where shadowy figures moved above their storerooms and cow byres. The street bustled with villagers returning from their work in the fields, some of them bringing in a few cows for the night. Passers-by looked at him in friendly curiosity, and pungent smells of cooking and cow dung floated on the evening air.

**** ****

Pearson stood, irresolute, examining a black Humber staff car in the courtyard at battalion headquarters. In the fading daylight he could see a film of fine dew on the shining paintwork of the car. He was alone, and the sound of laughter floating from the open windows of the house increased his sense of isolation. He trailed a finger across the car's bonnet, leaving a tell-tale pattern where the moisture mixed with the day's dust. He took a deep breath to steady his nerves and went into the house to a blaze of electric light.

Fighting back a desire to run, Pearson hesitated beside a group of officers chatting in the salon where stewards served drinks. Colonel Hartwell, large and avuncular, came over to greet him. A pink-faced man with a neat moustache, his body filled his uniform, straining it at the seams.

"Good evening, Doctor. Welcome to the battalion. All settled in? And your equipment?"

"Everything's fine, thank you, sir."

"Splendid. Come and meet the others. Anson and de Courtney over there command 'A' and 'B' Companies. And this is the adjutant, Captain Cazenove." He took Pearson over to a small, neat man wearing round spectacles.

"Welcome to the mess," said Cazenove, looking like an

owl. "What will you have?"

"Whisky and soda, please."

"I'll get the steward. Oh, and this is Mansell. 'C' Company."

Pearson warmed to Major Mansell from the start. He strode into the mess, exuding humour. His heavy, dark eyebrows jumped up and down when he talked, and his black, curly hair, cut just within regulation length, gave him a mildly rebellious air.

"Bloody warm in here," Mansell said. "All that hot air, I expect." He laughed, showing white teeth in a suntanned face. His black eyes sparkled beneath the heavy brows. He took Pearson round, introducing him to his fellow officers, some like him in their late twenties, others like Smith-Fenton, straight from Sandhurst.

It was as if he were at a cocktail party, standing in a room of strangers. Light conversation, with the participants sizing up each other to see where there might be common ground. It was, he realised, the test his father had warned him about. Who is this new man? Let's see if he's one of us, or might he send the port round the wrong way? de Courtney, a shy, quiet man with hair swept back in a central parting, asked him about his training.

"Medicine at Cambridge," Pearson told him. "At Jesus. Then medical school at Millbank. And a couple of years general hospital duties." He smiled at them. "Don't worry. As long as you don't catch some obscure tropical disease, I should be able to cope."

"Not much chance of that here," said Hartwell. "But why RAMC? Instead of practising at home?"

"Military background," said Pearson. "My father wasn't pleased, I'm afraid. But I always wanted to be a doctor."

"What was your father's outfit?" said Anson.

"21st Lancers."

"General Charles Pearson?"

"Yes."

16

"I saw the notice of his retirement. Smashed his leg out hunting?"

"Yes. He was frightfully disappointed."

A ripple of appreciation, of relief, ran round the room. The new man was going to be all right. It was clear that he came out of the right drawer.

"Bloody silly sport, though, hunting," said Anson. "Shaw was quite right. 'The unspeakable pursuing the uneatable'."

"It should be 'the inedible'," said Cazenove. "Proper English, you know."

"You hunt, Pearson?" said Anson, ignoring the adjutant.

"A bit. But I'm more of a fishing and shooting man."

"Only happy killing things, eh? Bit rum for a doctor." His neck swelled red above his collar.

Mansell took Pearson to one side. "Don't let them get to you. They mean well enough."

"It's all right."

"Anson can be a bit chippy sometimes."

"I noticed."

"He was miffed when Hartwell got the battalion, and reckons his chances of commanding the regiment took a knock. He's a bit of a loner, and a stickler for routine. He fell out with our last MO. Kept chasing the old boy around to keep him up to scratch. Like a terrier after a chicken."

Pearson took a pull at his whisky. "How many of you have seen action? You all seem so young, apart from Hartwell and Anson."

"They were in South Africa. The rest of us have been flying the flag, mostly. Why do you ask?"

"It's just that I can't imagine what it's like being shot at."

"That's what my wife says. I should think it will scare the hell out of us. Are you any good with a revolver?"

"Hopeless. I couldn't hit a barn, let alone the door."

Mansell threw back his head and laughed. "Nor me. But that's the point. No one can shoot with a revolver. You're probably out of breath and the damn thing waves about like a spoon in a jelly. Apparently what you've got to tell yourself is that anything that comes whizzing past almost certainly isn't aimed at you. It's just the result of some chap from the other side firing off into the blue. Talk to some of the old sweats in the sergeant's mess. I've got a couple in 'C' Company. They're frightfully good for morale. Incidentally, that girl in our billet's a beauty." His eyebrows shot up and down.

"And that from a married man," said Pearson.

"Yes. I take it you aren't."

Pearson laughed, and shook his head. "No."

Pearson enjoyed his first night in the mess. Later, walking back to his billet with Mansell, they went quietly, guests in a foreign land, through the village silent under the stars. At the house a lamp burned on the kitchen table with a faint odour of paraffin, but there was no sign of the teacher or his daughter. Mansell blew out the lamp and they went up to their rooms by moonlight coming through the windows.

"Good night, old man," said Mansell. "You passed with flying colours."

"Good night. It's hard to believe we're in a war."

In his room, Pearson stood at the window, looking over the moonlit courtyard. One of the horses whinnied briefly in the stable, and pawed at the cobbles of the floor. He thought of the fresh young faces in the mess, flushed with enthusiasm and a little wine, as they toasted their king and prayed for the support of God. It was presumptive to think that God might take sides in the coming war, but surely the Entente had the stronger claim for His attention? A nation that clearly had violated the neutrality of another, could not credibly expect to have the divine ear. Leaving the window wide open to the night, Pearson undressed and got into his bed.

He lay on his back, his hands linked under his head, looking by candlelight at the wooden boards of the attic ceiling. He settled his shoulders into the horse-hair mattress. The mattress yielded with a soft rustling sound. He would find time tomorrow to write home with his news. He thought of the two airmen. They must have been some of the first casualties of the war. It was said that the 'plane ran out of petrol. What a pointless way to die, he thought. But whether it was a 'plane crash or a bullet in the head, the result was the same. You ended up dead. He wondered where the men would be buried.

Wednesday 19 August 1914

Pearson awoke to the soft sound of Agnès calling the hens in the courtyard. He jumped out of bed, pulled on a silk dressing gown, and went over to the window to watch her throwing corn. The sun was barely up, low in the east behind a thin layer of cloud. She wore a long coat, down to her ankles, and the hens scratched around her feet, pecking at the grains.

He heard a knock at his door and ran over to open it, expecting Mansell. The maid stood there, a diminutive woman in middle age, her greying hair tied in a bun. She held a jug of hot water in wrinkled brown hands.

"Bonjour, M'sieur." She came in to the room to put the jug on the table.

"Bonjour. What is your name?"

"Marie-Hélène, M'sieur."

"A lovely name. Mine is Pearson."

"Oui, M'sieur. Mam'selle Agnès has told me."

She smiled at him and left the room. Before she shut the door, Pearson noticed another jug on the floor outside Mansell's room.

He shaved, put on his uniform, and went down to breakfast where Alazard welcomed him to the sun-burnt smell of coffee. At the range, Agnès heated milk in a pan.

"Did you sleep well?" she asked, and Pearson felt his heart leap. She was as pretty as when he first saw her in the garden.

"Like a log," he said. "Very comfortable bed."

She brought coffee to the table with a loaf of bread, still warm from the baker. She cut the bread into thick crusty slices.

"We don't have bread like this in England," said Pearson.

"Why ever not?" Alazard said, chewing.

"Ours is different. It's softer. And usually brown. "

Alazard raised his eyebrows. He looked as if he was about to say something, and then changed his mind. "Do you play boules?" he said.

"I'm afraid not."

"Then I must teach you. We can practice in the yard here. The schools are on holiday, so I have plenty of time."

"Perhaps the war will wait a little too," said Pearson. He looked at his watch. "But in an hour there's a meeting at headquarters. We are hoping to find out what's happening in Belgium. And Alsace."

"Will you be able to tell us?"

"I don't see why not. It's your army that's fighting. In Alsace, anyway."

In the courtyard, when Pearson came out with Mansell, they found Watson and Mansell's servant, Phillips, waiting for them. They walked out through the gate where Agnès stood on an old chair, tying up the rose where the mule had pulled at it the previous evening. In the warm sunshine she had removed her coat. She smiled at Pearson, pushing a loose strand of hair behind her ear. The skin on her cheek and her arm looked wonderfully fresh and he felt a sudden urge to reach out and touch her.

"Until this evening," he said, saluting.

"Until this evening, mon Capitaine."

At one minute to nine, Pearson and Smith-Fenton stood at the back of the crowded room. Blue cigarette smoke hung in wreaths in front of large-scale maps pinned to the wall. The Intelligence officer, Captain Donaldson, went into a brief huddle with Colonel Hartwell and the adjutant. When a clock on the wall struck nine with a soft chime, Hartwell held up his hand.

"Good morning, gentlemen. I hope you found the billets to your liking?" He stabbed at the map with his cane, and spoke for fifteen minutes about the dispositions of troops, and Field Service Regulations for infantry training. Pearson leaned against the wall, trying to concentrate on the intricacies of military logistics. He thought of the way Agnès had stood on the chair when she tied up the rose. The skin on the back of her hands was brown from the sun and fine stretched over her knuckles.

Donaldson, a swarthy, stocky man, came to the front, pulling at the hem of his tunic. For someone of his appearance his voice was surprisingly light and high pitched.

"The latest information we have from Belgium," he sang in a light tenor, "is that the Germans have met stiff resistance at the fortified town of Liège and have had to call up heavy guns. If they are successful, which we think is in no doubt, they are expected to move on to Namur where..."

The room reeked of tobacco in the hot still air, and the voice of the Intelligence officer whined on like a mosquito. Agnès had an endearing habit, Pearson thought, of tucking strands of hair behind her ear. He hadn't studied ears much. Hers were beautifully rounded at the tip.

Pearson listened to the mosquito "... on your map. In the meantime, the French, who pushed into Alsace earlier, have had some success, heading towards Mulhouse and Colmar." The Intelligence officer paused, stretching his hands behind his back. "We believe that the French launched a second attack yesterday, in Lorraine. You will recall that they lost these territories to the Germans in the war of 1870. " He looked round the room. "You will appreciate that the situation on the ground can change rapidly... "

"Do we know anything of the strength the Germans might put up in the Mons – Charleroi area?" said Hartwell.

"Too early to say, sir. It depends how they deploy if they have an easy time in Belgium."

Smith-Fenton held up his hand. "Excuse me, sir, but as the BEF is only about seventy thousand men, it seems likely that we shall be heavily outnumbered by the Germans, doesn't it?"

Donaldson looked up as if uncertain how to answer.

Colonel Hartwell took over. "What we must never forget is that the British Army is the only one in this conflict that consists entirely of professionally trained volunteers. We have the Lee Enfield, unquestionably the best rifle in the world, and our infantry are trained to use it with deadly effect. That is a formidable force." He paused, a comforting figure, smiling at the junior subalterns. "Remember also that we are not alone in this. The French have huge numbers under arms."

"Quite," said Donaldson, tweaking his tunic again.

"Thank you, sir," said Smith -Fenton, blushing.

"Presumably the Belgians haven't a hope?" said Anson.

"I don't think so," said Donaldson. "Their army's small and once their fortress towns have gone, they'll be in trouble."

"So it might be only a week or two before the BEF is in action?"

Donaldson ran a finger round under his collar. "Assuming the Germans decide to attack us," he said, "I am afraid that is highly likely."

"And what do Intelligence have to say about the possible duration of the war?"

A ripple of laughter ran round the room. Donaldson looked flustered. His voice changed gear into falsetto: "The short answer is that we don't know. The situation is not helped by all the speculation in England that the war will be over by Christmas. I can see no evidence to support that."

As the meeting broke up, Pearson went over to the colonel.

"May I have a word, sir?"

"Of course."

"I need to set up my aid post. How elaborate will our positions be?"

"We'll dig in lightly at first. I really don't expect any action here. But you never know. Talk to the company commanders. They'll help you."

"Thank you. I'm going out to the camp this morning. I want to have a look at the kitchens and check the latrines. And I'd like to meet some of the NCOs and men, so they can see what their new medical officer looks like."

Hartwell regarded him with a shrewd smile. "I can see you've done your homework," he said. "Our previous doctor took a bit of a back seat the last year or two. Luckily he was too long in the tooth for active service."

"So they gave you me instead?"

"Yes," said Hartwell, looking out of the window, watching his men. He turned back to Pearson, smoothing his moustache with a thumb. "There's one thing I want to make quite clear."

"Sir?"

"You are new at this, and I wonder if you realise quite how important you are in the battalion."

"Well, I'm just one of many..."

"Wrong. That's exactly my point." He waved an arm round the mess. "Individually we are, as you put it, one of many." He prodded the air with a forefinger. "You're unique. One medical officer for a whole battalion. When the shooting starts, we are going to depend on you, and your first duty is to care for yourself." He tapped his finger on Pearson's chest. "If you get shot up, the rest of us are in trouble. Can't emphasise that enough."

"Yes, sir. I do understand that."

"Good man. Anything else?"

"Once we're dug in I'd like to organise some training for the stretcher-bearers. And I want to visit the hospital at Le Cateau. I've got an introduction to the doctor there, and it might be useful to talk to him to see if there are any local bugs to worry about."

"Excellent idea." Hartwell brushed a speck of dust from the front of his uniform. "You seemed at home in the mess last night?"

"It wasn't difficult, sir. You gave me a good welcome."

Pearson filled his water bottle and set off on foot with Watson to the camp. The sun shone on a lovely summer's day, with a light east wind ruffling the roadside grasses. Weaving their way through slow moving military traffic, they followed the road alongside the railway. Some mules ambled past, heads low as they strained in the traces, hauling field guns.

Dust swirled from the limbers' wheels.

They crossed a small river and walked through fields of wheat where sweating horses pulled binders. Farm hands followed, putting up the sheaves into stooks. Small boys, armed with sticks, chased rats running from the corn.

Sparse trees dotted the land where the battalion camped under canvas behind a low ridge commanding the ground to the north-east. A sharp tang of wood smoke drifted from the cookhouse. In a grassy hollow, a hundred yards behind where men were already digging in, Pearson discovered a small stone hut. The wooden door creaked open when he pushed it with his foot. The place would make a perfect aid post.

Later, he dismissed Watson, and walked down to the Sambre, the wide, slow river that protected their right flank. He leaned against an old willow tree and watched the river. Dace were taking insects from the surface and a big carp hung motionless in the sun- warmed water beside some yellow water lilies. He stood still, watching, and thought of the Hampshire river where he had gone with his mother barely a week before, after trout.

He had walked with her, in late afternoon, by the side of a field of ripening barley, with a parasol casting shade across her head and shoulders, and the dog running ahead.

"I wish you didn't have to go," she said.

"I wish none of us had to go. It all seems so unnecessary."

"Most war is unnecessary."

"I don't suppose Father would agree. War, or its prevention, has kept him pretty busy all his life."

"Yes," she laughed. "And at least you won't be in too much danger, John. As a doctor, I mean. You won't be in the thick of it?" She had tried to keep her voice light, but he heard the concern in her.

"Oh, I don't suppose so. We'll be away from things, I expect."

He remembered how she had come to the bench overlooking the river, sitting upright with her marvellous posture, stroking the dog's ears, as he cast his line upstream and the shadows lengthened. A flight of mallard had swung round over the old mill and landed on the water as the church clock struck six. On that summer evening on an English chalk stream, he had left home to go to war.

He felt a sudden twinge of homesickness for his parent's comfortable house with the croquet lawn, and Freddy running in the lane. God alone knew what the future held, he thought, but it was unlikely to be dull. And there was Agnès, now. Would there be much time to see her before the shooting started? Perhaps in the morning he could deal with any cases at his sick parade, and then they could go together to the hospital to meet the doctor. Alazard had talked of them taking the trap. It would be fun if it were a fine day, with the wind blowing in her hair.

In the late afternoon, Pearson walked back to the village. To avoid the traffic and dust of the road, he crossed to the other side of the railway line. A faint path ran there beside the sleepers, used by railway workmen inspecting the tracks. His uniform breeches brushed against the blue flowers of scabious, disturbing butterflies that fed there, and poppies grew in profusion.

As he reached the billet, Pearson saw that the door to Alazard's stable was open. Jacques came trotting down the stone steps to meet him, hackles raised, and growling. He bent, giving his hand to the dog to sniff. Satisfied, Jacques urinated on the corner of the bottom step, and Pearson said: "It's all right, boy, I know you're here. We're going to be friends."

He heard Agnès call the dog through the open door, and felt his senses quicken. His shadow fell across the doorway as he came into the room. He took off his hat. She stood at the big table, her sleeves pushed above her elbows, kneading pastry in a bowl.

"Still at work?" he said.

She laughed, tossing back her hair, and brushed the side of her chin with the back of one hand. "There is always something that needs to be done. My father has gone into Le Cateau to attend to some business at the *lycée* and I am preparing for him a *tarte aux pommes*."

"I thought the schools are on holidays."

"Yes, that is true. But you know, there is his papers that need him."

"Are his papers," he said, gently correcting her.

She looked up from the pastry to see if he were teasing her, and saw from his expression that he was not.

"Yes, thank you. Are his papers. It is difficult to speak English."

"I think you speak it very well." He pulled a chair out from the table and sat down to watch her. The dog came to him and rested its head on his knee.

"You have finished for the day?" she asked him, flashing a quick smile.

"Yes. Unless you have something for me here."

"What could you do for me?" she said, mischievously. "My father cannot do much for me. Why should you be different?"

"My father doesn't do much to help my mother in the house. But that doesn't mean I don't. When I was a boy, my mother used to make me help. I have a young brother of twelve. He has to do things to help."

"But you have servants in your house in England?"

"Yes. But there are still other things that must be done."

She cut up apples, with swift, deft movements of the knife. "What is your brother's name?"

"Freddy. It's short for Frederick."

"And much nicer. Nicer for a boy," she said. "Frederick is the name of an old man. Tell me of your parents." She looked at Pearson. "They are old?"

He laughed, delighted at her question. "Not that old. My

father is fifty-five, mother several years younger. He's a retired soldier and my mother is tall and fair and very beautiful. She has excellent...she holds herself very well. Very upright." He looked at Agnès as she laid pieces of apple onto the pastry. "You remind me of her," he said quietly. "It's the way you move. You are so graceful. My mother's name is Grace."

She straightened, standing at the table, looking at him, her face calm and still. She swept back a lock of hair, leaving a trace of flour on her cheek. "Grace," she said. "That is a beautiful name. My mother's name was Geneviève."

"You told me your mother died. What happened to her?"

"It was an accident with the horse, five years ago now. My mother liked very much to ride but the horse was frightened by something when they were jumping over a ditch and there was a bad fall. The horse rolled and my mother was underneath. Her back was broken and I think also her stomach." She brushed her hand over her eyes, as if sweeping away the memory. "There was nothing we could do to save her. She died within two days."

"I'm so sorry," said Pearson. "I hope she didn't suffer too much."

"Oh, she was in great pain. But my uncle made her as comfortable as possible." She smiled again: "The doctor uncle which you are going to meet."

She crossed over to the range and put in the tart to cook. She looked at the clock on the wall and came back to the table to sit opposite him, studying the tall, fair young man from England, with his spectacles and his smart service dress uniform with the polished Sam Browne belt. Their eyes met, and she held his gaze.

"What is your name, Captain Pearson?" she asked. "What may I call you?"

"John," he said, but it didn't come out well. He cleared his throat. "John. My name is John."

She leaned forward cupping her chin in her hands, her

elbows on the table. "And how old is John."

"Twenty-six," he told her.

"I am twenty-two."

"It's not much." He waved his arm around the room. "It is not much, to be the mistress of this house. You seem...I thought you were older than that."

"It is enough. In our army there are many young men who are still boys of eighteen. They are old enough to die for France."

"Yes," he said. "It's true. It is the same in our army."

The dog moved, suddenly alert, and ran outside, his toenails clicking on the floorboards. A moment later they heard the horse.

"That is my father returning," said Agnès. "If you are not in a hurry to go to your mess, could you stay for a little to tell him of your meeting this morning? He is very anxious for information."

He watched her tidying her cooking things from the table.

"There's no hurry," he said. "But there isn't much I can tell him. Is your father very demanding?"

She looked at him, uncertain of his meaning.

"Is he...does he expect a great deal from you – in the house?"

"I think it would be difficult for him to manage if I were not here. But it is not very demanding, as you put it. He spends a lot of time in Le Cateau, at the *lycée,* and...he has some friends there."

There was something in her voice that made him look up, and he sensed her relief when her father came up the steps into the room. Alazard threw his coat onto a chair and ran a hand though his hair.

"Please sit down, Monsieur. What can you tell me from this morning? There are rumours we are in Lorraine again."

"Yes, it's true. Also, your army in Alsace has advanced towards Colmar. The Germans are withdrawing but we hear there are many casualties on the French side. The Belgians are being pounded with heavy guns, and we don't expect them to hold out for long."

"And then? What will happen then?"

Pearson spread his hands wide, shaking his head, wondering how much he could tell the man. "I don't know. The British are linking up with your forces near Charleroi, and if the Germans attack there we shall try to stop them."

"Mon Dieu," said Alazard. He scrubbed his head with his fingers. "Charleroi is not far from here. Forty or fifty kilometres at most." He stared at Pearson, before fetching a bottle of cognac from the table. He splashed cognac into the glasses. "Incidentally, I have talked with my brother, and he will be very pleased to see you in the hospital. You can call there any time you wish. *Santé!*" He raised his glass.

"Santé!" said Pearson. "Perhaps I can see him tomorrow when I have finished at the camp." The raw liquor burned his throat.

"I will take you," said Agnès. "And I want you to see the church. It has a very fine interior with a beautiful tapestry."

In his room, before he went back to headquarters and the mess, Pearson sat by the window, writing to his mother. Always, from his school days, he had addressed his letters to her alone, mainly because his father had spent so much of his time away, wherever his duties took him. Later, he had found it a difficult habit to break and, because he knew that his father was always given the letters to read, it seemed easier to carry on in the same way.

He knew that his mother would long to have news from him, and he wrote in detail to tell her of his journey into France, of the camp, and of the messing arrangements in the farmhouse. He also told her about some of his fellow officers and about the house where he was billeted. And, because it gave him pleasure, he told her a little about Agnès.

31

He read through the letter, sealed it in its envelope, and looked out of the window into the dusk, thinking of his conversation with Agnès. She was wonderfully easy to talk to, and so different from the girls he knew at home. She was already a woman, running the house for her father, supervising the maid, efficient in her dealings with him and Mansell, and the billeting arrangement.

At home in England, his contact with girls was cocooned in traditional society. Cucumber sandwiches for tea in the conservatory; games of tennis, the players all in white; formal cocktail parties or balls, seldom far from the jaundiced eye of a chaperone. But here, in a French village house, he could sit across the kitchen table from a girl and talk with her while she made an apple pie.

He had noticed the change in her voice when she was talking about her father in Le Cateau, and she seemed relieved when Alazard arrived and the conversation moved on. It was just a little change, a nuance, and he only noticed it because it had not been there before. He shrugged, and got up from his chair. Probably she thought Alazard spent too much time in the town. Or perhaps he had some friends she disapproved of.

A wave of exhilaration swept over him from their conversation in the kitchen, sharpened by an awareness of the clock ticking away the time they might have before the war swept them apart. The smell of evening, of dew and fresh hay, drifted through the window. And Donaldson had said it might only be a week before the British were in action.

Pearson heard footsteps running up the stairs, and Mansell poked his head round the door.

"Will you come down to HQ with me?" he said. "They've been harvesting like mad, and the cook's got some rabbits."

Thursday 20 August 1914

Pearson sat in his aid post, surveying his little kingdom. With the help of Watson and one of the orderlies, the hut had been swept and cleaned. The interior shone with new light, and a table and a couple of chairs stood by the window. A lock had been fitted to the door, and a shelf on one wall held a selection of medicine and equipment brought in from the headquarters' store. He looked out of the window and was surprised by the number attending his first sick parade. He quizzed Rowntree about it, a grizzled corporal who wore the South Africa campaign medal.

"No, sir," Rowntree told him. "Nowhere near this many usually. I think it may be a try-on. They probably just want to see what their new doctor looks like."

"But surely their platoon leaders would rumble that?"

"It's the first parade since we arrived, sir. They're probably going a bit easy on the men."

"All right, Corporal," said Pearson. "Fall them in outside and I'll talk to them." He put on his hat and went out.

"Good morning," he said as the parade stood at ease. "I can see that some of you are here with fairly obvious aches and pains." He pointed to a man with his arm in a sling. "That man for example. Others are perhaps just feeling a bit under the weather? I would like all those of you in the first category to fall out and stand over there." He pointed with his cane to the side of the hut. "The rest of you stay where you are." Five men went to stand by the hut, leaving about a dozen behind.

"Now," said Pearson, addressing the remainder. "You are all probably feeling the effects of the journey, and perhaps the change of rations. Is there anyone who feels worse than that?"

One man put up a hand. His face looked like dough. "I was sick four times in the night, sir."

"Very well, Private. Go and join the others. Now, the rest of you probably need a damn good dose of salts to clear out

33

your systems. There's nothing like it. It will probably give you the runs for a week but you won't need to see me again. I can either give it to you now, or you can wait until tomorrow's sick parade. If you come back tomorrow you may need a double dose. Tell the corporal what you decide. In the meantime I will see the other group, starting with the man with the sling."

When the last of the five patients had left, the corporal put his head round the door. "No more, sir," he said, grinning.

"They've all returned to duties?"

"Yes, sir. I think you won that round, if I may say so."

Pearson laughed: "That's good. The first round is usually the most important."

He felt like singing. One sick parade was only a small thing, but it was a start. He walked up into the camp feeling ten feet tall. Everything seemed in order, the work of a highly professional army, in accordance with the training manuals that he had studied. At the top of the ridge where the men of 'C' Company were digging their defensive positions, he found Mansell.

"Ah, the good doctor," said Mansell. "Rumour has it you've got some potent medicine in your AP." He roared with laughter. "The CSM told me a couple of our chaps were back here at the double."

"Well, there can't be much the matter with your lot. I can't believe they've dug all this since yesterday."

A network of shallow trenches ran along the side of the ridge, complete with traverses and angles to protect the whole system from enfilading fire, and a communication trench had been started leading rearwards towards the camp.

"You have to dig fast," said Mansell. "I expect they'll dig even faster if we get shot at."

"When you've finished, could we set up a bit of training for the stretcher-bearers?"

"Tomorrow suit you? How realistic do you want it? We can put out some casualties in no man's land." He waved his cane over the ridge beyond the trenches. "You could have the casualties out there for a bit while we let off some small arms fire over their heads. Perhaps a bit of smoke too, and then you can send your chaps out to bring them in."

"Can you arrange the shooting bit?" said Pearson.

"Yes. I'll clear it with the colonel." He laughed, pushing back his hat: "You'll probably find half the battalion comes along to watch."

The church clock struck midday as Pearson returned to his lodgings. The dog ran out to greet him and he followed it up into the house, where Marie-Hélène swept the steps with a besom.

"Mam'selle is waiting for you," she said.

"Thank you. Is she indoors?"

"*Bien sûr,* M'sieur."

Agnès held a small flatiron, working at the table. Another stood heating on the range. She wore an ankle length cotton dress, gathered at the waist, with long sleeves and frilly cuffs. Her hair was coiled neatly on top of her head, held in place with long pins, showing her ears and neck.

"I am afraid I have kept you waiting," he said. "There was more for me to do at the camp than I expected."

She shook her head. "It is nothing. And, as you can see there is always something to do here. You will eat before we go?"

"Would you have lunch with me? In the town?"

"In a restaurant?" She blushed a little and fiddled with her hair.

"Yes, if you would like that."

"Oh, yes. I should like it very much."

"Do you know somewhere?" he asked.

"Yes. I hope you will like it. My father goes sometimes." She blushed again and put a hand to her cheek as if to feel its warmth. She looked at the clock on the wall. "But we must hurry if we are to be in time. They serve lunch at half past twelve."

"But once we are there, we don't have to hurry?"

She shook her head. "No, no. Once we are there it will be all right."

"Thank heavens." Pearson laughed. "I wouldn't want to rush our first date."

She put the irons to the side of the range and picked up a hat, tying it under her chin. He followed her across the yard where he helped her with the harness, and she backed the pony up to the trap. He noticed that Alazard's horse was not in its stable. Agnès got into the trap and he stepped in, feeling the springs move as he sat down beside her. The dog jumped in and she made to push him down, but Pearson said: "We can take Jacques if you like."

"You do not mind him?" she asked.

"Of course not. But will he be all right when we have lunch?"

"If you want him, he can come too."

"To the restaurant?"

"Why are you surprised?" She laughed, flicking the reins, and the pony pulled them out into the lane.

"English restaurants aren't very good at dogs," he said lamely, and thought that in England it was not, perhaps, usual for an army officer to drive into the local town with a pretty girl he had known for two days and take her out to lunch.

"Would you like to drive, John?" she said, turning to him. "I should have asked you." It was the second time she had used his Christian name. She pronounced it in the French way, the 'J' softer than in England.

"No. You drive. I prefer it that way."

"But in England you would drive?"

"Yes, perhaps."

"Or do you have a coachman in your home?"

"No. But there is a man who does the gardens. Sometimes he will drive if necessary."

36

"And a motor car? You have a motor car?"

Pearson laughed: "Yes. My father bought one at the beginning of the year. He has a bad leg from a hunting accident and finds it difficult to walk. He thought the motor would be easier. My mother won't go with him. She says he drives too fast."

"The hunting is for foxes?"

"Yes."

She pulled the trap to the side of the road to allow a column of horse-drawn supply wagons to pass in the opposite direction.

"I should very much like to go hunting after foxes," she said. "I have seen photographs of the English hunting. It is very colourful, and the jumping will be great fun. My mother would have loved to hunt as you do in England. She was so happy on a horse."

"I would have liked to have known your mother."

"My mother would have liked you, too."

"Too?"

She turned towards him. "As I like you, John."

"From only two days?" He smiled at her: "It's not very long."

"The time is not important. It is how I feel that matters."

He wanted to say: 'Yes, you are right. Time is nothing, really, and what is it that you feel, and maybe it is the same as me?' A lock of hair had escaped from under her hat, curling down her neck and he said: "We may not have very much time left, before the war comes."

"I was speaking of the time that has gone, the time that is passed. That is the time that is not important. You are speaking of the time that is to come."

"Yes. Today, and tomorrow, and the days after. That is the time there may not be much of."

"I know this. It is very cruel that you should be allowed to come into my life at this time."

"It's the same for me," he said. "It is a very precious time."

37

"Then you feel it too?"

"From the moment you came through from the orchard with the eggs."

She turned to him again, her eyes dark and serious. "But there will be girls that you have left behind in England." It was more a statement than a question.

"Yes, there are many. But none that takes my breath away."

"And I do that to you? Take your breath away?"

"Yes."

"Then we are both in danger of suffocating!"

She laughed, happy as sunshine, and when one wheel of the trap fell into a pothole, she was thrown against him and he put his arm round her shoulder, pulling them together. Later, when they reached the outskirts of the town where the gravel road gave way to cobblestones, he moved over to his side of the seat and watched her, sitting very upright with the reins in her hand, looking ahead into the town. Her lips were slightly parted.

Plane trees cast deep shadow over the road, and she drove up into a small square where they could leave the pony in the cool, tied to a rail near a stone water fountain. She pointed to a restaurant at the side of the square with some tables set outside in the shade.

"This is the place," she said. "The food won't kill us, and we can see the pony."

She led him across the square. The few people eating looked up at Pearson, curious yet welcoming to the English officer in his uniform.

"Bonjour," said Agnès, acknowledging them, and to Pearson: "We can eat out here, or inside if you prefer."

"I like it here, if you are happy," he said.

She looked at him, smiling, and his heart ached at her loveliness.

"I am very happy," she said.

She put Jacques under one of the empty tables, and they sat down.

"I wish you could take off your hat," he said.

"You do not like it?"

"Yes, but I cannot see your hair."

She leaned towards him over the table: "And I cannot see yours."

He removed his hat and placed it on the table, looking at her. A shallow dent circled the hair at the back of his head where the hat had pressed.

"It is easy for you," she said. "Perhaps indoors I could do the same, but it would not be right outside. You are very fair. Is it normal to be so fair in England?"

"Yes, quite normal. My mother is blonde, like this."

"Will you take me to England one day, John?"

"Do you think your father would allow it?"

"Yes, I think so."

"I would love to take you there. In six months or so I will get some leave." He watched her and thought how Freddy would love to show her round the house and garden.

The waiter came over. "Bonjour M'sieur, Mam'selle. You would like to eat?"

"Yes," said Pearson.

"Le menu du jour ?"

"Yes, please."

" You will take an apéritif?"

"Would you drink an apéritif, or perhaps some wine?" he asked Agnès.

"Just a little wine, please."

"No apéritif," he said to the waiter. "Two menus du jour, and a carafe of red wine."

"C'est bon," the man said, producing cutlery from the pocket of his apron. Pearson put his hat on one of the spare chairs.

"I believe your French is better than my English," said Agnès.

"No. It is much more limited. Ordering food is easy," he said, laughing. "Is your father in Le Cateau today? I noticed he had taken the horse."

"I think so, yes." She looked down at her hands. "He is often here at the moment. He is very concerned about what may happen if there is much fighting. He likes to talk to his friends about this." She looked up again and Pearson said:

"Is there something about your father that worries you?"

"Why do you ask that?"

"Because sometimes when you are talking of him, I can hear it in your voice."

"I have told you that he is a lot dependent on me, since the death of my mother. I do not mind this so much, and I want for him to make his own life again, with his own friends. But …I am not sure if we should discuss this…"

"We don't have to," he said. He reached across to where her hands lay on the edge of the table, covering one of hers with his. "You don't need to tell me if it is painful for you."

She turned over her hand so that their fingers intertwined, and their eyes met. He thought she might cry.

"No…it is just that there is a woman that he goes to see. I do not know if she is very good for him. She is a teacher at the *lycée*."

"Why should she not be good for him? It is natural for your father to want to see a woman." He added something in French.

She laughed at his sudden use of her language. "Yes, he has plenty of vigour. But I am afraid the woman is interested also in his money. That is the only reason I am worried."

The waiter returned with a tureen of vegetable soup, a small basket of fresh bread, and a carafe of wine.

"Bon appétit," he said, placing it all on the table.

Agnès served them both, filling white china bowls from the tureen with a ladle. The square slept quietly through the hours of lunch, soothed by the calling of doves. The possibility of war seemed to belong in another time, another place.

"Have you always been close to your father?" he asked her.

She put down her spoon, pushed the bowl away a little, and pressed a napkin to her lips. "For all my life, since I can

40

remember. He is very good to me, a natural man with children."

"And you are the only one? His only child?"

"There were two others after me. They both died when they were babies. After that, the doctors said that my mother must not have any more."

"I'm so sorry. Were you old enough to know the others?"

"The first one, no. I think I was less than two. But the other – she was also called Geneviève like my mother – she came when I was four. I used to play with her all day in the garden. We loved her. It was her heart, they said. It was not properly formed. I do not think my parents ever got over this. And when Maman had the accident, my poor father was inconsolable. You would say that in English?"

"It's exactly the right word."

"Thank you. So you see it is natural that my father and me are very close."

"And that you should be worried about him. But I expect he knows how to look after his money. He'll want to keep it for you in your turn." He poured some wine, and when he replaced the carafe, a few drops ran down the side. He watched her collect the drops on her finger and put it to her lips.

He tried to keep his voice even. "How long has he known this woman?" he asked her.

"Maybe two years, since she began at the *lycée*. But only for a few months like...like it is now."

"And he understands how you feel about her?"

She shrugged: "Some of it, but perhaps not enough."

"I expect he will come to it. Your father is an intelligent man."

"And you are a good doctor. You have ...what do you call it? The bedside manner?"

"But you are not in bed."

"No," she said quietly. " I am not in bed, but that doesn't prevent me from knowing that you are good at listening. And that you understand."

The waiter came to clear away the soup, and he brought them green beans with some salad and, afterwards, lamb cutlets cooked pink with a sauce of red wine and pepper.

Pearson sat across the table from her, and when he stretched out his leg, he felt her foot against his calf. She didn't move when their eyes met, and she asked him: "What made you decide to be a doctor, John?"

"Do you mean instead of being a soldier?"

"Why? Is that what your father wanted?"

"He would have liked it. My grandfather was a soldier too, so I would have been the third generation."

"Did you fight with him about it?" She leaned her chin on the back of her hand, her elbow on the table.

God, he thought, you look beautiful like that. "Not really," he said. "He realised that we are different. That we come at things from different angles. Anyway, my mother would never have allowed us to fight."

"You are more like your mother?"

"Yes," he said. "I suppose I am."

"You haven't said yet why you became a doctor."

"I wanted to read medicine at university because I found it a very interesting thing to study. And I enjoyed it. So, it seemed the natural thing to do. To be a doctor I mean."

"And you wanted to do good? To help people who were suffering?"

"That came later."

"Later?"

"When I had learned about medicine. What the possibilities are. It embarrasses me a bit that it wasn't the other way round. You know, to start with wanting to do good. Most people start from there."

"But you have come to it. I can see that." She reached across the able and touched the back of his hand.

At the end of their meal, the chef wandered amongst the tables, talking to his customers. He came to stand beside

42

Pearson, holding a clean white napkin.

"Monsieur le Capitaine will permit me to offer a glass of cognac? I have heard that there is a large army of the British at Bazuel. You are most welcome for the fight against the *Boche*."

"It is not such a big army," said Pearson. "Perhaps another time for the cognac. We have an appointment at the hospital."

"The captain is a doctor," said Agnès. "I am taking him to meet uncle Gaston so that they can make some plans."

The chef spread his arms in a gesture of resignation: "It is difficult to make plans with the uncertainty of the war."

"Yes, but it's better to make them anyway," said Pearson.

"Perhaps," the man shrugged. "Do you think the Germans will come here?"

"I hope not, but it's difficult to gauge."

The chef flapped his napkin at an imaginary fly. "If they come, I shall close the restaurant."

"Then let us hope they don't come. We've had a very good lunch."

The chef bowed deep. "Merci, Monsieur. To the next time."

Pearson paid the bill, and Agnès said: "The hospital is on the other side of the town. We should take the trap."

They crossed the square with the dog and set off down narrow streets, the sound of the wheels echoing loudly off tall buildings.

"Thank you, John, for taking me to lunch," she said. "I felt very proud to sit there, in that place, with you. And to have you beside me now."

"Perhaps we will have time to go again."

"The time we were talking of on the way here?"

"Yes, the precious time."

"We must make it, John. Every day we must make it a little. It is too precious to waste."

"Yes. I don't have to dine in the mess every evening, you know. Perhaps I could eat with you and your father one

43

night?"

"You would do this for me? Give up your friends for an evening?"

"It is not much to give up for a beautiful woman."

"Do you really find me beautiful?"

"I have never met anyone more so."

"Except your mother. You told me that she is beautiful."

"I also told you that you remind me of her. And she is beautiful to me because she is my mother. You are beautiful to me because I am in love with you." The words were out before he realised it.

She stared at him for a moment, before nodding as if in affirmation.

Her voice was a whisper. "How do you love me, John?"

"Do you mean why? The 'how' I hope to show you later."

She blushed slightly. "Tell me why."

"Because I love to look at you, to listen to your voice, and because my heart sings when I am with you."

"It is the same for me," she said, simply. "But when you say it, it is like listening to a poem." She turned the pony through a gateway into the hospital's courtyard. "Now, we are here. I hope there will still be time for the tapestry afterwards?"

"There will be time," he said. "And if there is not, we'll find it. It's a new resolution I have made for us."

She left the trap in a corner of the courtyard, out of the way of other traffic, and told the dog to wait. It settled down on the seat, watching them.

The grey stone of the hospital gave it a gloomy appearance under a slate roof, and it was smaller than Pearson had expected, but scrupulously clean, with an appropriate smell of disinfectant. Agnès introduced him to Gaston Alazard, a thin man in a white coat, older looking than his brother, with a neatly trimmed beard and pince-nez spectacles.

"You are most welcome, Monsieur," he said, shaking Pearson by the hand. "It is a great honour for me to have a

44

visit from a doctor in the British army. If there is anything you would like to know, do not be afraid to ask."

Pearson followed with Agnès as Gaston took them on a tour of his wards. They stopped by the bedside of a young woman recovering, with her baby, from a Caesarean birth; a workman whose leg was in traction after falling off a roof; an old fisherman who had caught his eye on a fish-hook; and a little girl of twelve whose hands and arms had been scalded by boiling water. As far as Alazard knew, there were no infectious bugs in the area, and he would be only too pleased to offer the hospital for the treatment of casualties should Pearson request it. Agnès was a competent assistant nurse and would be a great asset in the event of many wounded soldiers needing help.

At the end of an hour, Pearson thanked him and made their excuses for leaving.

"Agnès would like to show me the church before we return to Bazuel," he said.

"You are lucky to have a good guide. And I expect she makes you comfortable with my brother?"

"Yes. Thank you."

"Au revoir, Monsieur. Please come again if you think I can be useful. And let us pray that the war will not reach us here."

They came back up into the centre of the town, the pony clip-clopping over cobblestones, and stopped in the shade near the entrance to the church. The church was set back from the road behind a wrought iron fence and a small courtyard, bright with pots of geraniums. Ornate stonework shone in the afternoon light with the colour of honey, and the spire rose tall behind, with a curious onion dome.

Pearson followed her into the church's cool interior, a refuge from the heat of the sun. They stood for a moment, adjusting their eyes to the light. Baroque pillars soared up to the vaulted ceiling, and sunlight from the stained glass windows streamed into the interior. The air sang with the scent of incense.

"I hadn't expected this," said Pearson. "It's as big as a cathedral."

"It was part of a Benedictine abbey," she told him. "Until the revolution. Much of it was destroyed then, leaving just the church. There is nothing like it in this part of France. Come."

She led him up the nave and stopped in front of a tapestry, hanging on the wall. In exquisite embroidery, a man wearing a red robe sat writing in a book, under the dome of a blue sky. His face shone with sorrow and piety as if lit from within by some holy fire. Flowers tumbled down the sides in a riot of colour.

Pearson stood, transfixed by its beauty.

"Do you like this?" she asked.

"It's wonderful. I've never seen such feeling in a tapestry. It's like a painting. Who is he?"

"St. John, I think. A tapestry like this is very special to us in France. It would have hung in the abbey here. I have loved it since I was a child. I helped carry it once or twice, in processions. No one knows the history but my father says it is very valuable. That it should be in a case, behind glass."

"But it wouldn't be the same in a case. It should be free, alive as it is now. Like butterflies. You shouldn't put them in a glass case stuck through with a pin. I wish I had seen you carry it."

"It was some time ago. When I was fifteen." She giggled and told him: "I used secretly to be a little in love with St. John." She pointed to the figure. "You can see that he is very handsome there."

"I hope you mentioned this in the confessional," he said.

She smiled, pushed back her hair, and took him to a pew. They sat down, and looked at the stained glass, breathing in the atmosphere of the building. The church was empty, apart from the two of them and an old woman, in widow's black, kneeling by the altar, her arthritic fingers busy with a rosary. The smell from votive candles mingled with the incense in a heady mix.

"Do you come here to worship?" Pearson asked her.

"Sometimes, but more in Bazuel. And not every week I am afraid." She looked at him with a little smile. "My father does not go to mass much since *Maman* died. He was very angry that God had let her die too, after the babies had been taken."

"That's a perfectly normal reaction."

"And you go to church in England with your family?"

"Yes, sometimes. But we're a bit different in England. You know that most of us are not Catholic there?" He laughed quietly. "For many of us it's a matter of habit. To be seen in church has a certain importance. Sometimes it has very little to do with our religion. A part of Sunday routine, before roast beef for lunch."

"But you are not without faith?"

"I have faith in myself, as a doctor, to try to do the right thing. I have faith in my family. Perhaps in my country too. I am not sure that I have much faith in God. Are you shocked by this?"

She shook her head. "No. It is what my father would say."

"And what would you say?"

"I think I would be afraid to have no faith in God."

He put a hand on her knee. "That is good, Agnès. You must hold on to that." He could feel the warmth from her body, and a sensation of lightness inside his head. "If we were not in a church," he said, " I would ask if I might kiss you."

"Then it is a good thing that we are."

On the way out, they stopped again in front of the tapestry. A priest had come into the church and he went over to stand with them. He looked very young, with a smooth face, untrammelled by anxiety.

"It is Mam'selle Alazard, surely?" the priest said.

"Yes, Father." She smiled at the priest. "And this is Captain Pearson."

"I am Father Albert," he said. "You are in the English army, Monsieur?"

"Yes."

"The captain is a doctor," Agnès told him.

"A doctor? That is most interesting. Tell me, as a doctor, do you not feel a conflict between your vows to heal and the requirement for a soldier that he must be prepared to kill?"

"Of course. I can't prevent the killing, but I can hope to comfort the wounded."

"Then we have much in common, you and I. But I am frightened of what may happen if the war comes here. I am afraid of what may happen to my church and my people. And I am very concerned for this tapestry. It is a fragile thing, some say woven in the fourteenth century. But no one knows for certain. It is of St. John the Divine. You can see he is writing the Book of Revelations."

"It's truly magnificent," said Pearson. "I have never seen anything like it. Perhaps, if the Germans come here, you should take it down and hide it somewhere safe."

Father Albert shrugged: "It will be difficult to find a safe place if there is much fighting."

They came out from the cool interior of the church to the sound of Jacques barking. The dog stood with his front feet on the seat, hackles raised at a small troop of British cavalry circling in the street, the horses hooves clattering on the paving stones. Agnès quietened the dog, and the cavalry trotted off, cheered by passers-by.

"18th Hussars," said Pearson as they got into the trap. "I wonder what they're up to."

"They are not from your camp ?"

"No. We have horses for some of the officers, but those aren't ours."

They drove out of the town and met a motor car coming at speed in the other direction, pulling a spiralling cloud of dust, a hint of red tabs on the occupants' uniforms.

"Staff officers," said Pearson. "Something's going on."

The road teemed with traffic, and they had to pull over frequently, with the pony mounting the verge, and the wheel of the trap falling into drainage gulleys.

"There is not usually so many people and horses," she said, and then added with a laugh: "No, that is wrong. There *are* not usually so many. You see, I have learned this."

"That is something else about you for me to love. That you are so quick to learn."

"I have a good teacher."

Alazard's stable was still empty when they returned to the house, and there was no sign of Mansell. Agnès backed the trap under cover and Pearson helped her unharness the pony. He led it into the stable and she gave it a net of hay and some fresh water, and threw a handful of corn to the waiting chickens.

He followed her up into the kitchen and called her so that she turned towards him. He put his fingers on the ribbon of her hat, undid it, and put the hat aside.

"You are so beautiful," he said quietly. He traced her lips with the tip of one finger. "May I, now we are not in the church?"

"Yes," she whispered.

He kissed her very softly on her lips and over her eyes, and then her mouth again, more firmly, and she swayed in towards him, holding him with her hands linked behind his neck. And after a little she put her hands on his arms, pushing him away.

"Yes," she said. "Yes, John. But not now, please. The others may return soon."

"Yes."

"You do not mind?"

"No, because you are right. Listen."

The horse came into the yard at the canter and they ran out to the top of the steps as Alazard dismounted, scattering the chickens.

"Mon Dieu," he said. "They have taken my school and now I've got the horse all lathered up."

49

"What has happened to the school, Papa?"

"It's to be the headquarters of the British army. A squadron of cavalry came into the town and their officer requisitioned my school. And then a motor car arrived with some more senior officers. They were polite, but very persuasive. Thank God the students are on holiday. Help me calm the horse."

The atmosphere at battalion headquarters that evening was rife with speculation. Donaldson, in his sing-song cadences, told Intelligence that Sir John French would advance to meet the expected German attack between Mons and Dinant, on the river Meuse. There was a rumour that French would set up his general headquarters in Le Cateau.

"I think I can confirm that," said Pearson.

"You seem unusually well informed for a doctor," said Anson. He sounded terse, as if military movements were not a matter for a medical officer.

Pearson shrugged. "I heard it from the teacher. They're taking over his school. It gave the poor man a frightful scare."

Hartwell stood up. "Gentlemen, we had better be ready for anything with GHQ down the road. I'd like to see all the company commanders before you go."

Pearson left the mess and walked back alone to his billet under the stars. The house was quiet, as if asleep. He could see no sign of Agnès or her father apart from an open bottle of brandy on the table. He left the lamp burning in the kitchen for Mansell, and went up to his room. He lit a candle, undressed, and lay on his bed listening to the silence of the night.

Friday 21 August 1914

When he awoke, Pearson looked out of his window and felt his heart leap at the sight of the trap in the cart lodge, swirling memories of Agnès from the previous day. The orchard trees stood in light mist, casting long shadows from the rising sun, with no breeze to stir their leaves. It was going to be another fine summer's day. He put on his uniform and looked at himself in the mirror, thinking how lucky he was to have been put in this house, with this lovely girl to share his breakfast.

He ran down the stairs and found her making coffee at the range. He went to her and she put down the coffee pot and took his hands. She wore a simple long sleeved white blouse and a cotton skirt that came to her ankles, and she had arranged her hair in the same way as on the first day they met; long, tied back with a ribbon. He kissed her, and she smelled of morning dew on roses and he felt his insides turn over with his longing. He brushed his fingers down the skin behind her ears and round her cheeks. There was no sign of Mansell.

"You smell of shaving soap," she said.

"It comes from a shop in London. It's frightfully expensive. A present from my mother. Is your father not awake yet?"

She shook her head. "He had a late night after you went upstairs." The cognac bottle, nearly empty, stood on the table.

"He should sleep well after that," Pearson said, pointing at the bottle.

"He was upset by them taking his school."

"I'm sorry they chose that building for their HQ."

"Actually, you know, I think he is quite proud in a way that they should choose his school. Does that seem strange to you?"

"No. And it will give him something to talk about when... when this is all over. But it will be annoying for him not to be able to work there."

"He says he will move his papers to the house of the woman I told you about."

" That seems a natural thing to do."

She looked at him with a smile. "Are you always so reasonable, John?"

"It's easy to be reasonable in the early morning, when the day is full of promise. You are as beautiful as I remember from my dreams."

"And you must have your coffee. Marie- Hélène will be here in a moment with the bread."

He sipped coffee, black and sweet, watching her, loving the way she moved and she came over to him to make a small adjustment to his tie and collar, standing close in front of him, in a moment of great intimacy. He breathed in her scent and listened to a light singing noise between his ears.

"If there is time," she said, "when you have finished your work, perhaps you will come with me in the trap. There is a pretty place by the river I would like you to see."

"I am sure there will be time. There is the resolution we made, remember."

At 'C' Company's trenches, the men had been digging hard since dawn, stripped to the waist and sweating. The front line had been deepened, with the addition of machine gun emplacements, and new soil heaped up on the revetement. The communication trench led rearwards to a second line of trenches, complete with dugouts. Pearson walked down the trench. The air there was cool from the damp walls of fresh dug earth. He tried not to think of it as a grave. The whole network seemed surprisingly permanent.

"It looks like you're planning on settling in for a while," he said to Mansell.

"Orders have changed. Since the GHQ rumour, we are now the defensive right flank."

"That sounds awfully important. I wondered why you

weren't at breakfast. Will you still want to do the exercise? Your men must have had enough."

"Oh, they're looking forward to it. The stretcher-bearers have been told, and I've detailed a couple of platoons to do the shooting. All we need are some casualties."

"I've volunteered Watson. I thought perhaps you might lend Phillips."

Pearson was hungry for lunch when he came in after the exercise. It had gone well and he felt like singing again. Watson and Phillips had entered into the spirit of the thing for all they were worth with shouts and curses emanating from deep scrub where they had hidden themselves.

The smell of roast chicken, as good as bacon frying, wafted through the canteen. He sat with Mansell and Pollock, one of the platoon commanders, in the shade of an oak tree, and listened to bugles down the line, bringing men to their meal.

"Bravo, Doctor. That went well," Mansell told him. "Your casualties were superb. Very vocal too."

"You heard that?"

"Couldn't help it. The rich language of Hampshire."

"I liked the bit with the Lewis guns shooting up the trees, and all those bits of branches and stuff flying around," said Pollock. "Very realistic smoke, too. Whose idea was it to block the trench like that?"

"Mine," said Mansell. "I wanted them to see what happens when you can't get wounded men away quickly. For stretcher-bearers to come out into the open like that would have been suicidal. You've got to have enough room to work stretchers round all the corners. And keep your head down at the same time."

"I think they got the point," Pollock said. "Incidentally, who found the chickens?"

"One of the cooks. Thompson. He's made friends with a woman in the village. A farmer's wife. She's taken a shine to him."

"*Vive le sport.* I hope the farmer hasn't noticed."

"If he has, Thompson might find himself head down in a water butt."

"I'm giving 'C' Company a half holiday this afternoon," said Mansell at the end of lunch. "They've done bloody well here since we set up camp."

Pearson stretched, stifling a yawn. "I'll tell Watson to. I think I might, too."

"With that pretty girl?"

"She wants to show me a place up the river."

Mansell laughed, his black eyes twinkling: "Make the most of it while you've got the chance." He gestured round the table. "It can't last like this you know."

Pearson left the camp and hitched a lift back to his billet on a motor lorry taking supplies through to GHQ in Le Cateau. Alazard's horse and the pony both had their heads out over the stable doors. He stroked the pony's ears and put his face to the powder puff skin of its nose. Jacques came trotting across the yard and Pearson followed him through the rose hedge into the orchard. The trees were well cared for and heavy with fruit, some already ripe.

He saw her at the far side, in open ground beyond the apple trees, gathering mushrooms into a fold of her apron, holding it up with one hand. She looked up as he came to her, and the distance between them evaporated. He put his arms round her, and she said: "If you do that you will break all the mushrooms."

"It's because they are between us. I don't want anything to come between us."

He helped her for a while, picking mushrooms and placing them in her apron.

"I've taken the afternoon off," he said. "Will you show me the river?"

"Yes. We can go now if you like."

"Is your father here? I saw his horse in the stable."

"No. He went to the school. An officer took him in a motor car. He has gone to tidy his things there to prepare for your army."

"They sent a car for him?"

She shrugged, an expression of resignation: "I think they wanted to make sure he would do it quickly."

"If he were here, would he mind us going out in the trap together? Going to the river?"

Agnès laughed and put a hand on his cheek. "No, he does not mind. He likes you. And I have told him that you make me happy. There is something else, too." She brushed her hair back behind her ear. "I believe he thinks it will be easier for me to accept his woman if he allows me to be with you."

They walked together back to the house and she put the mushrooms in the cool. Pearson went up to his room to change. He took off his uniform and put on a pair of grey flannel trousers, an open neck cotton shirt with long sleeves, and an old corduroy jacket. He rummaged in his wardrobe and pulled out a tweed cap that he wore for shooting.

She looked at him, smiling, when he came back to her. "This is the first time you are not in uniform," she said.

"Do you still like me? Some girls are supposed to be attracted to a uniform."

"Come here and let me see."

She looked closely at him, dark eyes searching, and kissed him.

"It is all right," she said with mock relief. "It is the same man under the clothes."

Houses along the street seemed to crouch in the heat, their shutters closed, burnished under the weight of the sun pressing down from a cloudless sky. She turned off the street onto a track that Pearson had not noticed before, winding through vegetable gardens, out into the fields. Cut corn stood in stooks, and they passed a horse-drawn wagon with men loading sheaves with pitchforks. Cornflowers, darker than the sky, grew from uncut headlands of the fields.

The track descended to lower pastures, fenced against cattle, where the grasses at the side grew long, ablaze with other flowers that Pearson could not name. They drove down into the valley, deep into the green womb of France, through a plantation of poplar trees, high pruned in rows, like the nave of a cathedral, casting cool shade.

The river lay beyond a narrow strip of meadow from which hay had been taken, the new grass fresh and green. Agnès left the pony tied in the shade of a willow and took Pearson by the hand, leading him by a little-used footpath to the water's edge, where a big pool curled on a bend of the river, fringed with reeds and water plants and yellow water lilies, open to the sun. The path led to a wooden jetty where a boat floated at the end of a short rope.

It was a secret place, screened on three sides by reeds and, on the far side, beyond the lilies, by thick woodland. Blue damselflies hovered over water weed at the edge of the pool and the current flowed deep and slow.

"It is my father's boat," she said. "He comes here sometimes to fish."

"I would like to do that one day," said Pearson.

"You are a fisherman too?"

"I like very much to fish."

They stepped onto the narrow planks of the jetty. Through gin-clear water, the bottom showed until it shelved steeply away, lost in the depths.

"I fish at home," he said, thinking of the Test. "It is a different sort of river, shallow and fast-running, perhaps a bit manicured."

"Manicured? That is a surprising thing to do to a river."

He laughed: "It is done by the water bailiffs. They look after the banks of the river so that fishermen can cast without getting the fly caught up in the long grass." He mimed casting with a fly rod.

"That will be for the trouts?"

"For the trouts, yes." It was not an afternoon for exercises

56

in grammar.

"There are some trouts in the small streams higher up." She pointed to low hills in the north. "But this river is not suitable for them. Here there are carps and perch and...we call them '*brochet*'."

"Pike. *Quenelles de brochet*."

"You know this dish?"

"Yes," he laughed. "It isn't one of my favourites. But perch are very good to eat. I have eaten them cooked straight from the water, on a grill over a fire. Perhaps with some herbs too, if you have any, and a lemon."

They returned to the river bank and he took off his jacket so that she could sit down. She removed her hat and shook out her hair, and he sat beside her.

"I should have brought a rod with us," she said. "I did not know you are a fisherman and a cook."

"I don't need to fish. It's so lovely here, and peaceful. Perhaps we can come again another time to fish when the war is over."

"I do not want to think about the war today." She lay back, her head on the grass, with her eyes closed against the sun.

"No. No war today."

He found a feather and stroked it against her cheek and over her eyelids, looking down at the smooth skin of her face and throat. A pulse was beating there, showing its rhythm through the skin and, from habit, he picked up her wrist to check her heartbeat. She was so beautiful, lying still, her stomach flat and the rise of her breasts swelling under her blouse.

"Will I live?" she asked dreamily.

"It's difficult to say without some further examination."

She lay quietly, smiling, her eyes still closed, and the sunlight on her eyelids darkened as his shadow fell across her face. He kissed her lips, wondering if he dared explore a little, and put his hand on her breast, tracing its fullness as she rolled against him, holding him tight, pressing her mouth to his. He lay beside her on the grass, cradling her head on his shoulder, his hand caressing her chin and her throat.

Small clouds had come up with the afternoon, floating high above in the blue sky. She held up her free hand and watched the clouds drifting slowly past her fingers.

"If you were a painter, how would you paint those clouds?" she asked.

He studied them, as if seeing clouds for the first time, and said: "I would put some white paint on the blue, and mix the colours a little at the edges."

"But do you think the clouds are really white? Look at that one. It is darker underneath, so you would need some other colour."

"Yes...I would have to put some grey there."

"The darker is in shadow. The shadow made by the top of the cloud taking the sunlight."

"You are not only very beautiful. You are also a teacher. Perhaps you get it from your father." His hand played with the collar of her blouse.

"Perhaps. But you must tell me how you are going to put grey into the cloud."

"I will mix a little black with the white. That will make it grey."

"But that sort of grey will not sing. You can make warm greys with red and blue added to the white. Or a little yellow ochre to cool the colour."

"How do you know all this?"

"Because I studied painting at school. Henri Matisse was born in Le Cateau. Do you know his work?"

"No." He fumbled with the top button of her blouse. "But I have heard of him."

"He is one of the *Fauves.*"

"And what is a *Fauve*?"

She laughed happily. "It means a wild beast."

"That's a strange way to describe a painter." The button of the blouse did not undo easily, so he moved his hand to her breast again.

"It is because they use colour as it has not been used before. The paintings are alive and free."

"Then I am sure I would like them because they would remind me of you."

" You are a difficult man to teach, John Pearson. You do not take it seriously enough." She turned her head and nuzzled his ear with her teeth.

"It is hard to be serious if you do that. And the sun is too warm."

"We could swim if you like."

"In the river?"

"Of course. I come here often to swim when it is hot like now."

"Well, I …it would be lovely, but I haven't brought my..."

"And nor have I." She sat up laughing, looking into his eyes. "I always swim with nothing on. No one ever comes here. And if they did, Jacques would let me know."

Pearson felt as if he were weightless, floating on air, lifted suddenly to a life that could not really exist. Yet there was a girl beside him who rose to her feet on the grass and began to undress, smiling at him as she did so, holding his eyes in a wonderful mixture of challenge and encouragement. He felt a pulse beating rapidly somewhere between his ears, and pulled off his boots and socks. Agnès stood naked before him, dappled shade from a poplar tree making a pattern of light and dark across her body, her eyes still watching his.

Astonished, he got to his feet to pull off his trousers, stumbling off balance when one of his feet caught in his braces, and she came to help him remove his shirt. He wanted to speak to her, to say everything that was in his heart and his head, but she put a finger to his lips, turned away, and stepped quickly onto the jetty, leaving him with a fleeting impression of her hair swirling across her breasts, and a dark ' V' below her belly.

For a second she stood, silhouetted against the dancing

sunlight reflected from the water, her feet tight together and the light shining through little gaps between her legs, at her ankles, her knees, and at the top of her thighs. He watched her spring into the air and dive into the river. Ripples spread across the pool, reaching the water lilies on the far side , making their yellow flower heads bob up and down. Pearson ran onto the jetty and dived in. The water was warm as milk on the surface, with cold patches deeper where they trod water together, laughing, unashamed in their nakedness.

"Always before, when I have swum here, I have been alone," she said. "It is lovely to swim alone, but better that you are here with me." She kissed him quickly. He felt the cool of the water from her lips.

"I had forgotten how it feels to swim naked," he said. " I have not swum like this since I was a small boy."

"It is better, don't you think?"

"This is so different. I can feel the water over all my skin. It's like swimming in silk."

"It is how it should be. With nature. How well can you see without your spectacles?"

"Well enough to see that you are very beautiful. Really, they are for long distance."

"So you can see me clearly now?"

"Yes, but even better when you come close, like this."

"Like that I think perhaps we would drown."

"'That I may drown in thee.'" He sang, watching her hair, fascinated, where it flowed over her breasts in the water.

"That is a song?"

"It's part of a madrigal. He is singing to her because he is in love."

She moved away from him a little, floating on her back, making small movements with her hands to hold her position. He could see her toes and her nipples awash, and her chin held up, her head well back in the water. She began to sing in a clear soprano voice, the sound lifting over the reeds, up into the trees.

"Plaisir d'amour, ne dure qu'un moment.
Chagrin d'amour dure toute la vie..."

He swam to her and held her as if he were a life saver, with her head up on his chest, her back against his belly.

"I know that tune," he said. "But I have not heard it in French. In the English version the pain only lasts a whole night, not all your life."

"Then I think it is better in English. I do not want to have pain all my life."

"I couldn't bear to cause you pain."

"You will not be able to prevent it, John."

"You believe the song?"

"I know it is right. I feel the pain already a little."

"For me it is not yet a pain. It is like a lightness in my body, as if everything has left me except my soul. I am living outside myself. Does that sound ridiculous to you?"

"No. But I think it is the beginning of pain. Someone told me that song was written over a hundred years ago."

"And you tell me this while we swim naked in a river?"

"I am telling you because it helps me keep things in perspective."

"There is a problem with perspective," he laughed. "With true perspective the lines never meet. We would always be apart." With unimaginable courage, he cupped her buttocks in his hand.

"And if you do that," she said, "we will definitely drown." A light breeze stirred the treetops, rustling the leaves, satin against fine paper, and brought a faint fragrance of balsam from the poplars.

When they came to the jetty, she climbed out, lithe and graceful as a panther, and he followed her, drinking in the beauty of her movement. She was like pale honey, all over her body in contrast to the stark whiteness of his own skin. She bent to gather up her clothes and he examined the linc of her vertebrae where they disappeared into the spread of her hips. She stood with her back to him and he watched as she

61

struggled to pull the clothes over her wet body. The thin cotton stuck to her skin.

He put on his underpants and trousers and made her sit down on his coat and he knelt at her side, stroking back her wet hair and kissing her ear. They lay back together on the grass, drying in the sun, and he ran his hand over her breasts, feeling her nipples hardening through the material of her blouse.

Later, when her hair had dried, he stood behind her at the water's edge, holding her to him, one hand under the swell of her breasts, the other at the top of her thighs. She leaned back against him, her head under his chin, and he could smell the river in her hair, feel the warmth from her body. He closed his eyes and the lightness came to him again, in a wave so that he thought they might fly together.

He began to sing to her, and as soon as he started she joined in:

"Plaisir d'amour, ne dure qu'un moment.
Chagrin d'amour dure toute la vie..."

He could feel the resonance of her voice blending with his as he held her in his arms, and he knew for certain that, whatever might happen in the clamour of the coming war, his life had been changed for ever. In the trap on the way back to the village she pressed herself against him, as if they were one.

Saturday 22 August 1914

Pearson sat in his pyjamas, writing, when Agnès knocked on his door. As he rose to meet her, she put a jug of hot water on the floor, and he took her in his arms, feeling her warm and lissom under his hands.

"I could not sleep last night," she said. "I wanted to see you when you got back from the mess." She stroked the light stubble of his chin.

He shook his head: "It was very late. I wanted to see you, too. The lamp had gone out when we got home and I thought you would be asleep. And I was frightened I might wake your father. The colonel held a meeting of all the officers after dinner. There has been some fighting on the border." He felt her stiffen against him, and saw the fear in her eyes.

"Some of our cavalry were involved," he told her. "It's all very uncertain, and I love you more than I can say."

"I have been saying it all night."

"Tell me how you said it."

"Que je t'adore. Comme je t'adore."

She looked up at him and he saw there were tears in her eyes. He wiped them away, very gently, with his thumbs.

"I have been saying it too, but it isn't so good in English."

"Say it to me, please."

He told her and she stood back a little, drying her eyes with a handkerchief. "It is good enough for me, if you say it like that. Now, you must use this while it is still hot."

She picked up the jug, carried it over to the corner of the room, and put it on the table beside the mirror so that the steam would not rise over the glass.

Pearson took off his pyjama top and began to shave, working a thick lather of soap onto his face. She came to stand behind him, kneading the muscles of his shoulders with her fingers, watching his eyes in the mirror.

"I do not want to hear if the fighting has started with your soldiers," she said. "It makes me very frightened for us."

"It frightens me, too."

He rested his hands on the edge of the basin, holding the razor, their eyes still meeting in the mirror. She leaned on his back.

"Why have you stopped?" she asked.

"It's the first time I have shaved in front of a girl," he said. "And I prefer to look at you." He began to shave again.

Agnès laughed, and kissed the back of his neck: "I used to watch my father shave sometimes when I was a little girl, but it was not the same as this. This is much more fun."

"I wish I could have known you as a little girl," he said, working the razor round his top lip, stretching the skin tight.

"Why do men make faces like that when they are shaving? My father used to do that."

"I expect he still does."

"Yes, but you have not said why."

"To hold the skin tight. You cannot shave close if the skin is all loose." He opened his mouth, stretching the skin tight across his teeth. "Like this you can shave very close, if the blade is sharp."

"But you cannot talk properly with your face like that," she giggled into his shoulder.

"I don't normally talk much when I am shaving."

"And I am talking too much. I must go and prepare the breakfast."

She raked her fingernails down his back and round his belly, under the cord of his pyjamas.

"If you do that," he said, "no one is going to get any breakfast."

He finished shaving when she had gone, and put on his breeches and his service dress tunic, checking his tie in the mirror. He sat on the edge of his bed to pull on his leather boots which Watson had polished like glass. He thought of the reports of fighting. It might only have been a skirmish between cavalry patrols, but it could surely only develop into something worse. And if the Germans launched an all out attack, it seemed likely that the relatively small number of British infantry would be pushed back.

He wished fervently that Le Cateau were further away, safer from a sudden German advance. The thought of enemy troops infiltrating Bazuel and spreading through the surrounding countryside turned his stomach sour. What on earth could he do to protect Agnès and her father? A sense of panic seized him. His duty lay with the battalion but his desire urged him to think of Agnès. What would Alazard do if the Germans came? Surely he would run, taking Agnès with him to safety? He had better talk quietly with Alazard, he thought. He couldn't say much, but just enough to find out what the man was thinking. Thank God the schools were on holiday, so at least he wouldn't have his pupils to worry about. But what about Alazard's woman? He could hardly ask him about her. He didn't even know her name, and perhaps it was better not to. But if she wanted to stay and take her chance, what would Alazard do then? Would he stay in Le Cateau with her? Perhaps with his brother, too, in the hospital? And might Agnès run on her own?

He fought down the panic in his head, trying to think of a way to take Agnès with him if the battalion withdrew. God, he thought, you can't do that. You can't have officers sheltering their lovers on a retreat under fire. It was impossible to contemplate, and anyway it would be absurd to subject French civilians to a danger probably far greater than they would face staying behind under an occupying army. But what might happen to a beautiful young woman with an invading army strutting about, looking to taste the spoils of victory? There were rumours of German behaviour with the civilian population in Belgium that he would rather not have heard.

He stood up and strode across to the window. The chickens were pecking frantically at their food, scratching in the dust. She must have just been there to feed them. He saw Phillips ride into the yard leading another horse, and tie them to metal rings on the stable wall. Mansell must have obtained them from the pool at headquarters, he thought.

He heard Mansell bang his bedroom door shut and clump down the stairs in his boots. Mansell wouldn't panic. All right, Mansell had not fallen in love with a French girl, but he would have other things to worry about, and anyway, he was a professional army officer, and not a medical volunteer.

He had better pull himself together, he thought, and not show them he was scared stiff. And he was scheduled to give a lecture to some of the men from 'A' Company in the morning. Perhaps the trouble in Belgium would trump that, but he had better be prepared anyway. He checked his appearance in the mirror. Everything seemed reasonably normal, so he went down to breakfast, leaving his misgivings in his room.

Agnès came out into the yard to see them off. With Watson holding one of the horses, Pearson adjusted the stirrups. He wanted desperately to talk to Agnès but it was difficult with Mansell and the two batmen working round the horses. He caught her eye and she came close to him as he was preparing to mount. He held the reins in his left hand and turned to her.

"Take care on your horse," she said quietly.

He knew that she was thinking of her mother. "I haven't got far to go," he said. "Just to the camp, and back again this evening."

"Perhaps you will be able to dine with us here tonight?" she asked.

"I'll try. But if it's not possible tonight, then I will make it so tomorrow."

He put his left foot in the stirrup and swung up into the saddle. The horse fidgeted, its hooves scraping the gravel. He wheeled about and, with Mansell, rode out onto the road. In the gateway, he looked back and saw Agnès standing proud and erect, watching them. He touched the peak of his hat with his cane, and she made a small movement of acknowledgement with her hand.

It felt good to have a horse under him again. The saddle creaked and he breathed in the smell of leather and horse sweat. "How did you find these mounts?" he asked Mansell.

"Phillips told me about them. He's pretty good at horses. Should have been in a cavalry regiment really. He thought they would be useful, to save time getting out to the camp. You look as if you ride a bit?"

"Not a lot now, but I've done it all my life."

"I've never done much," said Mansell. He tipped his hat back over his bushy hair. "Always felt like a sack of potatoes on a horse. My wife likes it but I belong to the 'dangerous at both ends and uncomfortable in the middle' school. But I thought Phillips would be rather disappointed if I turned them down. What are you on today?"

"Sick parade and a quick look round the kitchens. Then I'm giving a lecture to the men on hygiene, and the importance of avoiding VD. I'm starting with some of 'A' Company. If anyone turns up, and if it goes all right, I'm going to work through the whole battalion."

Mansell laughed: "Oh, they'll turn up all right if you make it nice and juicy. Anson will bully them into it anyway. He's keen on a spot of personal hygiene. It was pretty hot and sticky under those uniforms on the veldt."

"I hope he won't try to bully me."

"Don't let him rattle you, and you'll be fine."

They rode past battalion headquarters at the farmhouse, and joined a throng of traffic on the road out to the camp. Several platoons marched along the roadside, and other groups worked in the adjacent stubble fields, volunteered by their company commanders to help with bringing in the harvest.

"Look," said Mansell. "There's some of my lot." The men attacked sheaves of wheat with pitchforks, as if undergoing bayonet training, and hurled them up to French labourers on the wagon, cheering each other on with wild cries. "There's a practical demonstration of the '*entente cordiale*' for you."

"They might be doing it for real soon, do you think?" said Pearson.

"It's bound to come. You've heard that the Germans have counter-attacked in Alsace?"

"Yes."

"The French have been forced to give ground. They'll be back on the Moselle before long. And God knows what's happening in our sector up on the Belgian border."

"The RFC must know something," said Pearson.

"Not a thing. They were grounded by low mist yesterday, and when they did get up later, a couple of their aeroplanes were shot up. The poor sods had to come down the wrong side of the lines. Incidentally, how's your pretty girl?"

"I am afraid I have very much fallen for her."

"You don't need to sound so solemn about it."

Pearson brought his horse close alongside Mansell's. "It's just that I'm worried sick about what might happen to her if the Germans break out and overwhelm us."

"Well, for a start it's not at all certain that that will happen. It's on the cards of course, but they would get plenty of warning. There would be time to run."

"I'm not sure she would want to leave. There's her uncle too, at the hospital. I think he would probably stay, and her father. She wouldn't run on her own. And there's nothing I can do to take her with us if we have to retreat." He looked across at Mansell, hoping that he might somehow contradict him.

But Mansell shook his head. "No," he said. "I'm afraid there's nothing."

The men from 'A' Company waited in the shade for Pearson's first lecture. He had rehearsed his talk frequently in his mind, and he stood, comfortable and relaxed before them. It would be good to do the lecture, he thought, to take his mind off his worries.

"Please sit down, and smoke if you wish," he began.

Away from the heat of the day, the men were happy to have escaped from the training ground. They sat on the hard, dry earth or leaned against tree trunks, under the watchful eyes of their NCOs. The sound of small arms practice carried from the far side of the wood, reminding them that the business of war was not far away. Horses whinnied from the lines in the low ground.

Pearson smiled at the rows of faces in front of him and began: "I expect you all know the old saying, 'Cleanliness is next to Godliness.' I am not going to lecture you about your souls. That's the chaplain's job. But the thing I want you to remember about cleanliness is that it can make the difference between whether you live or die. There were two men at sick parade this morning with the runs. Not life-threatening perhaps, but a soldier can't shoot properly if he has to keep taking down his trousers."

Laughter ran through the audience.

"The point is," Pearson continued, "that when the shooting starts, our chances of survival are going to be much greater if we are healthy. The men with the runs probably drank contaminated water. There's no excuse for that here in the camp. Please remember only to drink water that has come from the regimental water carts. That will be fresh and clean. Tell your friends about this. It's very important.

"Now, lice. Some of you, particularly if you were in South Africa, will have met these little nippers. For those of you who haven't, here's a brief description. A louse is a small wingless insect, with a flat body, up to an eighth of an inch long." Pearson held out his hand showing a small gap between his thumb and forefinger. "He lives in your clothing, and lays eggs there, close to your skin, and when he gets hungry, he comes out and feeds off your body. He will make you itch like hell and scratch yourself sore. But the thing about body lice is that they don't like clean clothes. The dirtier and smellier you are, the more they will like you, so try to change your clothes as often as your mother would make you back at home."

Renewed laughter rang out, but Pearson held up a hand and the men fell quiet, alert and interested.

"It won't be as easy to change your undies when we are in action as it is here. Some of you will inevitably get lice, but do the best you can and remember that the little blighters die if you can wash your clothes in very hot water. Or burn them, if you think the quartermaster isn't looking." He raised his hand again to silence them.

"There's another sort of lice that you may meet up with if you are foolish enough to get involved with ladies of the night. I'm talking about pubic lice, otherwise known as crabs. They have little claws with which they cling to pubic hair, and are spread through sexual contact. On very hairy men you might find them on anal hair or even, God help you, in your beard, if you have been engaging in, ah, below the belt manoeuvres."

A riot of hoots and catcalls broke out, and Pearson quelled them again with his hand. "On second thoughts," he said, "that last remark is more applicable to the Navy."

More laughter followed and Pearson thought he had better try to keep this a bit more serious. It was not, after all, a joking matter. He remembered attending lectures at medical school. Some had literally bored him to sleep, but the best ones had always been those where the scientific dough had been leavened with a little light-hearted yeast. He looked at his watch. He had better get on, he thought, wondering what Agnès would be doing. A sudden thought struck him. What on earth would she think of what he had been saying to these men sitting on the ground around him, listening with appreciation to his talk?

He cleared his throat and began again. "If you think you've got pubic lice, you had better come to see me but remember that with all these things prevention is much better than a painful cure. The same goes for VD. And you all know how to avoid that, I hope.

"Syphilis and gonorrhoea are both spread, almost exclusively, by sexual contact. Not by sitting on lavatory seats. If you get VD it means you've been a naughty boy. Syphilis is caused by bacteria penetrating broken skin or mucous membranes in or around your genitals. You can catch it from kissing, too. What is the risk? About a thirty percent chance in just one contact with an infected person. Symptoms? You have to wait a bit for these to appear. Three to four weeks is the normal incubation time and then quarter inch sores appear.

"Now, these sores will heal in a month or so and you may think that's that. But, no, it isn't. You will be entering the secondary stage." He paused, noting that he had the full attention of his audience. "Stage two rears its ugly head with a conspicuous skin rash, with round pink spots. Headaches, loss of appetite, fever, fatigue, hair falling out in clumps. That sort of thing. The third stage can take years to develop, and involves tissue destruction of the palate, nose, and tongue. Finally you may fall victim to brain damage and paralysis. Any questions so far?"

An arm was raised, with a sergeant's three stripes: "Excuse me, sir. What is the cure for this? Er, the men will want to know." A titter of nervous laughter ran through the audience.

"I am sure they will," said Pearson. "The fact is that until very recently there was no effective cure. A few years ago a German scientist started experimenting with various arsenic compounds on rats which had been infected with syphilis bacteria. At first all he did was kill the wretched rats, but eventually he found the right formula. This stuff has been used on humans, and some have been completely cured. Others have not, so it is by no means foolproof.

"Now, before I finish, a word about gonorrhoea. You have all heard of the 'clap'. This is quite different from syphilis, except in the ways you catch it. The incubation period is very short – from as little as two to ten days. How do know if you've got it? It will hurt like mad to pee, and there will be a nasty discharge.

"It's a horrid disease and the only cure I know is a series of painful injections of mercury into the tip of the penis. I can see that some of you are looking pale suddenly, and I would just remind you again that prevention is better than cure. The best way to be absolutely certain of avoiding VD is to keep your dick inside your trousers. Thank you very much for your attention, and if there are any further questions..."

"Thank you for your little talk," Anson said to him later. A heavy sneer of sarcasm in his voice made Pearson turn to look at him. Anson stood with his legs apart, his hands clasped behind his back. "I hear you're a showman."

"Well, I wanted to make it a bit light-hearted for them."

"Trying to curry favour?"

"No. I thought it would make them listen better. They would probably lose interest without the odd joke."

"See yourself as a psychiatrist, do you?" His jaw jutted at Pearson.

"No, I..."

"Look, Pearson. You're new here. You don't need to fanny about with my men. Hygiene is an important matter. I've seen the need for it in action. Don't do the comic bit. Just give it to them straight. They'll respect you better. It's like at school. Some masters had the knack and others hadn't a clue, riots all round the classroom. Soldiers are like schoolboys. They know they can get away with murder with one officer but wouldn't dare try it on with the next." He waved a forefinger under Pearson's nose. "You need to toughen up or they'll run rings round you. They aren't like a bunch of medical students. You understand what I'm saying?"

"Well..."

"Think about it. You'll be in the mess tonight? There are all sorts of rumours coming in from the border."

"I was thinking of having a quiet night in my billet."

"God, don't tell me you're a mummy's boy. You can do that another night. Tonight you might learn what it's like to be in a war. The colonel was called into GHQ today so something's up. And the Squeaker will be there too."

"The Squeaker?"

"Donaldson. The Intelligence officer. Voice like a girl's."

Pearson rode back alone to Bazuel on a road more crowded than ever with military traffic, and farm carts loaded high from the harvest fields. It was a strange mix, he thought, to see the everyday life of a farming community going on side by side with the activities of a foreign army. He must not, he knew, allow himself to be rattled by Anson. Mansell had warned him. The man was obviously a bully. Anson had the habit of leaning forward when he spoke, bunching his shoulders like a prize fighter, as if preparing to take a swing at an adversary. Anson might be a bully, but Pearson had quickly come to the opinion that Anson was the sort of bully that was unlikely to back off in a confrontation. He was debating this as he rode past the butcher's shop and heard the sounds of a small boy crying. The boy was surrounded by a crowd of villagers, and clutched his right hand in front of him, one finger sticking out at an angle. A woman held him to her while berating another boy. Pearson stopped his horse and looked down into the crowd.

"May I help? I am a doctor."

The woman looked at him with suspicion. "A doctor, in the English army?"

"Yes. What has happened here?"

"My son was kicked by the boy there, and he has broken his finger. They are always fighting."

"It was not a real fight," said the other boy. "We were just playing. I didn't mean to hurt him."

"It hurts," wailed the boy with the finger, "and it is broken."

"It is always the same with boys," said the butcher from his doorway.

"Can someone hold my horse, while I look at his hand?" said Pearson, dismounting.

"Give me the horse," said the butcher. "I will tie her to the ring there. Sylvie, show him the boy's hand."

"Monsieur is the boy's father?" Pearson asked him.

"*Bien sûr*. As far as I know."

Laughter ran round the crowd and Sylvie brought the child to Pearson.

"What is your name?" Pearson asked him.

"Jean," said the boy, between sobs.

"That is my name, too." He squatted down, to the same level as the boy. "Now, Jean, let me see." He took the hand and examined it. Onlookers crowded round, curious to observe the English doctor at work. He looked up at Sylvie, still holding Jean's hand. "It is not broken, Madame..."

"But certainly it is broken," she shouted. "You are a doctor and you cannot see that it is broken?"

Pearson stood up, facing her. "The finger is not broken, Madame. It is dislocated. The joint in the middle of the finger is dislocated. It is not at all the same thing. A dislocation is simple to put right."

"So I didn't break it," said the other boy cheerily.

"No," said Pearson, "but it is painful. You should be more careful in future." He turned to Sylvie. "Perhaps we can take Jean indoors and I will fix the finger for him."

In the back room, Pearson said quietly to Sylvie: "This will be quick, but there will be some pain. You must trust me. I have done this small thing many times."

"It is not so small for Jean. It is the first time he has broken anything."

"It is not broken. I have already explained this."

"It is most painful," said Jean. "Even if it is not broken." He held up his hand. The finger stuck out at a sharp angle. "Anyway it looks as if it is broken."

74

Pearson held the boy's elbow. " Now, Jean. You are a brave boy, I think. Perhaps even more brave than your father?"

Jean looked up at him, smiling for the first time. "My father is a brave man. He is afraid of nothing. Not even my mother."

"Good boy. Now, I have to straighten your finger again. It is a simple thing to do but it will hurt for a little while I do it. Afterwards it will be as normal. I will be as gentle as possible, because I am a little frightened of your mother."

"That is as it should be," said Sylvie. "My son is very valuable to me."

"Give me your hand again, Jean," said Pearson. He took the boys hand. It was small and warm like a little animal. "What is your favourite pastime?"

"Skating on the river when it's frozen over in winter," Jean told him.

"But it's summer now. What do you like to do in summer?"

"I like to walk by the river and think how it will be in the winter."

"Then think of the river in winter." He held the boy's hand, and with great care, took hold of the finger. "Think of ice on the river, and you are on the bank wondering if the ice is thick enough yet to bear you, and you put one foot on the ice and lean out. Then you put the other foot there too, and when there is no sound of cracking, you know the ice is thick enough so you can skate and..." he pulled the finger in a long smooth movement, and the boy cried out briefly with the shock of it, and the finger was straight again.

Jean held up his hand to his mother. "Look," he said in wonder. "And it really did not hurt at all."

"I am sorry I doubted you," Sylvie said. "I should have had more faith. Thank you for helping us."

"It's nothing," said Pearson. "It must be strange for you to have your village full of British soldiers. I am afraid we must

75

be an awful nuisance."

"I find it exciting," said Jean. "Yesterday the cavalry were here, and big guns. May I go outside again to play, Maman?"

"It would be better not to play at catching balls," Pearson called to him. "It will take a little time to settle."

"Thank you, Monsieur. I am going to be a doctor when I grow up."

"Is that better than being a soldier?"

"Oh yes. There are lots of soldiers but not so many doctors. I think it is more special to be a doctor. Au revoir, Monsieur."

"You have other children?" Pearson asked her when Jean had gone.

"Two boys. The elder is already in the army. In Alsace. The other is seventeen. He is helping with the harvest now but I think the army will take him too. It is no time to be a mother with sons."

"I am afraid that is what my mother thinks too."

"And you have brothers?"

"Yes. One. But he is still a boy, like Jean. So he will be safe."

She shook her head. "No one is safe here. Belgium is not far away and my husband says we will not be able to stop the Germans if they attack us. How can we stop them? There is nothing, no natural barrier. It is open country, with fields and small woods."

"It is not so easy to attack across open country. There is no cover, and they will be easy targets for our rifles and machine guns."

"Do you believe that, really?"

"Perhaps not all of it. Tell me, if the Germans come, will your family stay here ? You have some relatives to go to?"

"Marcel would never leave his home. No. If the Germans come we will stay and make the best of it. If we left this house, what would become of it?"

Pearson straightened his hat. What indeed would become

of their house, he wondered? He said goodbye to her, and in the shop the butcher caught him by the arm.

"Thank you, Doctor. My son is a lucky boy. I have wrapped a shoulder of lamb for you. It's a little gift."

"But really there is no need..."

"Tomorrow is Sunday. You are lodged with Monsieur Alazard? Agnès is a good customer here. She will be happy if you take this home." He pressed the parcel into Pearson's hands. "I have kept an eye on your horse. It is good for my business if people think the English army come here for meat. Excusez-moi, Monsieur. I must attend to my other customers. Au revoir."

Pearson put the meat into a bag behind his saddle and rode off up the street. He hoped Agnès would like it. The butcher would know she had not yet bought meat.

He felt strangely relieved that Sylvie had told him they would not leave the house if the Germans came. There were already rumours of refugees flooding out of Belgium. And if the worst were to happen in Bazuel, and if Agnès and her father stayed, then it would surely be easier for them all if there were enough people left for them to be able to comfort each other.

In the yard, Pearson left Watson to deal with the horse, and ran up the stone steps with Jaques sniffing the parcel in his hand. Mansell sat at the table in the kitchen with Alazard and Agnès, drinking vin de noix. She rose to meet him. She had tied her hair up, exposing the full line of her neck. He wished very much that the others were not there.

"Good evening, mon Capitaine," she said in mock seriousness. "You have had a busy day?"

"Busy enough, and too much talking. This is for you, for the house." He gave her the parcel.

"What is it?" said Agnès. "It looks like the wrapping paper from the butcher."

"It's a shoulder of lamb. A present from Marcel."

"Marcel", she said, laughing, mimicking his accent. "You

have made friends with Marcel Boulanger?"

"His boy dislocated a finger, and I fixed it for him."

"And he gave you this in payment?" she held out the parcel.

"I would have refused but he was very persuasive. He said you would like it. Because it's Sunday tomorrow."

"You must have been very good with Jean," said Agnès. Her eyes were unfathomable pools. "Marcel is not known for his generosity."

"Marcel is so tight they say his head squeaks," said Alazard. "But it is very nice of him to give us some lamb." He stood up and walked over to the window, standing with his back to them. "Major Mansell has been telling us that things are not going well in Alsace, and that fighting has started on the border with Belgium." He swung round to face them again. "I do not like the sound of this at all."

"No," said Pearson. He looked at Agnès, wishing he did not have to say this. "The colonel has been at GHQ this afternoon. We'll hear about it tonight. I am afraid it may be bad news."

"And you should be there to hear it?" she asked, holding his gaze.

"I think so."

"We will all need to be there. All the officers," said Mansell.

"Yes," she said, standing close in front of Pearson so that he could smell the sweetness of the wine on her breath. "You must go to the meeting and tomorrow you can tell us what is going to happen."

**** ****

Fine drizzle fell from a still sky as Pearson walked back up the village street with Mansell after the meeting. The atmosphere at dinner had been subdued, quiet voices talking over the chink of cutlery, and Hartwell's talk did nothing to lift their spirits. They picked their way up the road, avoiding gullies seeping with the smell of drains.

"What did you make of all that?" Pearson asked.

"I had the impression that Hartwell was treading carefully. Anson knows Smith-Dorrien, and he says the meeting at GHQ must have been explosive."

"The general losing his wick?"

"Almost certainly. Apparently Hartwell was pretty tight-lipped when he was dropped off at the farmhouse. He's far too loyal to say anything of course, but reading between the lines, I should think headquarters morale is pretty low."

"Who'd be a general, eh?"

"Not me, if the balloon goes up." He chuckled and took hold of Pearson's arm. "You had better sharpen your knives, old man. You may be using them before long."

They closed the heavy wooden entrance doors of the gateway behind them and went into the yard. A smell of fresh horse manure and hay hung in the air, and in the dim light they could make out the shadowy shape of heads looking over the stable doors. A faint glow of light came from the window of the loft. Watson and Phillips would have turned in, Pearson thought. He wondered what they knew about activity on the Belgian border.

At the top of the steps, Jacques came out to meet them, pushing his muzzle against Pearson's hand. In the warmth and light of the kitchen, Agnès stood at one end of the table, ironing, and at the other Alazard sat reading a newspaper. Anxiety showed in his eyes as he ran a hand through his short-cut grey hair. Agnès straightened from her work, holding the iron above the table. Her hair was still pinned up on the top of her head, and she wore a light woollen cardigan around her shoulders, open at the front.

"Bonsoir, my friends," she said. The soft thump of her ironing started again.

"What will you have?" said Alazard.

"I can make some coffee," said Agnès.

"We have had a little cognac in the mess," Mansell said, laughing.

"And another will do no harm." Alazard poured from the bottle. The viscous liquid clung to the glasses, amber gold in the lamplight. "For you too, *cherie*," he said, pouring some for Agnès.

She placed the ironed blouse on top of a small heap of other clothes, and Pearson breathed in the biscuity aroma from hot cotton.

Agnès put the irons back on a shelf over the range and sat down beside her father. She held the brandy in front of her on the table, warming it with both her hands, looking expectantly at Pearson.

"So," she said, "what can you tell us?"

Mansell looked at Pearson, raised his eyebrows, and said: "I am afraid it's bad news. Your army has been pushed back from Charleroi across the Sambre." He shook his head. "There are reports of heavy casualties and roads blocked with refugees. Charleroi is in flames. It's all very confused and unfortunately the French retreat has left some of our forces exposed. We will almost certainly have to withdraw too, to prevent being cut off."

"Charleroi gone?" said Alazard. "I can't believe it." He sank back in his chair, defeated by the news.

Mansell arranged his cane on the table, making a diagram with some cutlery. "The British are now on a twelve mile front on the canal between Conde and Mons," he said, adding a ruler. "There's fighting on the far side of the canal and we are expecting a German attack. It's a difficult place to defend, with all those bridges and locks, and we're going to be heavily outnumbered. The *Boche* are at full strength after smashing the Belgian army."

Pearson watched Agnès as she listened attentively to Mansell, sitting upright without moving, taking in his words, understanding the gravity of what he was saying. Alazard leaned forward again on his elbows, his lips pursed in concentration. In the little silence, the clock on the wall ticked away a few seconds.

"I know the area by the canal," said Alazard. "I'm no soldier but I think it will be a difficult place to fight in."

Mansell nodded. "If we have to surrender the canal, there's a plan to form a new line just to the south of Mons." He moved the cane a few inches across the table.

"What about your camp?" Agnès asked him. She looked anxiously at Pearson who started to speak, but Mansell interrupted.

"Nothing for the moment. Our battalion is still in reserve. But things may change fast." He shrugged his shoulders and drained his glass. "Tomorrow even, things may change. It is, I am afraid, the nature of war. All we can do is wait." He laughed, spreading his hands in a gesture of resignation. "And sleep while we have the chance." He got to his feet, and gathered up his possessions. "Good night, and thank you for the cognac."

"He would make a good teacher," said Alazard when Mansell had gone.

"He's a good leader," said Pearson. "It's infectious. He's popular with the men and they'll follow him anywhere. People like that are very good for morale."

"I find it strange that he can be so cheerful. After what he told us," said Agnès.

Pearson shrugged. "He's a professional soldier. He's trained to know about danger. He knows how to keep things in perspective."

"'With true perspective the lines never meet. We would always be apart,'" she quoted to him.

"Where did you hear that?" said Alazard.

"It was something I told her," said Pearson. "I am not sure it is scientifically correct." He tried not to blush as a wave of nostalgia swept through him, thinking of her body in his hands in the water. Panic flashed into his mind in case her father questioned them too closely about their trip to the river.

But Alazard laughed: "It must be accurate. Artists talk about the vanishing point. But it's like railway lines going into the distance." He spread wide his arms. "They are always apart, like this." He reached for the bottle to refill their glasses. "Tell me, Doctor, what do you really expect to happen here?"

"I honestly don't know. I've heard that if the Germans force us back, they will have problems with their lines of communication. But I wouldn't bet on that. They might try to push on towards Paris."

"To Paris?"

"It's not that far. Listen. I have thought what it would mean to you and Agnès. The roads are full of refugees fleeing from the war. Some will have relatives to go, to but some of them will find it very hard. They may they have lost their houses in the fighting and are forced to run. I can't bear to think that might happen to you."

"We have thought about this too," said Alazard. "My brother won't leave the hospital, and I can't leave my students."

"What if this house is destroyed?"

"We can go to my brother."

"The Germans might smash the school."

"Then we would have to repair it. The new year starts in two weeks, and the school must go on. The children are more important than anything else in this. It's not their fault that countries fight each other."

Pearson was struck by the man's quiet dignity, by his determination to do the right thing for the children in his care. "And you," he said to Agnès. He reached across the table and took her hands. "What will you do if you have to stay, with the Germans occupying your country?"

"I will work with Uncle Gaston at the hospital. I will be safe there and I will think of you, that you will not be so far away."

Pearson looked at Alazard, wondering how much he knew,

but the teacher's eyes gave nothing away, and Agnès said: "It's all right, John. I have told my father that I am in love with you."

"I did not need to be told," said Alazard. "I am not blind. I understand my daughter well enough to know when she is happy. But I am afraid this war will make it difficult for you both."

"But if there were no war," Pearson said, "I should not have come to stay in your house. And then what Agnès and I have found together would not have happened at all."

"You see, Papa," she said. "I told you he is a philosopher."

Pearson thought of Alazard's lover. "You have friends in Le Cateau," he said. "What will they do? And in the village here."

"I think most of us will stay."

"The butcher said he wouldn't go," Pearson said.

"Marcel said that?"

"It was Sylvie. She said Marcel would never leave his home."

"And the peasants will always stay," said Alazard. "They cannot leave their land. It's all they have. Generally, people will stay if they have enough to eat."

"Invading armies take a lot of food."

"That is always a problem with war."

"Aren't you afraid?" Pearson asked him.

"Yes, I am afraid, but you know we have a long history of war. It has become a part of our lives to have foreign armies stamping through our streets every half century or so. Your Duke of Marlborough was here two hundred years ago in the war of Spanish Succession. Malplaquet is just up the road. And Wellington too! That's only a hundred years......"

"Papa, this is not a schoolroom. John does not need a history lesson." She stroked her father's cheek to take the little sting from her voice.

"No, of course he doesn't." He laughed suddenly and rocked back on his chair. "But I was going to say that I can just remember the war of 1870. I was nearly five years old. So you see there are many older people here who know about war, and how to survive it. It is in our blood." He pushed back his chair and got to his feet, smiling. "And now, as your friend said, it is time to sleep while we have the chance. Goodnight, Doctor. Will you turn out the lamp?"

"I will do that Papa, in a minute when I go to bed."

Pearson sat on the edge of the table and she came to stand between his legs, pulling his head into her chest, her fingers deep in the hair at the back of his neck. He stood so that he could reach her, kissing her upturned face and her throat in a passion of ecstasy, clinging to her, aware of her lovely softness in his arms, driving away the shadow of war.

"Tell me about your day," she said at last. "How was the horse?"

Pearson lowered himself onto a chair and she sat on his knee with her arms around his neck. "It was good to be on a horse again, but I haven't ridden for a month or so. I will be stiff tomorrow."

"Like this?" she said. She bit his bottom lip and placed her hand in his groin.

"No. Not quite like that. That is a sign of something else."

"Tell me about it please. I am not very familiar with this. I would like to learn."

"You seemed quite familiar with it at the pool. I wish we could be alone like that again."

She kissed him, rolling her tongue over his lips, breathing into his mouth. "Tomorrow," she whispered. "Tomorrow after lunch. My father always goes to Le Cateau, to see his woman after lunch on Sundays. You must eat the lamb with us and then we can be alone. Will you be able to do this, do you think?"

Pearson felt the lightness come back to him, floating him with her in the air. God, he thought, please let it be possible for me to do this. Please let there be no military emergency tomorrow.

"I am sure it will be all right," he said, with a thickness in his voice that he had not intended. "I will make it possible."

She sat back, holding his shoulders, gazing at him. "You are a very handsome man, John."

"I thought it was St. John that you found handsome."

She laughed, deep like a bell. "Yes, it's true. He is another."

"I could become jealous."

"But he is a man of thread, on a tapestry. And you are real."

"The tapestry is real," said Pearson. "And beautiful."

"Yes, and I love it, too!" She ran a finger lightly across his eyebrows. "It would be nice to make you a little jealous. How was the lecture?"

He did not want to talk to her about the lecture. "It went very well," he said. "They listened to what I had to say. It was not an interesting subject. It was all about how to stay healthy, and not drink bad water. And to keep clean and avoid lice."

"What is lice?"

"In French, *des poux*. Why are you laughing?"

"I thought perhaps it meant bad womans." She put a hand over her mouth, giggling.

"No," he said wearily. "But they came into it as well."

"Bad womans?"

"Women," he said. "One woman, two women."

"Of course. I knew that really. What did you say about bad women?"

"I told you this isn't an interesting subject."

"To me it is most interesting that you should know about bad women. What did you tell them?"

"Only about medical problems. The ones that happen if you don't take care with women like that."

She laughed again. "Now you sound like a doctor."

"You don't want me to talk like a doctor?"

She rubbed her nose against his. "It is all right, but I prefer to listen to you as a lover."

Sunday 23 August 1914

Dawn came late to northern France from a sky heavy with low cloud and drizzle. Over the Belgian border in Mons, the faithful went to mass, walking quickly on wet flagstones, sheltering under their umbrellas and smiling nervously at British troops resting in the Grande Place.

Twenty miles to the south, John Pearson locked up his aid post after morning sick parade. There had been few takers, perhaps because of the weather. Everything seemed normal in the camp, the men lying low, keeping out of the rain. Pearson wrapped his cape around him, dismissed Watson for the day, and set off to the village on his horse. He called at battalion headquarters, with the smell of cooking drifting from the kitchen, and he could hear the click and rattle of dice where Smith-Fenton and other subalterns played backgammon.

"I'm going home," he said to Mansell. "An invitation to lunch from the teacher."

"And his daughter, I hope?" said Mansell, teasing him. "Make the most of it, I would. There are unconfirmed reports that the shooting has started in earnest up on the border."

Pearson rode quietly up the village street. Few people were about on account of the rain, but shoppers came and went at the boulangerie, and small groups gathered around the market stalls. As he passed the café, a fug of *Gauloise* smoke wafted from the open door. The midday angelus rang out from the church tower. He wondered what Mansell had heard from the front, feeling sick with fear that the rumour might be true. Everyone had been saying for days that it could only be a matter of time.

He watched raindrops running down the backs of his horse's ears, and knew he was getting windy at the talk of action. Was it fear of being killed or wounded, he asked himself, or was he scared that he might get in such a funk that he would botch his work? He had not much experience of dealing with fear, the real fear that can suddenly turn your guts to water.

At the age of fourteen they had made him play at full back in an inter-house rugby match because someone had said he had a safe pair of hands. But Elliot was the captain of the other team, and Elliot was an enormous second row forward in the school 1st XV. He remembered going to bed the night before the match, and all night long this huge boy, big beyond his years, came trampling through the mêlée with nothing but a raw fourteen year old between him and the try line. At morning break, he had crept unseen into the chapel and prayed that he would do his duty and not get hurt. He had not been able to eat any lunch that day, and then he was out on the field, and before long someone from the other side lofted the ball high into the sky towards him. But the ball fell short and bounced, hanging in the air for Elliot to take at full speed.

He had a moment to focus on the massive legs, clad in school colours, churning towards him like a steam engine, topped by shoulders wide as a house. From the safety of the touchline, a voice shouted: "Take him low, Pearson," and he shut his eyes and went in, folding his arms round thrashing boots, and the giant came down with a terrible crack, spilling the ball wide, and sat up nursing a broken collar bone.

Pearson laughed at the memory, and he had never again been frightened of the tackle. But a game of rugby was not the same as being shot at and, no matter what Mansell had said about bullets not being aimed specifically at you, he had to admit that he dreaded being under fire.

He was not sure what to do with the horse when he rode into the yard of the teacher's house. The rain had eased so he removed the saddle and harness and put them on a rack under cover near the trap, and led the horse on a halter to turn her out in the paddock beyond the orchard. New mushrooms grew there, white and plump in the grass where Agnès had gathered them in her apron. The thought of her swept through him, an ache in his belly, and he hurried back to the house and ran up the steps, shaking rainwater off his cape and hat.

She stood at the kitchen range with her hair long, tied back with a ribbon. Alazard welcomed him at the table, and Jacques lay on the floor under the window, thumping the boards with his tail.

She came to him, taking his wet clothes, smiling calmly from her dark eyes. "So, you have been able to join us for lunch," she said. "I have been very much afraid that something would happen to prevent it." She hung his cape to dry.

"I told you that I would make it possible," he said, trying to forget what he had heard earlier from Mansell. "The camp was quiet this morning. There was nothing for me to do there."

"The lull before a storm, perhaps," said Alazard. "Is not that what you say in English?"

"Yes, we do have that saying. Sometimes it happens like that."

"An apéritif, Monsieur, before lunch?"

"Thank you. But I must change out of my uniform first." Pearson smiled at them. "You have invited me to your house, and I would like us all to forget about the war."

He went up to his room and took off his service dress and his shirt. He stood before the mirror in his underpants, looking at his reflection. How white he was, compared with the tanned body of Agnès at the pool.

He washed and dressed in the clothes he had worn with her to the river, and looked again at himself in the mirror. That's better, he thought. Now, at least you don't look like a bloody soldier. He stood at the window. The rain had stopped and he thought of Watson, hoping that he would be able to enjoy his day off. Perhaps they would be playing boules in the village later. God, he thought, what if Alazard decided they should all play instead of him going to Le Cateau? Panic rose, tight in his chest. But surely the teacher would not wish to disappoint his woman there? Agnès had assured him that her father always went to see her on Sunday afternoons.

She had cooked the shoulder of lamb slowly in a casserole with onions and garlic, white haricot beans and a little red wine, and when she brought it to the table, Alazard lifted the joint out to carve it on a large platter. The meat was sweet and tender and she had cooked young green beans from the garden.

"My only regret about living in this part of France," said Alazard, " is that we have no wine here. Possibly we could grow some white grapes in a hot summer like this, but for red wine you have to go further south. Down to Burgundy. I have always felt I should like to grow some vines when I retire."

"Would you be happy to leave here?" said Pearson.

"I think he would miss his friends," said Agnès.

"Perhaps some of them would come with me. Would you come, *chérie?*"

Agnès shook her head. "With your friends you would not need me," she said with a laugh, looking at Pearson. "And I am still too young to want to grow vines. Growing vines is something to do when you are settled."

Alazard said, "I am afraid you have had to become a little settled already, looking after me."

"It's difficult knowing when to settle down," said Pearson. "There are so many factors to think about."

Alazard poured more wine. "I have always taught my students that we seldom can control our own destinies. The best you can hope for is to learn, and read so that you are mentally charged up. Then, when opportunities arise, you can take advantage of them. You also need to learn that life is full of surprises that will catch you out when you are least expecting them. Living is at times a lottery where you don't control the dice. And, mon Dieu, with dying it is always a lottery."

"You are thinking of Maman and the babies?" Agnès said.

"You know about this?"

"Yes. Agnès told me."

"It is a perfect example," he said with a shrug. He took a mouthful of wine, rolling it round his tongue. He caught Pearson's eye. "And you, my friend, are another."

"Another example? Of what?"

Alazard leaned forward across the table. "Of being taken by surprise."

Pearson sensed a warning in Alazard's voice. A tickling sensation crept over his scalp. "I am not sure that I follow you," he said, playing for time.

"Oh, come now. You have been in France for less than a week. You cannot have expected to find yourself... ah... let us say emotionally involved, quite so soon? Is it not a surprise to you?"

"Well, yes, of course it's a surprise. It's a surprise to be at the beginning of a..." He saw that Alazard was watching him, like a cat with a mouse. But Agnès smiled encouragement. "And I am not sure where it will lead," he added, looking at her.

"Then perhaps you should think carefully until you are more certain," said Alazard, his eyes wide, challenging him.

Despite himself, Pearson felt crimson flush his cheeks. "All right," he said. "Let me tell you what I am sure of. It began when I first came to your house and Agnès walked out of the orchard. That was the beginning, and now we are very much in the middle of it. I am in love with her and I have never been happier." He looked at Agnès, hoping he had not said too much, and the teacher gave a small wry smile over the rim of his wine glass.

"I appreciate your honesty," said Alazard. "And I hope you will understand the natural protective instincts of a father."

When they had finished the lamb, Agnès cleared away their plates, taking them over to the sink in the corner. Pearson followed her with his eyes, thinking how beautifully she moved. It was extraordinary how the simple act of walking across a room could be imbued with such gracefulness. She's like a ballet dancer, he thought. A ballet dancer who has not been regimented at school, but allowed to run free like an antelope.

She brought a *tarte aux pommes* to the table, placing it in front of her chair. It was as neatly made as if it had come from the patisserie that morning, slices of apple arranged in interlocking circles under a caramel glaze. Pearson remembered watching her make one the day after he arrived at the billet when she had a dusting of flour on her cheek. It seemed an eternity ago.

"It is my father's favourite," she said to him. "But this one I have made for you too. The apples are from the orchard."

After coffee, Alazard walked over to the window. Sunlight sparkled on raindrops hanging in a spider's web beyond the glass.

"It's good," he said. "They will be able to play this afternoon." He turned back to face the room. "And I shall not get wet riding to Le Cateau. I normally visit friends in the town on Sunday afternoon. If it rains later, I will perhaps stay the night and return in the morning. I hope you will excuse me." He put on his coat, and kissed Agnès on both cheeks. "An excellent lunch, my dear," he said. "Agnès will look after you, Monsieur, and the major."

He shook Pearson's hand, told Jacques to stay, and went down the steps towards the stable. He had said nothing, Pearson thought, that could be interpreted as either encouragement or disapproval. An admonishment, to show he was not blind to his daughter's well-being, was a perfectly natural reaction. Pearson wondered if he were supposed to know about Alazard's lover and came to the conclusion that it would make little difference either way.

From the window he watched Alazard lead his horse from the stable, mount in one fluid movement, and ride out into the street. He turned back into the room where Agnès cleared away the remains of lunch.

"Don't look so worried," she said. "That was just his way

of testing you."

"To tell me I should think carefully about us?"

"Yes. And it was meant for me too." She kissed him quickly on his lips. "Anyway, you passed."

"I hope so."

"Oh, yes. Did you notice how he dropped the subject? With him that is a sure sign. The teacher made his point, and got his answer."

"Agnès, if your father returned suddenly for some reason and found us together, I should never forgive myself."

"I know that, John. And I love you for it. I could not forgive myself either. But I know he won't come back until tomorrow. I know he will stay the night in Le Cateau."

"But I don't want you to have to deceive him."

"He will not question me about us. So any deceit is something private that I will have to live with."

"I have no right to ask you to do this for me."

"I do it for myself, too. Because it is what is right for us."

With a feeling of pressure rising in his chest, Pearson helped her as she washed the dishes with hot water from a kettle. He stood close to her, acutely aware of their proximity. When they had finished, she took the cloth she had been using, wrung it out and placed it to dry by the range. Pearson held out his hands to her and she came to him, her eyes searching his face for reassurance.

"Now may I show you how I love you?" he said.

She looked down at their hands. "I am a little *timide*, John. What is your word for that?"

"Shy. We would say shy, in English."

"Shy?" Her eyes were on his again. "How do you spell that? It is a strange little word."

He spelled it for her, and she said it again for him.

"You did not seem shy when we were together by the river," he said, remembering her nakedness. "You do not need to be shy with me now."

"By the river we were just swimming with no clothes."

"And in the water, when I held you like that? And after swimming, on the bank?"

"After the swimming, we were drying in the sun," she said, teasing him a little. She took his face in her hands, looking at him with serious eyes. "Now we are at the beginning of something different."

"Are you frightened of it," he asked her. "Or of me?"

She shook her head a little. "No, I am not frightened. I have not done this before, but... but I know something of it."

At the very edge of his hearing he caught a sound as of distant thunder, the faintest throb, a pulse beat in the air.

"You have a friend who has told you?" he guessed, straining his ears to catch the sound again.

"Yes. I have a friend who is married, in Le Cateau. We know each other very well. We are almost like sisters. She has told me all about it."

"All about it? I believe there is much to learn."

"You believe? You do not know it all then?" she giggled.

He laughed with her. "Some of it I know from being a doctor. A little, just a little, I have found out for myself."

He kissed her very slowly, and he felt her tongue searching his teeth, while he listened for the sound he did not want to hear.

"Did your friend tell you about kissing like that?" he asked.

"Yes. And other ways. She says that our bodies are to be enjoyed when we are in love."

"She must be a very good teacher. Listen, Agnès. When people are in love there is nothing they can do together that is shameful so long as they both do it willingly. It's natural for us to be shy to start with. But it will go when we have..."

"When we have practised together?"

"Yes." He heard the far-off pulse of sound again, and prayed that it might be the thunder of a distant storm. "We may have so little time, Agnès. If I could have one wish for the rest of my life, it would be that we could have more time

94

together." He pulled her to him, pressing her body to his, and spread his fingers up the back of her neck, behind her ears. "The war is bound to come here," he whispered, "and you and I will be pulled apart."

"I know this, John. It is why I want us to have something to hold onto for when the bad time comes. You think it will be soon, don't you?"

"Yes." The thunder came again, rattling the window, and he knew then for certain that it was not thunder but the sound of gunfire. She heard it too, and he felt her stiffen in his arms, her eyes huge and questioning. "Yes," he said. "It's a long way off, but the north wind is bringing it to us. It's the sound of artillery."

"Then we have no time to lose," she said, simply.

"But if I have to go tomorrow? What if the battalion goes to fight tomorrow? If they go, Agnès, I have to go too. You do know that, don't you?"

"Yes, I know that. It is why I want for us to be together now." She looked at him imploringly.

"It will make it harder, in the morning, if we have to say goodbye."

"Everything is always different in the morning."

"I did not say it would be different, just harder."

"It cannot be harder than saying goodbye to you now."

"No," he said. "Nothing could be as bad as that. I don't think that I could do that now." He held her to him again and she came without resistance, swaying in his arms.

"Love me now, John. While we still have time."

"Yes. But it may be the last chance until the fighting finishes and I can come back for you. I promise you that if I live, I will come back."

"You don't need to promise."

"No, but I do anyway."

"Then please make sure you live. Oh, for God's sake, live."

She led him across the room to the door that led to the

apartment she shared with her father.

"Shouldn't we go upstairs to my room?" he said.

"It's not necessary." She laughed into his chest. "Even if it does not rain, my father will not come back. And if Major Mansell returns, we are more private in here."

He had not seen the room before and was enchanted by its femininity, with her little possessions on the dressing table, and her nightgown hanging on the back of the door. She drew the curtains, shutting out most of the sunlight and came to stand in front of him. He traced the line of her cheek and the side of her neck with his fingers and began to undress her, all the time watching her eyes, their pupils enlarged in the half-light, trusting him implicitly.

They stood naked together and he breathed in the scent of her; a warm, musky scent, mingling with his own desire, and he took her to her bed and lay down with her and they began to practice and to learn some of the things for which there would be so little time.

The church clock struck three, and they lay quietly together in her bed listening to traffic on the road outside from motor lorries running to the camp. They had made love, nervously at first, but with increasing abandon and delight in each other, and she lay on her side, temporarily turned away from him. He pressed up against her back, her buttocks in his lap. With his free hand he caressed the line of her torso where it dipped from her shoulder to the narrow of her waist before it flared up over her hip. A lorry stopped outside the house, leaving the engine running, and the sound of the cab door banging came into the room. She turned her head to him.

"Why has it stopped, John?" She sounded breathless. "Do you think they are looking for you?"

He sat up resting back on his elbows. "I don't think so. Not in a lorry."

"Why are you whispering?"

"I don't know."

"I'm going to look from the window."

She got out of bed and opened the curtain a little so she could see out. He watched her stand on tiptoe, leaning forward, her hands on the window sill so that her back was arched away from him, her shoulders high. Her hair hung between her shoulder blades, and he thought he must remember how she looked like that. He must add this image of her beauty to the others from the orchard and from the trap, and when they were at the river. She leaned, peering down from the window so that the weight of her upper body was taken on her hands, placed slightly apart on the windowsill, and he felt his pulse quicken at the glimpse of dark tufts of hair under her arms. He could not imagine, somehow, such animal magic adorning the pale society creatures he knew at home. She moved back suddenly as the cab door banged again, and he heard the grate of gears as the lorry moved off. She was smiling as she came back to him in the bed.

"What was it?" he said.

"It was nothing. Just the driver making himself comfortable."

"What? Do you mean he was having a pee?"

"Yes," she laughed happily. "A pee-pee."

"Against your house?"

"No, no. Against the wheel of the lorry."

"And you watched all this?"

"I could not help it. I was thinking of you."

"Of me?" He buried his nose in her armpit.

"Yes. Of you, here." She knelt over him, holding him in her hand. "Is this all right, John?"

"Yes... yes. Very all right." He felt himself swell under the touch of her fingers, and her hair swung against his belly.

"Take me into you like that," he said.

She leaned forward, lowering herself over him, brushing his lips with her nipples and he put his hands on her hips, pulling them together.

97

Afterwards, he lay with her beside him and he knew from her breathing that she was asleep. They were both naked, with no bed covers over them for the room was warm from the heat of the day. She lay with her head on his arm, her face turned towards him and her left arm over his chest and he watched her breasts rise and fall with her breathing. Five days, he thought. He had been in this country, in this house, for five days. She said that time was not important, and, in a way, he could see that it was so. It was not the length of time that mattered, but what you did with it.

He heard the distant boom of the guns again and a deeper roar of a far-off explosion. They must be blowing the canal bridges, he thought, imagining desperate men running for cover as the last troops came over the water. They must be falling back to the new defensive position that Hartwell had talked about. If he had been posted to one of the other battalions he would be in the thick of it now instead of lying in the arms of this impossibly wonderful girl. He inhaled her scent, looking down the length of her body where it touched his, to her feet curled by his shins. She lay on her back, her belly flattened before the slight rise to her pubic bone and its darker covering.

Tomorrow, he thought. Could they be granted another day like this? But why should he have that comfort while other men were fighting and dying nearby, and he was not, solely because of the lottery of military planning? She stirred in her sleep, pressing against him, and he felt again a surge of longing for her. But if we cannot have tomorrow, he thought, at least we have the rest of today, and perhaps tonight too if we are lucky. A lock of her hair had fallen over her lips and he moved it away with his fingers.

Why could she not come with him if they were forced out of Le Cateau, he wondered again? She had worked in the hospital there and her knowledge would be useful in a casualty clearing station. There must be precedents for foreign civilian nurses working with the army overseas. But

98

an army retreating under fire was not a hospital, and he knew he could not subject her to the awful perils of shellfire in open ground.

What if he deserted, though? He could go missing in the streets of Le Cateau if it came under fire. She could shelter him and they could lie low for a few days in someone's loft until the immediate danger had passed. And they could run over the border to Belgium and cross into Holland and make their way...his mind raced with the possibilities before the desperate reality of running as a fugitive brought him to his senses. Sooner or later they would catch up with him and he would be shot as a deserter. Perhaps they would shoot her too. And how could he live with himself, even if they did not shoot him, for having left his post and the battalion without a medical officer?

What would Mansell, Watson, the boy Smith-Fenton, all the men of the battalion do without a doctor to dress their wounds when the shooting started? And what on earth could he say to his parents? 'I ran away because I had fallen in love?' He smiled grimly to himself at the chances of the old general accepting that as a valid excuse. And Freddy? Freddy would never forgive him and he could not possibly let Freddy down.

She moved again, stretching, and nuzzled his ear. "Have I been asleep?" she said.

"Only for a while."

"But you have been awake?"

"Yes. I have been thinking how lucky I am to be here. With you."

"You were not sleepy too?"

"A little. But I was happy to be thinking of you. And watching you so that I will be able to remember how you look when you are asleep." He brushed his hand across her breasts, down to the flatness of her belly. A faint scratching sound came from the door.

"That is Jacques," she said. "He can hear our voices."

99

"I don't mind if you want to let him in."

"It is better if he stays there." She leaned over him, kissing him and letting her breasts swing against his torso. "He would certainly be jealous if we let him in." She fell back again, putting a hand onto his over her stomach. "Will you tell me something about you, John? About your childhood? I know so little of you. Tell me about your home."

"It's a big square house, red brick, at the edge of a village..."

"Like this?"

"A bit like this. But further out of the village. There's a long wall between the garden and a roadway, and you come in from the road through gates onto a gravel driveway. The house is at the end of the driveway with rose beds on both sides and a big lawn with a copper beech tree at the end. My father planted it when I was born, and it has turned into a beautiful tree. The leaves come out pink in spring before turning to copper in midsummer. It's big enough now for a hammock and you can swing in it on hot afternoons. My father had a little metal plaque made. It says 'John's Tree.' I love it. Beyond the tree there is a kitchen garden, a *potager* you would call it, and an orchard.

"It sounds very much like this," she said, "but larger, perhaps?"

"Larger, yes. But the idea is the same."

"Houses in England have ideas?"

"No. It is a figure of speech."

"And the village? It is like Bazuel?"

"There is a big difference between villages here and in England." He sought a way to explain it to her. "In England the houses are more spread out. More separated from each other. Also they are usually set back a little from the road, with a garden in front as well as behind. And there are hedges or fences, and sometimes walls between each house and the next."

"It sounds as if the English do not care much for their neighbours." She turned his hand over, interlocking their fingers.

"It's not that we don't care for our neighbours, but that we value our privacy."

"And inside your house. Tell me how it is inside."

He thought of the house with its hunting pictures in the hall; the wide carpeted stairs rising to the first floor with the brassy glint of polished stair-rods; the morning room, and the drawing room with its mahogany furniture; the rather cold formality of the dining room, and the passage to the kitchen with the green baize door. The comparison with the intimate simplicity of the teacher's house, where everything revolved around the comfort of its kitchen, struck him forcibly with a longing to stay with her. He turned towards her and pulled her to him. "It's so different," he whispered in her ear. "It's too big, and too empty, and too cold in its formality. It is perhaps a house more than a home. It's difficult to explain."

"But it has always been your home?"

"Yes, and of course I love it for that," he said, feeling remorse at the way he had described it to her. "It is perhaps disloyal of me to have talked of the house like that."

"Disloyal to your family?"

"And particularly to my mother. She wouldn't agree with me. The house is what it is because of her. She has made it the way she likes it, and for my father too. It's hard for me to see it as they do, because I've spent so little time there."

"But why, if it's your home?"

"There's a tradition in England. About education. Some parents don't send their children to a local school as most of you do in France. I was at boarding school from the age of about eight until I was eighteen."

"Boarding school?"

"You have some here. Where you are sent away to school. You go at the beginning of each term and you sleep there and do all your lessons there until the end of the term. It's your

101

life for most of the year."

"We have some like that. But not many children go. It seems unnatural."

"It's supposed to make us better leaders."

"I had not thought of you as a leader, John. It is one of the things that I love in you."

"I don't see myself as a leader. I find it better to flow with the current. The current of life. Anyway, you can understand now that I was only at home for the school holidays."

"And at school, you were happy?"

"It's easy to be happy at school if you accept it. If you accept the discipline and the routine."

"But did you not miss your family?"

"Very much at first. But you get used to it. And it helps if you are good at something."

"Let me guess the things you were good at." She sat up, looking at him seriously, covering his hand where he stroked her breasts. "Languages," she said. "You would have been good at languages. That is why you speak French. Perhaps some others?"

"Latin. I was good at Latin. And rugby."

"That isn't a language."

"No," he laughed. "And I didn't study it very seriously."

"You are a strange mixture, John Pearson. A speaker of Latin who plays rugby and is happy to drift with the current. I could learn to love that very much. Listen, there is the gunfire noise again."

"Yes. And they are blowing the bridges. That is the deep boom – there, you can hear it now. It is to try and slow the German advance. I don't think it will work for long."

"I do not want to think about that." She snuggled against him. "Tell me about your little brother. Is Freddy at one of those horrid schools?"

"Yes. And he doesn't find it horrid. He does well there. Better than I did. I think Freddy will make a good leader."

"But if he is only at home for the holidays, you will not see much of him."

"No, I'm afraid that's true."

"I don't think that is a very good way to make a family."

"It's how some people do things in England. It is to make men of boys so that they can go out to run our empire."

"We have overseas possessions too," she said.

"Yes, but not so many. France doesn't need so many leaders, you see."

"Perhaps you are right." She pulled on the hairs of his chest. "Have you travelled much round your empire?"

"No," he laughed again. "Not at all. I hope to, when the war is over. And I want you to come with me."

"But you said you would take me to England."

"We'll go to England, and to Scotland. And then down through Africa."

"Ah, then and I can show you some of our empire on the way. How shall we cross the desert?"

He played with the skin behind her ear. "We can go on camels in a caravan with the Tuareg or, if you prefer, we can go into Egypt and take a boat from Cairo up to the top of the Nile at Khartoum."

"And climb the pyramids, " she said. "I think that it will be better not to cross the desert. I am not very fond of camels."

"No, but I am not sure the pyramids are for climbing."

"Perhaps not. What shall we do when we get to the top of the Nile?"

"We will go to Omdurman and see the place where my father charged with the 21st Lancers."

"Oh! You haven't told me about this."

"No. It was sixteen years ago. In September 1898."

"It was a cavalry charge?"

"Yes. Against the Mahdi. The Lancers were ordered to clear a plain outside Omdurman where a couple of hundred tribesmen had gathered. So they galloped in, but when they arrived they found another two or three thousand tribesmen hiding in a hollow in the ground. It was too late to stop so they had to keep going and fight it out. More than seventy of the regiment were killed and over a hundred horses."

"But your father was not hurt?"

"No. An awful lot of the tribesmen were killed. It was a victory, but a rather sad one."

"What country are we in now?"

"In the Sudan."

"Yes, of course. It will be interesting to see. And after we have done that?"

"We will go to Khartoum, which is the capital, and then we'll follow the Blue Nile up into the mountains and go through to Abyssinia."

"But that isn't in your empire, surely?"

"No, but I believe it's very beautiful and I think we ought to go there. I'm not sure if there is a proper way through the mountains but we can find a guide to take us."

"But he will have to be paid."

"I'll cure his family of beriberi in payment. Do you know this disease?"

"No, but I have heard of it. Tell me what it is."

"It's inflammation of the nerves, and makes your heart stop."

"And Dr. Pearson can cure this?"

"I think so. You have to give them a lot of vitamin B."

"But perhaps they will not have the beriberi."

"Maybe not," he chuckled. " But you can be certain they will have something for me to cure."

"If we are in Abyssinia, will you take me to Addis Ababa please? I have always wanted to go there. It's such a good name."

"Of course. We'll go to see the Emperor. He will be very pleased to meet such a beautiful woman."

"We will make a beautiful couple."

"Yes. We can stay there for a while being beautiful, before we go down into Kenya to shoot guinea fowl. And then we'll go to the coast near Mombasa and swim in the Indian Ocean."

"I thought we were in Africa."

"Have I told you that I love you?" he said laughing, and she came to lie on top of him.

"Why does it have to be the Indian Ocean?" she said, breathing it into his mouth.

"It's difficult to get everything right when you have an empire as large as ours. Actually, I expect it's because we got to India first. Before Africa. But we can rename the ocean if you want. We'll call it the Lover's Ocean and swim there naked."

"But what if there are sharks?"

"We will shoot the sharks."

She lay on top of him, the light weight of her body warm and loving. He felt slowly down the length of her spine, counting the vertebrae.

"Going back to the guinea fowl," she said. "How will we cook them?"

"I'll make a fire. And you can put the birds on a spit, and rub them with fat from inside the body cavity, at the lower end. And you can cook them over the fire so they're still pink in the middle. Oh, I forgot to say that we'll have to gather some wild herbs from the bush which you can spread over the birds with the fat. We'll eat them with our fingers, by the light of the moon."

"Perhaps there will be lions and tigers wanting to join in."

"I am amazed at your ignorance. Surely you know there are no tigers in Africa?"

"I am a little confused because of the ocean with India. But the lions may be round the camp fire?"

"The lions I will shoot, too."

"It seems there is going to be an awful lot of shooting with these travellings."

"It is better English to say 'on these travels' since we are in the British Empire."

"Yes. We must be very careful of your beautiful language."

"English is not really such a beautiful language. It's your French that is beautiful. And the way you speak English. That is also beautiful."

"Thank you. I have forgotten now where we have got to."

"We are still in Mombasa. And from there we can go overland through Tanganyka into Rhodesia and then on into Nyasaland on the way to South Africa. I hope I've got all these countries in the right order. It's difficult to remember from school. Maybe it would be easier to take a steamer from Mombasa, and run down the coast of Portuguese East and go round to Cape Town." With his fingers he played with the little valley at the base of her spine.

"How do you know all this? And all these places?"

"I'm just guessing most of it."

"I want you to keep talking," she said. "When you are talking I cannot hear the sound of the guns."

"Shall I tell you about a discovery I have made?"

"Yes please. Is it connected with Africa?"

"No. It is to do with you."

"Oh..."

"It's here," he said, touching her back between her shoulder blades. "You have a mole here."

"That is not so interesting, because I already know it. I can see it when I twist round in front of the mirror."

"All right. But there's something else."

"To do with me?"

"Yes." He held her head between his hands, very close to him so that their eyes swam. " I have often wondered how it would feel to be in love. To be really in love. You talked about the pain, the *chagrin d'amour* when we were at the pool. I feel this now, Agnès, like a sweet knife cutting deep inside. It is terrible and wonderful and beautiful. I didn't know it was possible to feel like this."

"I am learning it, too," she whispered. She moved aside a little and stroked her hand down over his belly, feeling his tumescence under her fingers. The church bell rang five times.

"John," she called to him. "You must wake." The urgency in her voice swam into his brain. He sat up quickly and she bent to kiss him.

"What time is it?"

"Six. They sent a messenger for you and Major Mansell. I sent him away."

"Not Mansell?"

"No, no. The messenger. I promised him I would come to you immediately." She wore a dressing gown, with her dark hair loose and she smelled of sleep. "He said I must tell you to go to your headquarters as soon as possible."

"All right. Does Mansell know?"

She shook her head. "No, I came here first to tell you."

He could see the fear in her eyes, wide and dark, and he felt a knot tighten in his stomach. "I'll wake Mansell. Can you...dressed like that can you cross the yard and shout for Watson to wake him too?"

"Yes. What is happening, John?"

He got out of bed and led her to the open window. In the east, the first signs of dawn flamed soft and pink, and a slight mist drifted through the orchard trees. The rain had cleared away, promising another day of summer. They stood in the window listening to the guns, an abomination of sound violating the morning air.

"It's closer now," he said. "Closer than last night. We must be retreating still. That's why they want us. Come here so I can feel that you're real." He held her tightly against his chest, feeling her heartbeat. The countdown to the time of their parting had begun, and he saw that she was watching him closely. "Please go and wake Watson," he said. "And remember that I love you with everything that I am."

"Yes. I will always remember this, and the other from last night. Always."

Pearson listened to her footsteps receding down the stairs,

crossed to the window and leaned out as she ran to the stables. The memory of his time with her in her room swept through his mind, the feel of her body burning his hands. He strode out of the room and banged on Mansell's door.

At half-past six Pearson sat with his brother officers as Colonel Hartwell held up his hand for silence. Pink and smooth, with a neat moustache, Hartwell looked the epitome of everyone's favourite uncle.

"Good morning gentlemen, and my apologies for getting you out of bed. We're on the move. We were informed at five o'clock that II Corps has been ordered to retire to a line running twelve miles from here. Near Bavay. No doubt you have all heard artillery during the night. Our new position will be on the hill beyond Le Cateau.

"We'll dig in with the help of local civilian labour. As soon as we've had breakfast, we'll march out. It's about four miles. It's going to be hot, so make sure you remember to organise plenty of fresh water." Hartwell straightened his shoulders and clasped his hands behind his back, rocking on the balls of his feet. "We have enjoyed nearly a week of summer camping here, and now it's our turn to do some real work. I know I can count on you. Smith-Fenton has details of the new billets. Doctor, a word please before you go."

"Up before the beak?" said Mansell, with a laugh. "Come and join us when you're done."

Pearson waited by the door for his meeting with Hartwell, feeling like a boy at school outside the headmaster's study. But his commanding officer came to him with a smile and a whiff of shaving soap.

"Thank you, Doctor. I've been told to expect casualties from other units in the hospital in Le Cateau. We're short of medics, and the other battalion MO's are up to here in it." He held a hand under his chin. "Until we're in action, I want you to help out where you can. Don't neglect you usual duties, of course, but as you already know the hospital, you could be invaluable there. And still close enough to our new position if we need you. That all make sense?"

"Yes, sir. I'll get up to the hospital and see what I can do. And I'll move the RAP ." God, he thought, it's less than a week since I was a doctor in Hampshire, and I'm already talking like a soldier.

"Good man. You may find the first casualties coming in early tomorrow."

The atmosphere at breakfast weighed heavy with purpose and resolution. Clipped snatches of conversation rattled between men eating standing up, swallowing their too-hot coffee. At seven o'clock Pearson rode through the village, already feeling the heat of the morning sun. Marie- Hélène waved to him from a small queue at the boulangerie. Villagers stood about in small groups, talking earnestly. They can hear the gunfire, he thought, and now it's really beginning. For a few days he had lived in the unreality of a little time capsule, an eddy at the edge of the stream, but that was coming to an end now, and he was being swept out, helpless, into the current.

He rode into the yard in the bleak knowledge that it would be his last day there. Jacques came trotting over to see him as he tied the horse to a ring outside the stable where Alazard forked manure into a wheel barrow.

"Bonjour," Alazard waved his fork in the air. His cheeks, freshly shaven, shone with vitality. "What is the news?"

Agnès came down the steps, her dress swinging from side to side.

Pearson forced himself to look the teacher in the eye. "We're withdrawing. Back to Bavay and..."

"To Bavay?" Alazard exploded. "Mon Dieu, that is no distance from here. What is our army doing?"

"They're retreating."

"Can nothing stop the Germans now?" He pushed the

barrow out of the stable and slammed the door.

"I don't know. Perhaps later when we have time to regroup."

"And you?" said Agnès. "What will happen to you and your men out at the camp?" The fear in her tore at him.

"They're moving now," he said. "To a new position. Just outside Le Cateau. To the south of the Cambrai road. We...Mansell and I, have to go to another billet."

"Now? Today?"

"I don't know. Maybe not just yet."

"Where will you go, John?"

"I don't know. They'll tell us later. But they've asked me to work in the hospital. Until I am needed with the battalion."

"With Gaston?" said Alazard.

"Yes. I'm going now to see what I can do. Some of our wounded are coming here. The serious cases, the ones that are too bad to be treated at the front."

"I can come with you," said Agnès. "If there is work for me."

"There'll be things I don't want you to see."

She looked down. "I'll be all right," she said.

In the stables across the yard, Pearson could hear Watson moving about above, whistling tunelessly. He went up the stairs to the loft to find his batman tidying his quarters.

"The men are moving today," Pearson told him. "I want you to go with them. I've organised a mule cart for my stores. Take the AP furniture too, and you can ride with the cart. Scout around a bit for a suitable place for the new post. We might have to get a dugout made. I'll join you later this afternoon."

"Very good, sir. The *Boche* seem to have us on the run. Bloody guns kept me awake last night."

Pearson sat with her in the trap on the way to the hospital, his horse trotting along behind, attached by a long rope from its halter. She leaned close to him so he caught her fragrance.

"It's exactly a week since you came out of the orchard and I saw you for the first time." He stroked the back of her neck.

"I have counted the days, every day. And every day has been a blessing."

"Today may be the last, for a while."

"But I will see you in the hospital." She sat, calm and upright, holding the reins lightly, swaying with the motion of the trap. "I will work with you John, and help you."

He nodded, wanting desperately to hold her. "I thank God for that. That we may at least be together in the days."

"I thought you did not have much faith in God."

"When you need God very badly, it is easy to have some faith."

"I will tell you a secret. At dawn this morning, when you left me for your room, I prayed that God might grant us one more night together. I am not sure it is right to ask something like that of God, but it seems that it is going to be possible."

"Yes," he said, squeezing her arm. "I have been thinking about what you must do if the Germans come. When you worked with Gaston before, did you wear a uniform?"

"For nursing?"

"Yes, as a nurse."

"Sometimes. Why?"

"I want you always to wear it."

She smiled at him, coyly: "You would like me more in a uniform?"

"It is not possible to like you more. I'm trying to be serious. You're a beautiful young woman and very vulnerable with an invading army swaggering through the streets. But as a nurse in the hospital they will need you and respect you. I believe it will keep you safe. You must dress as a nurse before you leave the house in the mornings."

"Yes, John. I think you are right. I will talk with Gaston."

"I wish I could do more to protect you."

"There is nothing more. I will do as you suggest and be a

111

nurse. I am sure it will be all right."

In the town, dogs scavenged amongst fresh droppings from the mules and horses. The church door stood open and father Albert emerged, blinking in the bright light. Pearson waved, wondering if the priest had been able to find a hiding place for his tapestry. Father Albert acknowledged him uncertainly, shading his eyes against the sunlight. At the restaurant where they had eaten, a crowd of men sat at outside tables, talking earnestly, smoking, and drinking pastis.

Gaston listened quietly at the hospital door while Pearson explained the military situation. "I have only two patients at the moment," he said. "The child with burns and the man with his leg in traction. I will move them to a quiet corner out of the way. I don't want to upset that child. She has suffered too much already." He removed his pince-nez spectacles, put them into the pocket of his coat, and stroked a hand over his beard. "We have all heard the gunfire. From tomorrow, you say, we should expect the first casualties?"

"Yes."

"I am so pleased you will be here to help, even if it can only be for a short time. And don't worry about Agnès. She will be safe here, and very useful to us. You said it is the worst cases that will come?"

"Yes. The ones who cannot be treated properly at dressing stations. The seriously wounded. They will be suffering from severe and probably infected wounds. And shock from loss of blood. We'll need a lot of anaesthetic."

"We have plenty of ether. And chloroform. That could be useful, though perhaps dangerous for patients with severe shock. Ether will be safer, I think."

"Yes. What about locals?"

"Novocaine."

Pearson paced about the room, hands clasped behind his back. He stopped in front of Gaston. "Morphine," he said. "We will need morphine. We must not run short of that."

"I have some. But I will telephone Cambrai to arrange for

more."

"I will do that for you," said Agnès

"Give them your uncle's name," said Pearson. "Tell them it's urgent."

"You can telephone from my office," said Gaston. "While we are in the wards." He led Pearson down the hospital's main corridor.

"How many beds do you have?" Pearson asked him.

"Twenty that are made up. Eighteen of them free. I have another twelve which we can use in emergency. They are in the two wards at the end."

"Can you prepare them quickly, if necessary?"

Gaston nodded. " Yes. I will ask the nurse to arrange it this afternoon. You think they will be needed?"

"I don't know," said Pearson, shrugging. "There are several thousand men fighting out there. Of course not all the casualties will come here, but thirty beds doesn't sound much." He looked back up the corridor. There was no sign of the girl. "I must tell you that I am very concerned about Agnès's safety, but I believe she will be safe working here if the Germans come. They must surely respect a nurse?"

Gaston held out his hands, palms upwards. "They say that war brings out the best in people. And sometimes the worst. But she will be as safe in the hospital as anywhere. And if things get really bad I can always arrange for her to sleep here. And her father too if necessary."

"Thank you. You know Agnès means a great deal to me?"

"I am beginning to understand that," said Gaston with the shadow of a smile.

When he left the hospital, Pearson rode down the hill, over the river, and out onto the Cambrai road. He could feel the heat of the afternoon sun burning through his tunic, and flies swarmed over the sweating neck of his horse. Lines of infantry and horse-drawn artillery slowed traffic to a crawl. He came to a junction, with the old Roman road running straight as a ruler on either side, and recognised Anson and

Cazenove, dismounted, consulting a map.

"We're taking up our position here," said Cazenove, lifting the map for Pearson to look at. "You can see them over there, on that slope above the Cambrai road." He pointed down the valley with his cane. "The French are helping us, and by the sound of those guns the quicker we're dug in the better."

"I hope you're properly organised, Pearson," Anson said. "You'll have to do some hard work soon instead of poncing about with that girl."

"That girl, as you call her, is a nurse and is going to help in the hospital."

"Well, bully for you, Doctor. Look, you may have landed on your feet, but don't let a pretty face get in the way. If my men get their arses shot up, I don't want some lovesick medic with bags under his eyes cutting off the wrong bits."

"You don't seem to have a very high opinion of my ability."

Anson, red in the face, held the bridle of Pearson's horse. He looked round quickly at Cazenove who stood a few yards away, studying the hill ahead through binoculars. "I don't know anything about your ability," he said to Pearson in a voice harsh with menace. "I just hope you've got enough. Your old man might be a general, but you're on your own out here. Now, trot along and set up your new aid post." He smacked the rump of Pearson's horse with his gloves.

Men were digging in the stubble when Pearson rode up the edge of sloping ground to a low ridge, humped like a whale's back, at the top of the field. Mansell had warned him that Anson could be difficult, but the man's words smarted in his ears. He wondered what Anson knew about Agnès. Probably, he had heard that the two of them had been seen out in the trap together.

A network of firing trenches spread out along the front of the ridge, and the men had started on communication lines leading back to the other side. The metallic ring of picks and the scrape of shovels spoke of hard digging. To the rear, he saw Watson with a muleteer, manoeuvring the battalion's medical supply cart along a narrow track at the lower edge of the field, sheltered on both sides by thick hedges. He rode down to join them.

"I thought somewhere down here, sir," said Watson. He looked hot and very red in the face.

Pearson looked around. Watson was right. Access was good, down the track to the Roman road, with a high bank for shelter.

"It looks fine. Well done, Watson. I'll organise some labour to make a dugout in the bank. Get back to your mess when you've done, and wake me at dawn."

Pearson dismounted, and Watson took the horse to a ditch at the far side of the track where water ran. The horse sucked at the clear stream, its ears moving to the rhythm of its drinking.

The troops toiled through the heat, and by the late afternoon, the trenches were deep enough to provide reasonable cover except where the communication trench ran over the ridge. Smoke rose into the still air from cookhouse fires. The gunfire from the north sounded no closer and the camp had an air of calm.

Perhaps we are holding them, Pearson thought. Perhaps we have stopped them up there north of Bavay. Images of Agnès swept through him. Might they be given another night together before the wounded start coming in, he thought, and to hell with Anson?

There was nothing further he could do at the hospital, and no sign there of Agnès or the trap. Twenty or thirty beds did not seem much, he thought. But the church was a strong, sound building and might be safe, and not a target for the German guns. Perhaps it could be used to take in casualties if the hospital were swamped. He cantered up to Le Cateau, tied the horse to some railings, and went into the cool interior of the church. He stood by the pew where he had sat with Agnès, running his fingers along the smooth oak, feeling her presence in the air. Father Albert came out of the vestry carrying an altar cloth and Pearson went to meet him at the top of the nave.

"Bonsoir, Father."

"Bonsoir. I do not like the sound of all this gunfire."

"I can't tell you much about that, but there is something I hope you can do for me."

Father Albert placed the cloth on the end of the altar. "What can a poor priest do for you, Monsieur?" His expression was wide-eyed, open with honesty.

"I've come from the hospital," said Pearson. "We expect to take in casualties there but as you know, there's only space for a few. I was hoping to have your permission for others to be brought in here, if necessary."

The priest looked at him and Pearson could sense the man calculating the possibility of complications.

"I'm not sure we have all the facilities here that you would need."

"No, Father. But the same is true of other buildings. You have fresh water here? Water that is good for drinking?"

"Yes, of course, but..."

"And some electric lighting?"

"Yes, a little, and plenty of candles..."

"We wouldn't need much else. We would bring our own medical supplies, and these walls are good and strong. It would only be a temporary arrangement. And no doubt the Lord will approve."

Father Albert smoothed imaginary wrinkles from his soutane. "If you put it like that," he said, "I can hardly refuse you. But I shall pray that it won't be necessary."

Pearson looked across the aisle where the tapestry glowed with colour. He thought of Agnès, as a girl of fifteen, carrying it in processions, and he saw her again in her bed, loving him as passion overcame her shyness. She had told him that she loved the tapestry from childhood, and in the instant, he knew what he must do. He must save it for her sake. Soon, the time would come when he had to leave her, and he would protect the tapestry with his life. It would be a talisman to bind them together until he could come back for her. He coughed into his hand, wondering how best to put it to Father Albert.

"In exchange for the loan of the church," he began, "I have a proposition concerning your tapestry. Unless you have found a safe place to hide it?"

"Not yet. I have thought a lot about this. I am certain the tapestry cannot stay here if Le Cateau is attacked. It must leave this church and the town. Perhaps it could go to a farmhouse in one of the villages nearby."

"The Germans are burning villages."

"Yes, I have heard that. But they can't burn everything."

"No. But a farmhouse would be a big risk."

"I have thought of taking it to the hospital. No one will target a hospital, surely?"

"The hospital's a possibility," said Pearson. "But if the Germans drive us out of Le Cateau, they will take over the hospital. Would you trust them not to destroy the tapestry?"

Father Albert looked downcast. "No," he said. "I don't think so." He spread his arms in resignation. "You said you had a proposition?"

Pearson decided to jump in boldly. "Yes. That I take it for you."

Father Albert raised his eyebrows in astonishment. "But you can't do that! You are a soldier. You might be involved in the fighting. How could you keep the tapestry safe? I could not possibly allow it. You will forgive me, but you are not even in our army." His face became pink with agitation.

"Would it make a difference if I were?"

"Perhaps. I don't know."

"So, it is not the fact that I am a soldier that worries you, so much as that I am a foreigner?"

Father Albert looked distraught. "No, no. Now I am

afraid I have offended you."

"I am not so easily offended. Listen. We both know it will be impossible to find a building where the safety of your tapestry is guaranteed. But I have somewhere in mind."

"You can guarantee it?"

"As nearly as makes no difference." Pearson took a deep breath. "I will put the tapestry in my medical supply wagon. These wagons are some of the most important vehicles in the British Army. They are never put at risk because the contents are so vital. They are kept far back from the action and are always guarded. We take what we need each day forward to our aid posts."

"But I should never know where you had taken it."

"No, that is true. But you wouldn't need to know. All that matters is that the tapestry will be safe, with my supplies. And when the war is over and the Germans have been sent home, I will bring it back for you. You have my word on that. There is still some risk, of course. But it will be a smaller risk than anything else."

Father Albert smiled weakly, his face betraying his doubts. "I don't know. As you say, everything is a risk. But at least you are a doctor. They don't shoot doctors."

No, Pearson thought, they don't shoot doctors intentionally, but artillery fire was sometimes very haphazard. "Think about it," he said. "But don't take too long. The war is closing in."

"I shall pray that we do the right thing. But why should you want to help me? For you, the tapestry is nothing special, just a piece of pretty material."

"It's not so simple," Pearson said. "The tapestry is a beautiful thing. And valuable. But there's something else. Agnès Alazard has talked to me about it. It has meant a great deal to her, since childhood. And, because of that, to me too. If I take your tapestry, I would be doing it not just for you, but for her sake as well."

Father Albert clasped his hands behind his back and stood straight as if bracing himself to do God's work. "Tell me," he said, "the last two times I have seen you, you were accompanied by Mademoiselle Alazard. I have not seen much of her or her father recently. How do you find her?"

Pearson looked at Father Albert. The young fresh face, and clear untroubled eyes invited confidences. He thought for a second that the man would be comforting the other side of a confessional screen. "How do I find her? Let me tell you something, and you can judge for yourself. Since I came here a week ago, she has become my life. She is everything to me. Everything, you understand? She is the very air I breathe." He paced up the aisle towards the altar and came back to face the priest.

"Father, I have no idea what is going to happen here in the next few days. Most of it will be out of my control. If I have to leave suddenly, I can look after your tapestry, but I won't be able to protect Agnès. I have arranged for her to work with her uncle at the hospital as a nurse, and he will do what he can for her. Will you promise me to look after her if she comes to you for help?"

The priest took his hands. "Of course. Things become much clearer now. Thank you for telling me. I will pray for you both, although it seems in these dangerous times that God is going to be very busy. And I shall think about your offer."

To avoid the traffic on the edge of the town, Pearson took the horse down a steep bank and trotted alongside the road, the animal's hooves swishing through the stalks of wheat stubble. Once, he came to a wide ditch, and wondered briefly if it were the one that had killed Agnès's mother. He put the horse to it at the gallop, cleared it easily, and landed on the far side to cheers from the troops above. He removed his hat and waved it above his head in acknowledgement, slowing again as he approached the outskirts of Bazuel.

The teacher met him in the courtyard and helped him unsaddle the horse and turn it out into the paddock. A rolling boom of gunfire came to them on the north breeze, swelling to a heavy crescendo, throbbing on and on, in the still evening air.

"That's the closest yet," said Alazard. "It can't be more than ten kilometres."

Pearson thought of the long lines of troops he had passed on the road. They were coming from the north, away from the fighting. It was unlikely to be the British that were laying down a barrage, he thought. An army on the run would not have time to plan offensive action. It sounded like they weren't holding the line at Bavay.

He turned, hearing the low growl of a dog. Jacques came out of the house and was running down the steps with Agnès.

She came to him, soft and pliant in his arms. "What is it, John? It is closer now."

He held her, crushing her a little, breathing her scent. "Yes. Much closer."

"Will you still be here tonight?" she whispered, out of her father's hearing.

He felt his insides turn over, wishing he could be alone with her, without the teacher. "Yes. I've told them where I am. I don't think I'll be needed before morning."

"You expect the first casualties tomorrow?" Alazard called to him.

"Yes. I must be at the hospital early." Pearson smiled. "With my assistant here."

"Your assistant brought her uniform back from the hospital this afternoon," said Agnès. She held her chin high.

Alazard led them back into the house and lit the oil lamps. He brought a bottle of wine and some glasses to the kitchen table. Pearson watched her sitting, erect and calm, as he listened to the squeak of Alazard winding a corkscrew. Alazard put the bottle between his knees, pulled out the cork, and splashed wine into their glasses. *"Santé."* He raised his glass, shaking his head. "I can't believe we are retreating so fast. At this rate the Germans will be through here in twenty-four hours. I do not understand that we have not been able to stop them. The 5th Army is supposed to be one of our finest."

"We don't seem to be doing any better," said Pearson, turning the glass in his hands. The wine glowed dark in the lamplight.

"We have been thinking what we should do," said Agnès. "Before I left the hospital, uncle Gaston told me I could stay there if things get bad. I am going to take some things over tomorrow and live there for a while." She looked at Pearson confidently, knowing that he would agree.

Pearson covered her hand with his. "I am very glad you have done this," he said and turned to Alazard. "Will you go to Le Cateau too?"

"No. I am going to stay here. If the Germans come and find this house empty they are certain to take it. They will probably use it as a billet anyway, but if I am here there is a chance I can protect the place."

"They might turn you out onto the street."

Alazard shrugged in resignation. "If they do that I will go to Le Cateau."

"But could you live here with the house full of German soldiers?"

"I would not enjoy it. But I would do it if it were necessary. And perhaps it would not be for long. Anyway, there are the horses and the hens to feed." He stood up and crossed to the window at the sound of a wagon coming into the yard. English voices carried into the room and a moment later Mansell came in looking tired, but ebullient as ever.

"We're off," he said, removing his hat. "The town's full of our men pouring in from the north. They've been on the go since the Germans pushed us off the canal." He ran a hand through his thick hair. He turned to Agnès. "Would it be all right for my man to come up in a minute to pack my gear?"

"Yes, of course." She played with the collar of her blouse, looking at Mansell. "I am so sorry you have to leave us."

"Believe me, so am I. I don't expect ever to find another

billet like this. I've been very happy here. Thank you both for everything you have done for us."

"It is nothing," said Alazard. "I wish you good luck. Will you take a glass before you go?" He held up the bottle.

Mansell laughed. "Not this time, thank you." He went to meet Phillips and took him up the stairs to his room and later, when he had said goodbye, he called to Pearson to go with him down to the waiting wagon in the yard.

"It's a bloody shambles in the town, old man. The place is full of troops trying to find something to eat and lying down on the cobbles to sleep. Fighting a rearguard action on the run is one hell of a difficult manoeuvre. It's all happened so quickly. Just as it started to get dark the whole place filled up. It's been a rout, I'm afraid."

"Where's the line now?"

"God knows. Five or six miles away."

"But the battalion's all right where they've dug in?"

"Yes, so far. Try to get over early in the morning. Watson knows where we are."

"Any good?"

"I've only seen it from the distance. A scruffy old farmhouse. But we're lucky to have it. Those poor sods on the run haven't got anywhere to go. They're out in the open tonight, and by the look of it there's going to be a storm. Probably rain like hell later."

Just before midnight Pearson heard her soft footsteps on the stairs and the creak of a loose floorboard on the landing outside his door. He sat in his dressing gown, writing in a notebook by candlelight. The door opened, and she came into the room, barefoot, wearing a long white nightgown, with her hair down, pushed back behind her ears. He stood up, putting the notebook and his pen on the chair, and she ran across to him with quick light steps, coming eagerly into his arms. He held her head, pushing his fingers through her hair, holding her to him in an ecstasy of kissing. The warm contours of her body pressed against him.

"I am sorry to have been so long," she whispered. "I wanted for my father to go to his room and be asleep."

"I would wait for you for ever," he said. "How do you know he is asleep?"

"After you went upstairs he finished another bottle of wine. I could hear the snoring through the wall." She glanced at his notebook. "What have you been writing, John?"

"It's a poem, for you." He picked up the notebook, carefully tore out the page, and gave it to her. Her eyes were dark opals.

She held the paper to the light of the candle, her hair hanging forward like a curtain. In the silence while she read, Pearson stood at the window. Lightning flickered sideways across the sky. Agnès looked up at him, shaking her head, and read the poem again.

"I should have guessed you are a poet." Tears trembled in her eyes. "This is so beautiful. May I keep it?"

"It's yours. I wrote it for you."

"Then it is ours, together. It belongs to us both."

Lightning flickered again, strobing through the window, and a light rain began to fall. A long roll of thunder rumbled across the sky.

"That is a better sound," she said. "Better than those awful guns. Always I have loved the sound of thunder, even as a child."

Pearson laughed. "It used to frighten me as a small boy. I used to hide under the bedclothes. Come here so that I'm not scared."

He stood behind her, cupping her breasts in his hands, holding her as they looked out of the window at the rain of the coming storm. The troops on the cobblestones will be out in this, he thought. Water will be sluicing over the town square, soaking men already exhausted from the long retreat from Mons. And tomorrow those same tired men may have to fight again. He closed his eyes, trying to shut out the thought of war, and she pressed back against him, warm and full of loving.

"Come with me," he said, and led her over to the bed.

He undid the buttons of her nightgown, slipping it off her shoulders and she put down her arms so that the nightgown fell to the floor. She stepped out of it and, from the candlelight, the shadows of her movement leaped across the ceiling. She pulled the cord of his pyjamas and he kicked them away. Like pieces of a jigsaw, they rolled together on his bed, kissing and kissing in a crescendo of rampant abandon, while the storm broke and rain hammered with a roar on the roof and gushed unchecked into the courtyard below.

Later, she lay with her head on his belly and he traced the little hills and valleys of her face with his fingers.

"You are so beautiful," he whispered. "From the moment I first saw you. Why should it be me that can lie here with you, loving you? What is the matter with all the young men of France that you were here like an open flower, unpicked, when I arrived?"

"Perhaps we are like the birds," she said and he could feel the resonance of her voice in the muscles of his belly. "Like two swifts who choose each other out of the hundreds that arrive in spring and fly, screaming round the church tower."

"Did you know that swifts sleep on the wing? They even mate like that, flying through the air." He stroked the skin behind her ear.

"When you make love to me, John, I feel as if we are flying."

"I feel it too. Do you know when I first felt as if we might fly together?"

"Tell me."

"It was when we were at the pool. You said you sometimes swam there with nothing on. And then you began to undress, and for a second you stood in the sunlight on the jetty and I felt as if I had no weight in me, that I would float in the air with you."

"Perhaps we really are two birds. Will you come with me to the pool again one day?"

"Of course. Shall we do that or go to Africa first?"

She thought for a moment, searching his groin with her hand. "I want very much to go to Africa with you. I think we should do that first and then come back here and go to the pool. The river will always be here."

"And you think Africa might disappear?" He sighed a little, loving her.

"No, but I cannot wait to cook guinea fowl over a fire with you."

"I hope you haven't got too romantic a view of Africa."

"If I have, then it is your fault."

"Mine?" he laughed. "Why should it be my fault?"

"When you laugh like that it makes my head bounce up and down. It will be your fault because it was you who made it sound so romantic in the telling."

"We were talking about the young men of France," he said a little later.

"It was you that talked of them."

"Yes, but you haven't answered my question."

She moved up so that her lips brushed against his ear. "Is it not enough that I was an unpicked flower, as if waiting for you?"

He held her very tightly against him, feeling the length of her softness. "With you, nothing can ever be enough for me," he whispered.

Lightning split the sky and a simultaneous crash of thunder burst overhead. A gust of wind blew in through the window, swinging the shutters, and the guttering candle sent shadows dancing on the walls. Pearson wondered what it would be like out in the new trenches. They would not have had time to make proper dugouts and the rain would search out every corner. The men would be getting awfully wet. He was glad

125

that Watson had come back with Mansell and would be dry in his loft. He wondered what Anson would think of rain and of his men lying out in it.

"John," she said quietly. "You have gone away from me."

"No. I'm here." He found her hand.

"Yes, but you left me."

"How did you know? It was only for a second."

"Yes, but every second is important. What were you thinking?"

"Of the rain. The rain in the trenches."

"And your men there?"

"Yes. Of the men."

"Your men are fortunate to have you."

"No, Agnès. I am just an ordinary doctor who happens to have put on a uniform. It's me that's lucky." He sat up, leaning on one elbow, watching her. "Outside, men are crouching under makeshift shelters of tarpaulin. Some will have wounds from today's fighting. All of them will be exhausted and hungry and tomorrow they may have to fight again. And I am warm in bed, in the arms of the most lovely woman I have ever seen. But it is more than that. Much more. What we are doing is of little consequence to other people, or the war. But it is everything to me. Nothing is more important to me now than to be with the woman I love."

"But in the morning? What will happen in the morning?"

"In the morning I will still love you."

"Even if you have to leave me?"

"If I have to leave you, it won't stop me loving you."

"No. Nor me you. And if you go, I will still have that. That and hope. Do you think it is dangerous to hope?"

"Only if you are denied it."

"Can I ever be denied hope?"

"No. Hope only dies in prison when there is no possibility of escape."

"And I wouldn't be in a prison, John. Listen to me. Whatever happens, you are in here, in my head. And here, in my heart. And here." She took his hand and pressed it to the lower part of her belly. "You are in here with me, and no one, nothing, can ever take that away."

"No wonder I love you," he said. "Kiss me again."

She rolled on top of him, kissing his lips, probing with her tongue. He stroked the soft skin of her waist and out over the flare of her hips.

"I called at the hospital again on my way home, to see if you were still there", he said. "It seemed awfully empty without you. I went into the church too."

"To look for me, or to pray?"

"Both. And to see Father Albert."

"Father Albert?"

"I thought we might need to use his church if there are too many casualties for the hospital."

"Oh, John. Do you think it may be so bad?"

"I don't know. Perhaps. I told him I would take away that tapestry if the fighting gets any worse. He seems awfully worried about it."

She rolled off him and sat up, staring at him. "But John, how can you do that?"

"I'll put it in with my stores. It will be safe there."

"Why do you think that?"

He told her about the medical wagons.

"Oh. You would do this for Father Albert?"

"Yes." But mostly for you. Because of what I know it means to you."

"I love you, John Pearson." She thought for a moment, playing with the stubble on his chin. "What did Father Albert say?"

"He is going to pray. So he does the right thing."

"I am glad if you take it. I think it will be a good thing."

"Why, really?"

"Because I know you will keep it safe and it will be another reason for you to come back."

"I don't need another reason to come back. Not so long as

you are here. That is enough reason."

Gradually the storm moved away to the south leaving the night calm. The rain eased and the only sound from outside came from the slow drip, dripping of water in the courtyard below.

Tuesday 25 August 1914

The message came at daybreak. It was written on a piece of paper, delivered by a boy on a bicycle. Pearson read it and handed it to Agnès. She looked at the note and nodded, before giving it back to him.

"Thank you," Pearson said to the boy. "The doctor gave you this at the hospital?"

"Yes, Monsieur. I came as fast as I could."

"What is your name?"

"François, Monsieur." He looked down at his boots, turning his cap in his hands.

"Well, François, have you had any breakfast?"

The boy looked at a loaf of bread on the table. "No. There was no time."

"Give him some bread," said Alazard. "And some coffee. Do you like coffee?"

"Yes, Monsieur."

"I will make you *café au lait,*" Agnès told him, moving over to the range. "Sit down François. You can put your cap on the spare chair."

"Thank you, Mam'selle.*"*

"What is the road like?" Pearson asked him.

The boy shrugged. "Muddy. But it's all right on a bicycle because you can swerve between the carts and the motor lorries." He looked up, with his mouth full of bread. "They are saying that we shall push the Germans back soon."

"Did you see any wounded soldiers at the hospital?"

"There was a horse ambulance. I could not see inside. The town is full of soldiers. They are everywhere."

"Where is your home?"

"Near the bridge. Behind the hospital."

"Well, François, when you have eaten enough you must go back. Will your parents be there?"

"My mother is there." He sat up straight in his chair. "My father is fighting in Alsace. He is with our cavalry."

Pearson went down the steps with his arm round François' shoulder. "Tell the doctor we will come as soon as possible," he said. He watched the boy go, pushing his bicycle over the loose gravel of the yard before mounting it in the gateway, a small figure pedalling hard for home. The gunfire started up again, intermittent salvoes of artillery, booming in the morning air. After a night of rain, the grass of the orchard steamed in warm sunshine.

Pearson shouted for Watson and ran back up into the house. It was still too early for Marie-Hélène, and Agnès stood at the sink, her arms buried in soapsuds. Alazard had left the room and Pearson came up behind her and put his hands on her breasts. She leaned back against him. "The wagon will come for us at any minute," he said. "We can get them to drop us at the hospital. It may take a while if that boy was right about the traffic on the road."

"There is another way we can go," she said, drying her hands on her apron.

"Where?"

"There's an old track that used to be the road before the railway came. It's a little further but nothing uses it now."

"But we still have to cross the railway?"

"Yes, of course. It goes over the top, the other side of the embankment."

"I'll get Watson to pack my things," said Pearson. "You had better get ready."

She was dressed as a nurse when he came down. She wore a white nurse's cap and a long blue cloak with its hood turned down flat behind her shoulders, smiling, a little self-conscious. Jacques looked on uncertainly, his head tilted to one side, alarmed at the sight of suitcases. He began to bark furiously as the wagon arrived, drawn by two mules, crunching gravel as the muleteer circled in the yard below. Pearson took Alazard's hand.

"Good bye," he said, having sudden difficulty with the words. He had prepared himself for this moment, but when it came, his thoughts evaporated like morning mist, leaving him speechless. He owed so much to the teacher. What can you say, he thought, to a man who has sheltered you for a week in his house, provided you with every comfort, and with whose daughter you have fallen in love and taken to your bed? He cleared his throat. "Good bye," he said again. "I don't know how to thank you for everything you have given me. I shall never forget this week. I hope you will have your school back soon."

Alazard raised his eyebrows. "If I can keep the Germans out of it. And in the meantime make sure my brother looks after Agnès."

Watson saddled the horse for him and then climbed onto the wagon with Agnès, telling the driver that she would show him the way, and Pearson followed them out onto the road. In the gateway he wheeled the horse and called to Alazard: "Good luck with the vineyard, if you go south."

"Thank you. Perhaps one day we can take a glass of red together." He raised his arms high in the air, as if appealing to God, and Pearson put the horse into a trot.

François was right. Columns of cavalry and transport crawled along the main road to Le Cateau. French cavalry seemed to be going in one direction, the British in another. Pearson rode close behind the wagon as it lurched onto a track at the edge of the village, weaving through stubble fields until they came to the old road, following higher ground where they crossed the railway at the beginning of a cutting outside Le Cateau. He could see Agnès, sitting beside Watson, talking to him and once turning to smile at him, and he felt a small pang of jealousy that he was not with her in the wagon. His saddle creaked as the horse walked at the slow pace of mules, and the curious onion dome of the church spire rose into the sky ahead.

Le Cateau seethed with troops, making movement impossible. Ragged columns of retreating soldiers, exhausted from two days of fighting, poured in from the north. In the

131

square, men sprawled on the cobblestones trying to sleep, or queued outside the cafés, hoping to find something to eat. Pearson looked around, exasperated that he could see no sign of officers, no organisation of command. The wagon halted, its way blocked by the crowd. The mule driver turned round, spreading wide his arms in desperation, appealing for help.

Watson jumped off the wagon and came to Pearson, holding the horse's bridle.

"If you ride in front, sir, we'll get on better. The horse will clear the way."

"All right, Watson. Tell them we're going to the hospital." He rode to the front and heard Watson, now back standing in the wagon, bawling at the crowd.

"Come on lads. Move aside will yer. 'ospital supplies. Some of you will be needing them soon, so look sharp. Mind yer backs now."

Tired men, grey-faced and mud-spattered, stood aside in sullen resignation, allowing the wagon through to the far side of the square where a narrow side street led off to the hospital. House windows were shuttered as the occupants battened down in the face of the coming apocalypse.

To his horror, Pearson saw several horse-drawn ambulances standing in the hospital courtyard unloading stretcher cases. A tightness twisted in his stomach, drying his mouth with the sour taste of anxiety. He looked at Agnès, and was amazed as always by her serenity. This is where I find out if I'm any good, he told himself, as his horse fidgeted on the cobbles, tossing its head. He dismounted, trying to swallow his fear that his inexperience might let him down. He started to tell Agnès that she should get off the wagon but she was already stepping to the ground.

"Leave your case," he said. "I can bring it in for you."

"What about your luggage, sir?" said Watson.

"Leave it on the wagon for now." He turned to the muleteer. "What are your orders?" he asked.

"Only to collect you and take you to your quarters, sir."

"Nothing after that?"

The man shook his head. "No, sir."

"Can you wait here somewhere? It might be all day."

"I don't mind if it's all night as well. I've got food for the mules and I can sleep under the wagon."

"All right. Watson you had better take the horse and let the adjutant know where I am. And tell him about all these ambulances. You all right on a horse?"

"Not quite like Phillips, sir," said Watson. "But I won't fall off."

"Off you go then. And come back here later with the horse."

He swung Agnès's suitcase off the wagon, took her arm and strode into the hospital. It was amazing, he thought, how giving a few simple orders could make you feel more positive. He put down the suitcase in an alcove off the hallway where it would not be in the way, and stood aside to make room for some stretcher-bearers. A hospital orderly met them at the doorway to the first ward. He looked old and frail and very frightened.

"I need to speak to Dr. Alazard," said Pearson.

"The doctor is operating. There are many cases."

"I know. Dr. Alazard is expecting us."

"You will excuse me, but I must see some identification."

"I am a doctor, too."

"I will ask. Wait here please."

When he came back the orderly showed them into the operating theatre where Gaston, his pince-nez glasses sparkling in the light, bent over a patient, assisted by a nurse. A man, unconscious from anaesthetic, lay on the operating table, where Gaston attended to a deep wound in his chest. A strong smell of disinfectant filled the room.

"Thank God you're here," said Gaston, looking up briefly from his work. His eyes smiled over the top of his mask. "I was not sure the boy would find you. As you can see, we are very busy."

133

"Where can I be most help?" Pearson asked.

"In the first ward. On the left as you came in. They are putting the casualties in there for assessment. Monsieur Trichet is doing what he can." He waved a glinting scalpel through the air towards the orderly. "But it is not fair on him to be asked to prioritise the needs of patients. It will be a great help to us if you will work there. Agnès can assist you. She can bring you what you need. I will come to see you when it is quieter." He leaned forward again over the man on the table, excising the wound.

Of the ten beds on the assessment ward, six were already occupied. Daylight flooded in through tall windows giving the room a clean, fresh atmosphere. It was a place designed for healing. The silence surprised and worried Pearson as he made a quick tour, reading any notes clipped to the ironwork of the beds, explaining things to Agnès.

"They are probably suffering from shock," he said.

"Is that why they are so quiet?"

"Yes." He stopped by a bed where the hump of a body under a sheet seemed unnaturally short. He lifted the sheet and saw that both the man's legs were missing, cut off above the knee. Blood seeped through roughly applied bandages. The man was awake, his eyes burning like coals, staring in some faraway agony. Pearson picked up his wrist. "The pulse is too fast. Fast and weak. He will have lost a lot of blood and his blood pressure must be very low." He lay the man's wrist back on the bed, and picked up the clipboard. "Nearly two days," he said, shaking his head. "He's been like this for two days. It's shock. The body shuts down whole areas of circulation. Starting with the skin. See how cold and pale it is. Can you make up some saline solution? You know how to do that ?"

"Yes."

"It's his only hope. He's badly dehydrated. If we can raise his blood pressure it may be possible to save him."

"I will go and make some solution."

"Make lots. Some of these others are sure to need it too. Are you all right?"

"Yes, thank you. Why do you ask?"

"There was something in your voice."

"It's this man," she whispered. "With no legs. It was terrible for me to see this." She turned away and he heard her say: "I wanted to be strong for you."

He reached out to her and lifted her chin so that she looked at him. "A man like that is a shock to anyone," he told her gently. "I am so sorry to bring you into all this."

Pearson bent over the man, moving a hand in front of his face. "Can you see this? Try to follow it if you can."

The dark bloodshot eyes flickered briefly and his dry cracked lips opened a little but no sound came. Pearson looked at his card again. They had given the man enough morphine to lay out a horse. "We are going to get some fluids into you, and I'll be back later. The nurse will fix you up." The sideways movement of the man's head was almost imperceptible. He's lost the will to live, thought Pearson. That is what comes from forty-eight hours of blood loss, pain and shock.

Pearson moved from bed to bed, evaluating his patients, assessing priorities. Quickly he realised that it was not necessarily the most badly wounded that should be treated first, but those who seemed more likely to survive. He was going to have to play God, deciding whom to save and whom to let die. But who the hell was he to judge this? And how was he supposed to value the life of one man over another's? By age, or rank? They didn't teach that at Millbank.

There was only one theatre, and he would have to decide the order in which to send them. He would have to be professional about it. He could forget the question of age. That didn't really matter when they were all between eighteen and forty. And as far as rank was concerned, that didn't matter much either. Who was to say that a private in an infantry regiment was less valuable than a colonel of horse?

He went over to where Agnès attended to the man with no legs, watching her as she hooked up his drip. She worked smoothly, unflustered, inserting the needle with calm brown hands. When she had finished she stood up and looked at him and he was amazed at her composure.

"Is that all right?" she said.

"It's perfect. And I love you."

She blushed, and said to him: "You should not say that now."

"It gives me strength," he said. "Three of the other patients will need a drip. But not the one in the end bed, the one with abdominal injuries."

"And the last one, in the bed under the window?"

"He needs nothing now. I am afraid he's dead."

She put her hand over her mouth and her eyes were huge and very dark.

"I am so sorry, John."

"There will be others. The man with abdominal wounds. He is unconscious, with bad wounds here," he held the centre of his chest below his ribs. "With wounds like that there is nothing we can do. It is a miracle that he is still alive."

"About the other one," she said quietly. "Shall I tell Monsieur Trichet?"

"No. When the stretcher bearers come back I will ask them to take the body to the mortuary. Can you show them the way?"

"Yes."

"Then for the moment please arrange drips for the others."

Pearson thought quickly. Of the six men in the ward, one was dead, one was going to die at any minute, and the man who had lost his legs would probably die if they didn't operate soon. But an operation was impossible unless his blood pressure could be raised. So that left the other three. And any minute now more casualties could arrive.

He heard Gaston Alazard say: "I am ready for another case."

"Corporal Wilson, head wound," said Pearson. "He's conscious and seems to know what's going on. I don't think you can save his eye, but I'd love it if you prove me wrong."

"The others?"

Pearson told him what he knew and Gaston nodded, looking round the ward. "Thank you. This is a great help to me."

"With your permission," said Pearson, "I can look after the man over there who has lost a hand. I don't think you need to see him."

"That is better still," said Gaston. "Agnès can bring you anything you need." He hurried back to the theatre.

"You're a lucky man," Pearson said to the man with no hand. "Someone has done an excellent job here."

"The MO did it. Out in the open, behind a little wall." The voice was weak but clear.

"What is your regiment?"

"Nothumberland Fusiliers."

"Your doctor is a talented man. I'm going to tidy it up and put on some fresh dressings for you. You'll need a bit of local anaesthetic." He called to Agnès and she brought him what he needed.

"We took a pasting at the canal," the man said, holding up his amputated arm. "We were covering a bridge from an old farmhouse when a round of HE came in and wiped out the whole lot of us. Apart from me. Shell splinters and chunks of masonry flying everywhere. Dust and blood all over the place, staining the rubble. We got our own back later though. A *Boche* swam the canal to get to the swing bridge on our side. So he could shut it and let his mates over. We potted away at him in the water and couldn't hit him, but someone shot him from a loophole in a garden wall when he was working the handle and he fell into the mechanism."

"You must stop talking now so I can do this properly."

"Then we got caught by a machine gun south of the canal. They must have brought it up in the night. Blew the hell out of us in the morning. At least two never made it and several wounded."

"All right. Don't talk. You're going to need all your strength later." He injected novocaine.

"It must have jammed," the man said. "It suddenly went quiet and I thought if you hang around here it won't just be an arm they've hit, so I held it with the other hand and ran like hell for cover. The MO patched me up."

"Can you feel this?" Pearson pinched his arm below the elbow.

"No, nothing. Lucky it was an arm. I couldn't have run if it had been a leg. It's a funny sound you get from machine gun bullets. They're heavy calibre and slam into things like being in a shipyard." He sank back, exhausted by the memory.

"Look," Pearson said to Agnès. "This shows what a skilled man can do out in the open. I'm going to trim off that flap of skin and put in a few stitches. He was lucky to get it done so soon after he was hit. The longer you have to wait, the less chance you have. You can put a drip in, too, please."

Pearson worked on, oblivious of time, his concentration centred on the wounded. They must have trained me well, he thought as his early fears dissipated, and with growing confidence he began to believe in his ability to heal. The ability that Anson had doubted.

As he worked he became aware of Agnès's constant presence at the periphery of his vision. She had an extraordinary faculty to anticipate his needs. Always she seemed ready with the instrument or dressings that he wanted, and when a man was brought in crying out with pain and terror she went to him, soothing him with her comfort.

"You have learned well here with Gaston," he told her.

"I was lucky to learn when things were peaceful. When there was time."

"Yes. Do you know I was very afraid when we arrived here? I was not sure that I could cope. I was frightened that I would make some awful error of judgement. That someone would die because of what I did, or didn't do."

"I felt that fear in you, John," she said softly. "And I knew it would go away when you began to work."

But her confidence was tested later when they looked again at the patient who had lost his legs. He drifted in and out of consciousness, muttering incoherently.

Pearson took the man's blood pressure. "It's still dangerously low," he said. Can you help me with the bandages?"

He lifted the man's buttocks so that she could unwind the cloths and cut away the material where it stuck. He glanced at her, knowing that it would be hard for her. She had gone very pale and he saw little beads of sweat break out on her face. Her hands began to shake slightly, and when she looked at him, biting her lip, he was torn by her distress as she struggled to help him.

"I'm so sorry to ask you to do this," he said.

She unwound the last of the bandages until the exposed stumps wept blood like raw meat, and gave off a sickening sweet smell. She raised her head in horror.

"Oh God," he said, "I should have known."

"What is it?"

"Gangrene. Gas gangrene."

"The smell?"

"Yes. I should have taken off the bandages when I first saw him this morning. This is my fault."

"How? They must have been on for ages. Two days you said."

"Yes." He looked at the ward clock. "And now more time. Gangrene thrives in the absence of oxygen. I should have known."

She shook her head as if to clear it. "But what can you do?"

"All that dead and damaged tissue needs to be cut away. You need to make a large clean wound, open to the air. Then there's a chance it will heal."

"I can help you if you wish."

Pearson shook his head. "I dare not do it. He is so weak it will kill him."

"And if you do nothing?"

"He will die from toxaemia."

"Then you have nothing to risk by trying."

"Except the life of another patient. To do here what needs to be done would take a long time. It would have to be done with great care. And more casualties may come in at any time."

"Yes. Yes, I understand. I am sorry, I did not mean to argue." She put a hand to his cheek and he loved her for it with an awful longing. "You have so much to think about," she said. "I should not make it worse."

"Nothing could be worse for me than if you were not here. We ought to dress his legs again. With sulphonamide. It's the least we can do. I can get Trichet to help me if you like."

"No. I will do it."

He applied the sulphonamide and lifted the man again so that she could wind the dressings.

"Tell me, John," she said as she worked with the bandages, "What is the cause of this?"

"Of gangrene?" He paused, gathering his tired thoughts. "The fields here are full of animal manure. A soldier like this will have crawled, trying to protect himself from gunfire. His clothes will be covered in mud. If he gets hit by shrapnel, they go through his trousers, taking manure through his skin and into his flesh, cutting veins and arteries. Be careful there, do not wind it quite so tight."

"Like that? Is that better?"

"Yes," he nodded. "The point is that those organisms from the soil will be dispersed right through his legs. The incubation period is as little as twenty-four hours. The clock starts ticking early." The words came out in a torrent, leaving him breathless as she finished the dressing.

She stroked his forehead. "Do you know you have been working now for more than eight hours, with no food or rest?"

"So have you. And I couldn't have done it without you." He waved an arm as if to encompass all of northern France. "And some of our men out there have had no rest for more than two days. How can you expect men to fight like that?" He took a deep breath and said more slowly: "The main problem is the time it has taken to bring these men to a hospital. Look at that man whose hand we did. He had good medical care a few minutes after he was wounded. It makes all the difference, do you see? The difference between life and probable death."

Gaston came into the ward, exhausted, his face drained of colour. He removed his pince-nez and rubbed the heels of his palms into his eyes. "We can take no more," he said. "All the beds are full. What is happening out there?"

"We're on the run," said Pearson. "An army on the run."

"I have told Trichet that we can take no more casualties. Incidentally, he has heard that your staff officers have left the school."

"That can't be right," Pearson said, appalled. "They can't just leave."

But the doctor shook his head. "There is a school caretaker. Apparently the place was full of activity at lunchtime, but when he went back an hour ago it was deserted. Empty coffee cups lying around and ashes from burnt paper in the fireplaces. Oh, Trichet says there is a Private Watson in the courtyard asking for you."

Pearson went out to the fresh air of the courtyard, praying that he would not find more ambulances full of casualties. What on earth would he and Gaston do when more arrived? Perhaps they could put a few in the corridors. He remembered his conversation with Father Albert. They could take casualties into the church but he would have to arrange for some medical supplies to be sent there. It wouldn't be too bad up there for the lightly wounded but you couldn't send serious cases, men with no limbs or their guts blown open.

But the yard was deserted, bathed in the warm yellow light of late afternoon. The clamour of war rang much louder out in the open, away from the protection of the hospital walls. So, he thought, they've moved GHQ back. They must be getting windy. He could identify individual gunshots from the artillery now, and imagined the British rearguard fighting with the Germans snapping at their heels.

There was no sign of the mule cart. Perhaps the man had gone down to the shade near the river. He saw a horse at the far side of the courtyard, and Watson sitting on a low wall, smoking a cigarette in the sunshine. The normality of it, compared with the horrors of the ward, swept through him in a wave of nostalgia for ordinary times. Watson jumped to his feet and stamped his cigarette into the ground.

"You look done in, sir."

"It's been a long day. How are things at the battalion?"

"Pretty good, sir. They're mostly dug in."

"And the RAP? I ought to get down there." He ran a hand over his face, feeling the stubble.

"Captain Cazenove said to tell you there's no need, sir. Rowntree and the other orderlies have got all your supplies in, and the captain has sent the word round that no one is to turn up for sick parade unless they're dying. There won't be many volunteers for that," he added with a smile.

"No, I hope not."

"They've heard what it's like here. They don't need to be told you've got your hands full."

"I can sleep here tonight in a chair. Would you get some washing things from my case if you can find that mule fellow? And you can tell him he can get down to the lines with the rest of my stuff. You all right in the new billet?"

"It's not a patch on that loft but it's dry enough." Watson fished in the pocket of his tunic and pulled out an envelope.

"Major Mansell asked me to give you this, sir. He said to tell you there's no reply needed. Is there anything else for me when I've found your washing things?"

"No. You'll take the horse back? Look after her won't you. I've got rather fond of her."

Watson grinned in conspiracy: "Phillips has pinched some first class rations from one of the cavalry units. She wont go short."

"Thank you, Watson. Tell the adjutant if anyone needs me I'll either be here or in the church."

"The church?"

"Yes," he laughed. "Don't look so worried. They may take in some of the lighter casualties there."

"Very good, sir. I'm not very good at churches. I'll go and find your things."

Pearson went back into the building and found Agnès making coffee. There was no sign of Gaston Alazard.

"He is taking a rest," she told him. "While you were outside I went round the ward with Gaston. He has given some more morphine. Most of them are asleep."

Or dying, he thought, but he said: "I'll go again in a minute." He held her waist, pulling her to him, happy to see that some of her colour had returned.

"Look," he said, "I've had this from Mansell." He showed her the envelope and tore it open.

1630 hrs. John, the CO wanted to bring you up to date and I said I would do it. You may have heard that GHQ have done a bunk. That's not for general publication, you understand. Not very good for morale, that sort of thing. You won't have heard that Smith-Dorrien has decided to stand and fight here. It's a tough decision with an army on the run but I think he reckons the alternative is worse. If the blighters overtook us we really would be in trouble. Hartwell knows you are doing v. good work where you are. He wants you to stay there and will blow for you when you're needed.

*Everything all right here and we are keeping your bed for you
in the billet. Talking of which, give my regards to your pretty
girl if she's still with you. Can't for the life of me think what
she sees in you though.. Richard.*

Pearson gave her the letter and watched her as she began to
read. A frown of concentration brought small furrows to her
brow. She's got to the bit about Smith-Dorrien, he thought.
At the end, a smile softened her face again and she looked up
at him blushing.

"I will have to talk with Richard Mansell," she said.
"Blighters is a rude word for the Germans?"

"Not really. It's for anyone you don't like."

"And now there is going to be fighting in Le Cateau?"

"It looks like it. Perhaps not so much in the town, but in
the hills outside."

"Where your men are?" She handed him a mug of coffee.

He thought of the sloping ground south of the Cambrai
road, and of the track behind the ridge where they had put the
aid post. "Yes, maybe there. And on the hill this side of the
Roman road." He sipped the hot coffee. It was the hill that
was strategically important. The Germans might creep into Le
Cateau but they couldn't hold it safely without first taking that
hill. He wondered who was dug in up there, and was glad it
was not his battalion.

"What will happen to our patients if the Germans come?"

He heard her voice as if from a distance, pushing aside his
thoughts. "I hope there'll be time to evacuate those that can be
moved," he said. "It may be difficult. The roads will be
jammed."

"And the ones who cannot be moved?"

Pearson put down his mug and held her hands. "I want
you to stay here with Gaston to care for them."

She looked down at the floor and then up, staring into his
eyes. "I want to go with you, John. I am afraid to stay here."

"You don't need to be afraid as a nurse, caring for the

wounded. We have talked about this. You will be safer here with Gaston than anywhere else."

"I want to be with you."

He felt the anguish tearing through him, breaking him apart. "Listen," he told her, "I have thought so much of this, of us somehow running away together, hiding in lofts, escaping from the war. But we cannot make a life like that, based on deceit. I can't shirk my duties to my men and I can't take you with me into a battlefield."

"No," she said, and he saw the tears well up in her eyes. "Of course I know that. But I still want to be with you."

"You are with me for ever. As I am with you. This war can't go on. Maybe for a few months. Until the end of the year perhaps. Then I'll come back for you. Look, I want you to have this." He pulled his signet ring from the little finger of his left hand and held it out for her.

"It is for me to keep?" She looked at him in wonder.

"Yes, and for you to wear. I am not sure which finger it will fit." He felt the weightlessness come again, as if he could fly. "I want you to marry me, Agnès, when I come back."

Dawn, Wednesday 26 August 1914

At first light Pearson crept from his chair so as not to wake Agnès, still curled in sleep. He boiled a kettle and shaved, rubbing life into his face with a coarse hospital towel. He found Gaston in the ward and spoke to him quietly, confirming what they had decided the previous night.

He walked up the empty streets carrying his small suitcase, partly filled with medical supplies. The air throbbed with gunfire from artillery and the new, intermittent, menacing rattle of machine guns. He moved easily on the pavement, swinging the suitcase with his stride, his soul filled with an extraordinary sense of elation and invincibility. That wonderful girl had said she would marry him! The Germans might be about to push the British army out of Le Cateau but it would not last, and it could not be long before he would be able to come back to claim his prize.

They would get Father Albert to marry them, and Gaston would find work for him in the hospital. He could set up home with Agnès in Le Cateau or one of the nearby villages. A village house would be better, he thought, with a piece of land so she could keep hens and they would grow vegetables and fruit. And they would need a stable of some sort for a horse and somewhere to keep a trap. The trap would be useful for visiting his patients, and in the summer they could go down to the pool with its water lilies and swim naked in the clear water. Later, when there were children, they could take them out into the countryside and show them where the poplar trees grew in rows with tall grey trunks and, in springtime, breathe the sweet scent of balsam. They would speak in English some of the time so that the children learnt it properly, and could talk to his parents when they came to stay.

This is the hell of a thing to be doing, he thought, remembering his parents. Mother will be all right over it but Father might be a bit tricky with his general suspicion of foreigners. "I have a French daughter-in-law" was not the sort

147

of remark that would come easily to him. And the prospect of Catholic grandchildren would certainly raise his blood pressure. But his father would come round to it once he had met Agnès. He should write to them again, he thought, and tell them about Agnès. Not now perhaps but a bit later when things had settled down.

He came out of the network of narrow streets into the brighter light of the square, expecting to find it full of soldiers, but only rubbish remained, the detritus of men who had slept rough. He heard a flight of swifts fly overhead, black scimitars carving the morning air, indifferent to the foolish destructiveness of man.

He crossed the deserted square towards the church, and found the door ajar. The oak timber felt rough under his hand as he pushed it open and went into the cool interior. An old woman dressed in widow's black swept the aisle, banging her broom into the ends of the pews, sending specks of dust to dance like insects in beams of sunlight from the high windows. Pearson ran over to the tapestry, wondering if he should take it down. He wished Father Albert would come. The morning angelus began to ring out from the tower. An omen perhaps, but for what?

He went back outside, full of doubt. He had expected to find activity in the church, wounded men needing his help, but there was only an old woman with a broom. Yesterday they had had to force a passage across the square between exhausted and demoralised troops and now he stood there alone, an officer of the British army, holding a suitcase. Anyone seeing him would probably think he was a deserter on the run.

As the echoes from the angelus died away, he heard the crash of an artillery salvo. Immediately the air overhead split apart with the sound of shells tearing through the sky, followed by the whip-crack of high explosive, outside the town on the Cambrai road. Pearson put down his suitcase and stood, irresolute, his earlier feeling of invincibility draining away. He heard the clatter of cavalry as a squadron of hussars burst into the square and a young fresh-faced lieutenant rode up to him on a sweating horse.

"They've got some 77s up in the cutting by the railway," the young man shouted to him, looking up as another salvo of shells tore overhead.

"What are they shooting at?"

"Our positions in the hills. You on your own, sir?"

"I was expecting some casualties. We were going to use the church."

"Oh, I don't know about that." The young man looked around, obviously impatient to leave. "You may get some takers soon. We're falling back to the south." He wheeled his horse around to rejoin his squadron, leaving Pearson alone.

Hesitantly, he went back into the church. Perhaps the old woman might know something.

"What?" she said cupping a hand to her ear. "You'll have to speak up."

"I am a doctor," he shouted. "I have come..."

"No you're not! I know the doctor. He poisoned my husband. He went to see him and when he came home he was sick for a week. It nearly killed him. Who are you?" She challenged him with her broom and Pearson could not decide which he feared most, the broom or the bristles sprouting from her chin.

"I am a British doctor, Madame," he bellowed. "I was expecting to find..." but he knew there was little point in pursuing that line, and to his relief Father Albert ran into the church, his soutane billowing in his wake.

"My poor church," he said. "I have come to see if the tapestry is all right. And I heard shouting, even over the gunfire. It is very bad outside." He was breathless from running.

The old woman, appeased by the appearance of Father Albert, resumed her sweeping after a final flourish of her broom. "Do not mind her," he said. "She is a little deranged.

But always she is sweeping in here. It is her labour for God."

"I was expecting casualties here," said Pearson, beginning to feel foolish. Something had gone wrong. Plans must have been changed.

"I don't know about casualties," said Father Albert. "Everything is chaos, and the Germans are in the outskirts of the town." He wrung his hands.

"If they are that close, it explains why our casualties aren't coming in here," Pearson said. "They'll be taken further back, somewhere safer."

"Perhaps the Germans will bring their own wounded here," said Father Albert. "Or to the hospital."

"There's no more room in the hospital," said Pearson. "All the beds were full last night, with some cases lying in the corridors."

"Then they may have to come here."

Without warning, a shell burst against the spire, splitting the air with shock. Masonry collapsed into the nave in a tumbling violence of sound and clouds of grey, choking dust. The old woman came marching down from the altar, clutching her broom, surveying the devastation. Father Albert stared in horror where blue sky streamed through a jagged hole in the tiles.

A memory of his brief training on the gunnery range swept through Pearson. "They can't have been shooting at the spire," he shouted. "It's a mistake. Someone put in the wrong charge. It should have gone over the top with the others." His hands shook uncontrollably.

White-faced, Father Albert brushed plaster from his soutane. "May God protect us," he said, and seized Pearson by the arm. "Come quickly. You must help me take down the tapestry."

He pulled Pearson over to the wall where the tapestry hung. Dust from the explosion clogged the air and fallen plaster crunched under their feet. Father Albert stood on a chair and reached up, but the top of the tapestry was too high for him.

"A ladder," he gasped. He stared wild-eyed at Pearson. "Wait here. There's a ladder behind the vestry." He ran across the nave and disappeared behind the stone pillars.

Pearson stood, afraid and indecisive, thinking that if the Germans really were so close he ought to escape while Father Albert was looking for his ladder. He knew he should get back to the hospital and the battalion, but how could he tell Agnès that he had deserted the priest and their precious tapestry? With relief he saw Father Albert reappear, dragging a stepladder with one hand and holding a roll of paper in the other.

"Quick," said the priest. He climbed the ladder and unhooked the tapestry, scrabbling with his fingers at the fastenings. "This is God's work we are doing." He jumped down and kicked lumps of plaster from the floor. "Spread out the paper for me," he said to Pearson. The paper was coarse and brown, and Pearson used his foot to unroll it. The shock wave from a new salvo ripped over the town, and, sweating, Pearson shut his eyes, dreading further explosions.

Between them they rolled the tapestry and wrapped it in the paper. Father Albert pulled some white string from the pocket of his soutane. He bent to tie the parcel and when he had finished, he straightened and Pearson saw that his composure was returning.

"Here," said Father Albert. He thrust the tapestry into Pearson's hands. "It is the will of God. I asked Him for guidance and I know now that it is right for you to take it." He smiled at Pearson in the calm, fresh-faced manner of someone who has put his troubles into the lap of God.

"Thank you, Father. Please don't worry about it. It will be safe with me, and when I bring it back there's something I want you to do for me. And for Agnès."

"What can I do?"

"I want you to marry us."

Father Albert clapped his hands, a wide grin spreading

across his face.   "You have asked her, of course?"

"Yes."

"That is happy news on this terrible day. Go quickly now, before they shoot at my church again. I will stay here for a little and pray for us all."

With the suitcase in one hand and the parcel under his other arm, Pearson ran across the square, his ears still ringing from the explosion. The 77s were firing again but the sound of the shells seemed fainter, a harsh whisper, with a longer interval before bursting. They must have switched targets, he thought, as he paused for breath at the side of the town hall. He had been badly scared by the shell on the spire, the shattering noise with no warning, and the violence of falling stonework. But he had survived his baptism of fire.

He laughed, seized with a sudden elation as he recalled Mansell's words in the mess that night. "If something comes whizzing past, it's probably not aimed at you..." But there was something profoundly shocking about the haphazard randomness of death. And it was coming to Le Cateau where the inhabitants crouched in their cellars, or under their tables, holding each other for comfort, listening to the exploding shells and the insistent rapping of machine guns.

He ran down the narrow side streets, his footsteps echoing from the walls. She must not leave the hospital, he thought. She must stay there for as long as they are fighting for the town. And when it is over I will come back and marry her. No one, surely, would ever target this hospital? He burst, panting, into the courtyard. A horse ambulance waited there. God, he thought, they can't still be bringing in new cases.

But they were not bringing new cases. They were evacuating the last of those that could be moved. The driver cracked his whip and the ambulance pulled away into the street with a rattle of wheels on the cobbles.

He met her in the corridor, outside the ward where they

had worked together.

She had removed her nurse's cap and her dark hair flowed down her neck. Her eyes were filled with concern as he pulled her to him, turning her face up to kiss.

"What has happened to you?" she said.

"Nothing."

"But you are covered in dust." She brushed clouds of dust from his shoulders.

"A shell hit the church spire. No one was hurt, but some masonry fell near us." He showed her the paper parcel. "Look. Father Albert has given me the tapestry. And he has agreed to marry us."

"Oh John.." She clung to him, kissing him desperately, kissing the dust from his lips. "So that is what you were doing at the church," she said. "I thought you were looking after wounded soldiers. We were so worried for you. We heard the gunfire."

"They're shooting from the cover of the railway cutting. There aren't any wounded in the church. It's too close to the front now. I should have realised that. How many cases are left here ?"

"Ten, I think. It is as you said. They have taken everyone who could be moved. Two more of them died this morning and it is affecting Gaston very badly. He says it is impossible to treat severely wounded men so long after they were injured."

"Gaston is right. Where is he."

"In his office, writing up his notes."

"He's a good doctor. You should be proud of him." He watched her, wondering what it was that made some people so lovely to look at. "Has no one sent for me yet?"

She shook her head. Her eyes implored him that he might somehow make it possible for him to stay..

"It can't be long now," he said. "The guns are shelling the hillsides where our men are dug in. If there's no more for me to do here I must go and join them. There's something else I should do but I don't know how." He played with her finger where she wore his signet ring.

"What? Tell me."

"I should find your father and ask him if I may marry you."

"I will tell him. And so will Gaston. It will be all right."

"It would be better if I could ask him."

"Yes, but he will understand it was impossible."

"How can you be sure."

"I know him," she said with a lovely simplicity.

"It's not every day that a man's daughter tells him she has found someone she wants to marry. It will come as a surprise."

"No, it will not be too much surprise."

"Why do you say that?"

"Because I told him."

"You did?"

"The night before last. After you went upstairs. Before I came up to your room. I told him I would marry you if you wanted it. He is very happy for me, John."

Pearson kissed her, savouring her taste, dreading what he knew must soon come.

"Perhaps he forgot by the morning. You said he finished another bottle."

"He would not forget something like that."

He must, he knew, leave her and get back to the battalion. He was surprised they still had not sent for him. It was over a mile to where they were dug in, and he would have to carry the tapestry. Even through the stone of the hospital walls the vibrations from an intense artillery barrage reached them.

"Listen," he said. "You must promise me not to leave here while there is fighting in the town."

"I have already promised you that."

"Yes, but promise me again. I want to hear it so that I can remember."

"All right. I promise."

154

"Good. Now you must cover your hair."

"Now?"

"All the time. You are too beautiful like this." He gestured to her hair where it curled at her neck.

"The cap makes me ugly?" she asked as she arranged her hair and covered it with the cap.

"No. You could never be anything other than beautiful. But with the cap you have more authority. You will be in a better position to control things."

"Some men are supposed to like a woman with authority."

"If you're going to argue with me I won't marry you."

"I am not arguing, John. I am talking to delay the time when you will leave me." She bit her lip.

"Yes, I know. I must go now and say goodbye to Gaston."

He did not see her lip begin to tremble as he left her and went to find Gaston. She had talked about '*chagrin d'amour*'. Well, he thought, he had it now all right and it hurt like nothing he had ever felt before.

The old man sat slumped at his desk, drained with exhaustion. He looked up at Pearson, shaking his head in great weariness. "They have taken them away," he said. "All except the ones who will die."

"Get some rest. It won't be long before you are needed again. And I'm afraid it's time for me to leave."

" Was there nothing for you in the church?"

"No. It was empty except for the priest. And an old woman." He opened the case and put all the medical supplies onto the desk, pushing aside some papers to make room.

Gaston stood up and held out his hand. "Thank you, and goodbye. It has been a privilege to work with you. And do not worry about Agnès. She will be safe here with me." He winked with a little smile of conspiracy. "And everything will be all right with her father."

Pearson met her again in the corridor. She looked extraordinarily composed.

"Now?" she asked him. She held out his sponge bag with

his shaving things.

"Yes." He had to clear his throat. "Yes, now."

She straightened his tie, smoothing down the collar of his shirt. "Is it safe for you outside?"

"Yes," he lied. "There is a back way, a track with high hedges." He put the sponge bag into his case.

"I did not want it to be like this," she said.

"No. But remember we are together now. A part of each of us, together for all time."

"Kiss me, John."

She clung to him, her hands locked behind his head, pulling him into her as if to devour him, and when they came apart she said: "There is so much to say."

"Yes. So much. And now I have to go."

She shook her head as if to clear it. "There is so much to remember. Now, you go."

"Yes, to remember. Now."

"I know, and you are going."

He picked up the tapestry in its paper wrapping and threw it onto his shoulder, feasting his eyes on her, and the pain was really in him, pulling his insides away. He reached for her with his free hand, caressing the soft curve of her cheek.

"Now," he said. "It must be now." He picked up the case.

She tried to speak but the words would not come, and she stood before him swaying, rocking in her grief, her hands working at her collar. She began to cry, silver tears rolling down her cheekbones, and Pearson could only walk away in utter desolation as the whole of his life, his energy, the very core of his being was sucked out of him by the agony of their sorrow.

10.30 am. Wednesday 26 August.

Careless of his safety, Pearson walked out of the hospital to the edge of the town where the Cambrai road began. The roar and crash of artillery seemed to belong in another place, unconnected with the reality of his leaving Agnès, as he struggled to convince himself that he had done the right thing. But having to abandon her, leaving her to the mercies of the Germans? A wave of nausea swept into him, sickening him with anguish. For the rest of his life he would have to live with this if it turned out badly.

A sudden rattle of small arms fire came from further up in the town, and he heard English voices shouting. He crouched behind the trunk of a plane tree, peering back up the street, his cheek pressed to the rough, peeling bark of the tree. He watched in horror as a few hundred yards away, men in khaki took up positions, firing from the corners of buildings, or lying prone on the street, shooting back up into the town. He felt a spring of sweat run down the inside of his arms. The enemy were here, and men in grey would be infiltrating the network of streets, running from building to building, fanning out through the town.

Gripped by fear, he ran round the corner but he was brought up short by a sergeant holding a rifle with fixed bayonet.

"I wouldn't go that way, sir. The *Boche* are in the cutting a mile up the Cambrai road."

"I've got to get back to my battalion."

The sergeant glanced at Pearson's RAMC badges. "You're an MO, sir?"

"Yes. They're dug in on the hillside."

"You could try down the river a mile or so, then cut round to the right and come in the back way."

The track with its high hedges, thought Pearson. "Yes," he said. "That sounds better. What's the shooting back there?"

"We're the rearguard, sir. To hold them up as long as

possible while we get the rest of the transports away." He pointed down the valley. "Your first half mile might be a bit dodgy. Their 77s have been shooting it up along with the Suffolks on the hill above. You should be all right after that."

"You know there's a hospital? For God's sake don't let them shoot there."

Pearson left the man and scrambled down a bank to a path that followed the river where it ran through allotments heavy with late summer vegetables. A German aeroplane circled above the low hill on his right, dropping flares as markers for their artillery, and smoke from bursting shells drifted on the wind. It was all so different from the cosy exercises on Salisbury plain.

At the far side of a small poplar plantation the path widened to a track and came out into an open meadow, the grass still wet with morning dew sparkling in the sunlight. It should have been a place of peace but an RFA 18 pounder lay twisted and broken, its barrel pointing uselessly at the sky. A smell of fresh earth and high explosive hung in the air and the stumps of broken branches showed white against the dark soil churned by horses and the wheels of departed limbers. A shattered boot, laced tight around an ankle, rested under the gun. A confetti of body pieces and shreds of uniform lay on the surrounding earth or hung from nearby bushes, in an obscenity of decoration.

Pearson put down his case and the paper parcel and leaned against a tree at the edge of the river, overwhelmed with sickness. They must have taken a direct hit, he thought. Minutes before they would have been loading and firing, loading and firing, sending shells spinning over to German positions when without warning retribution arrived and blew them all to pieces. And he had deserted the woman he loved. Half blinded by tears, he picked up his possessions and walked on across the ruined meadow, oblivious to the danger from enemy guns.

At the end of the meadow, in the shelter of a copse of ash

trees, a horse grazed with its reins hanging over its ears, and a man lay smoking a cigarette, propped against a low bank. His left foot bent sideways. Pain had drained the colour from Watson's face, but he was smiling.

"I'm sorry about this, sir."

"What happened?" Pearson asked. He knelt beside Watson and forced himself to think..

"The horse threw me. A shell came in and she panicked."

"What hurts apart from the leg."

"Only my pride, sir. Phillips won't ever let me forget this."

"Don't worry about Phillips." He looked at Watson's tattered trousers. "No shrapnel?"

"No, sir. We went through some brambles before I came off."

"All right. Let's have a look at your leg."

He slid his fingers slowly over the puttees from Watson's knee towards his ankle. There was no sign of blood and he could find no evidence of bone splinters. "I don't want to uncover this out here and I think it's a clean fracture. How long have you been like this?"

"A couple of hours. A troop of gunners had just come past. They had been shot up pretty badly and told me to be careful."

"You were coming for me?"

"Yes." He fished in the pocket of his tunic. "There's a note here somewhere from Captain Cazenove. I think they want you back, sir."

"I was expecting it. How's the mare?"

"Seems all right. She likes the grass in there." He handed the note to Pearson.

Pearson read it quickly and put it in his pocket. "I'm needed," he said and looked at his watch. "God. This was written at seven. Four hours ago. We'd better hurry. Why did you come this way?"

"Major Mansell suggested it. He thought you might have left already. He hoped you wouldn't come along the main road because of the machine guns Fritz has put in the cutting.

He said I might meet you along here."

"So after you broke your leg you just waited?"

"Yes, sir. And had a smoke. I knew it wouldn't be too long."

"Thank God I didn't disappoint you. Now, let's get you back. You can't get on the horse like this so I'm going to strap your leg to the other one and we'll walk. It'll probably hurt like hell, and we'll have to be quick until we're round the corner."

"I don't think Fritz is going to worry about us. Those poor buggers on the hill are getting it all."

Pearson went over to the horse. It lifted its head, chewing grass, looking at him with sad eyes. It seemed remarkably unconcerned with the explosions and rifle fire. He stroked its muzzle and lashed his case and the parcel with the tapestry behind the saddle, hoping that the battalion had not yet been involved in any serious fighting. He cut a length of leather from the reins with his pocket knife, and then tied the horse to a tree with what remained.

"Think of something nice," he said to Watson, recalling the boy with a dislocated finger. "I've got to turn this leg in a bit." He wished he had not emptied everything out of the case in Gaston's office.

"I'll think of the wife. Oh... Oh, Christ that hurt." Watson's head strained back , the sinews in his neck tight as cords. "She'd give me hell if she could see me now."

"Straighten the other leg." Pearson bent the knee of the bad leg up a little so that the foot would keep clear of the ground and strapped them both together as tight as he dared. "What's your wife's name?" he asked.

"Florence. I've been thinking of her this last hour. You can get a lot of comfort from a good woman when things aren't going too well."

Yes, thought Pearson, Watson's got a part of Florence here with him, and that's what I have with Agnès. Together for all time.

He broke a heavy branch from one of the ash trees and brought it over to where Watson lay. "Time to get you up," he said. He came round behind and put his hands in Watson's armpits. "Take all your weight on the right leg."

It came as a surprise to him to find how light the man was to lift, and he held him with one hand while he reached for the branch. "Lean on this," he said.

He saw a hat lying at the edge of the brambles and went over to pick it up. He brushed earth off it and put it on Watson's head. Watson leaned on the branch, bent forward a little with his eyes shut. He was sweating, gasping in his pain. A shell burst, a hundred yards to their right on the side of the hill, and the horse looked up with startled eyes.

"Can you make it to the corner?" said Pearson.

"Yes."

"Put the other arm round my shoulders."

"I'm not much of a dancer."

"Don't worry. No one's looking, but let's get out of here."

They began to hobble through the still-wet grass, with Pearson leading the horse with his free hand. A salvo of shells burst overhead, leaving white puffs of smoke staining the air like small clouds.

"Hopeless," said Watson. "They've set the fuses wrong. That's much too high for shrapnel." They were almost at the corner where the hill would shelter them.

In the safety of dead ground, Pearson said: "You know where we are. How far is it to the Roman road?"

"Is that the straight one where you can see for ever?"

"Yes."

"About half a mile."

"And from there to our trenches?"

"Roughly the same."

"We can't do a mile like this."

"I can try, sir."

"No. Anyway it'll kill me. I want you to sit here while I ride in and I'll send a cart for you."

"First class cab service?"

"Believe me, Watson, you're worth it. You've got your cigarettes?"

Watson nodded, tapping the breast pocket of his tunic.

"All right. Lean on me and come over here."

He helped Watson to sit on an old tree trunk and left him a water bottle. "Nice cup of tea waiting for you when you get back," he said, mounting the horse. The colour had returned to Watson's face suffusing it with red as Pearson set off at the canter.

He slowed to a walk, cautiously approaching the Roman road, watching it where it rose to the ridge. A troop of RFA 18 pounders, deployed either side of the road, fired intermittently over the ridge. He skirted round behind the guns, entered the narrow track with its high hedges, and galloped up to his aid post. To his relief he saw the mule cart parked on the verge where the mule nibbled at the hedge.

"Welcome back, sir." It was Corporal Rowntree.

Pearson took a quick look round. They had made a fine job of the dugout in his absence. "Anything serious?" he asked.

"Not here, sir. But they've got some cases up the line."

"Can't they bring them in?"

"Not in daylight. We didn't have time to cover the communication trench and it's not deep enough for stretchers where it comes over the ridge."

"All right, Corporal. Watson's down the track with a broken leg. I'm sending the cart to bring him in. You'll have to put it in a splint if I'm not here. I'll be at battalion HQ if you need me. Look after this parcel, will you? Don't let anyone touch it. It's very precious. And my case."

Pearson packed some supplies into a bag, and walked up through the bivouacs towards the sounds of battle, praying that Agnès would be all right if the Germans had taken the town. He crouched low as he approached the headquarters where it was dug into the hillside, fifty yards short of the skyline. Mud from the recent rainstorm sucked at his boots.

Anson blocked the entrance to the dugout. His face was covered in ginger stubble. Behind him Pearson could see Hartwell and Cazenove studying a map, and at the far side Mansell and the battalion signallers worked on some equipment. Anson stepped forward into the trench and let a heavy blanket swing behind him, closing the entrance. He lurched towards Pearson, his voice low and ugly with violence.

"Where the hell have you been? Cazenove sent you a note hours ago. For Christ's sake man, for better or worse your place is here. Not mooning about with your woman in that bloody town."

Pearson balled his fists, fighting back a boiling need to strike out. Anger burst inside his head. "If we were not in uniform," he fumed, "I would box your bloody ears." He pushed past Anson and entered the dugout, his face white, desperately trying to calm himself. He owed Anson no explanation. The man wasn't worth it.

"I'm sorry, sir," he said to Hartwell. "Watson couldn't reach me. He broke his leg when a shell panicked his horse. I met him in the valley. I've sent a cart for him."

Hartwell stood up. "Good. Are you all right? You look done in."

Pearson took a deep breath. "I'll be fine. It's been a rough forty-eight hours."

"We heard you've been busy. I'm afraid there's work for you here, too." He ran a hand over his face as if to sweep away fatigue.

"Casualties in the firing line?"

"Yes. It's 'B' Company. They were badly mauled earlier this morning and the stretcher-bearers got peppered every time they tried to bring out the wounded. I'm afraid de Courtney and several others were caught by high explosives."

"Fatalities?"

"Yes. Captain Robinson has taken over."

"I'm very sorry, sir. Can I get in there?"

"You can crawl in but the bloody communication trench is too shallow to get stretchers out. The ground's solid flint where it runs over the ridge. We were still trying to dig when the Germans set up their machine guns. They've zeroed on the ridge so we can't do anything until after dark."

"What about other casualties?"

"Nothing certain. We're trying to set up a link but there's a fault with the telephone at the other end."

"We're making up a new receiver," Mansell called. "We'll test it here before we send it over."

"If someone's going in, I can follow him," said Pearson.

"You remember what I said to you back in that farmhouse," said Hartwell. "I don't want you getting shot up."

"No." But Pearson was thinking there were still several hours until nightfall. Several hours when those men could be treated. The patients in the hospital had waited for two days. And he thought of the nurse with her slim brown hands setting up saline drips on men too far gone to save.

"No, sir," he said again. "I wont forget." He went over to join Mansell. The eyebrows looked more bushy than ever and stubble darkened his cheeks.

"Thank you for the note," said Pearson. He kept his voice low. "How are things, really?"

Mansell shrugged. "Anson and I are in the cover trench. But 'B' Company took a pasting earlier. It's not so bad now. The *Boche* seem to be concentrating on the right flank."

"The Suffolks?"

"And King's Own Yorkshire..."

"I met some of them in the town."

"How was the hospital?" Hartwell called.

"Awful, sir. We lost several. Some of them could have been saved if we'd got to them earlier."

"It's bloody difficult if you're on the run."

"Yes. Can we hold them here?"

"God knows. It doesn't look good. They're all along the

Cambrai road and they've taken Bazuel. They're pushing in fast on our right flank. That's what all the shooting's about. Frankly, I'm expecting orders to retire."

So the Germans are in Bazuel, Pearson thought. And probably in the whole of Le Cateau. Alazard might have them all over his house, sitting at his table and dumping kitbags on his beds. And Agnès? He felt a cold sweat break out under his hat. She had promised him she would stay with Gaston in the safety of the hospital. He wondered what she might be doing, thinking of her comforting men who struggled for life.

"If we retire," he said, "We must arrange to get stretcher cases away early, before the roads jam up." And Watson too, he thought, and hoped Rowntree had been able to fix his leg.

"It's ready," he heard a voice say, and one of the signallers came over, packing the receiver they had made into a cotton haversack. He held a spool of wire.

"I'll run oot a new wire," the signaller said and Pearson followed him into the communication trench, wondering where in the Highlands the man came from. He bent over his case holding the medical supplies.

"You'll have to get lower than that," said Anson. "You'll have to crawl. On your knees and those lily-white hands. Here, drag the case behind you." He threw over a length of cord and Pearson attached one end to his belt and the other to the handle of the case. He did not look at Anson.

Pearson crawled along the shallow trench, trying to keep clear of the wire the signaller was laying out. Sharp flints dug into his knees and elbows as he hauled himself towards the top of the ridge, and the sun burned into the back of his neck.

It's like being a mole, he thought, hemmed in on three sides by raw earth. Except a mole would have the luxury of a roof. The crack and boom of gunfire became louder away from the shelter of the headquarters dugout, and he could hear machine guns slamming away without knowing whose they were until the earth above him jumped and shook, spattering soil onto him. Splinters of flint stung his exposed skin like hot needles. In front of him the signaller stopped, and Pearson lay flat, focusing hard on the soles of the man's boots, inches from his face. One nail was missing from the left heel, and the steel quarter-plate was loose. Earth worms reached out from the trench wall, questing uncertainly before dropping to the floor.

The swish-crack of bullets moved away and Pearson, shaking, heard the calm voice of the Highlander: "They canna have seen us. They're shootin' off at random."

"Well, they scared the hell out of me."

"Are ye a stalking man, sir?"

"I've done a bit."

"Would ye feel better if we were crawling up a burn after a bloody great royal?"

"God, I wish we were."

"Well, come on then. Lets get closer to the beast." He rolled onto his side, squinting back at Pearson with a grin. "Look where the sun is, behind ye. It's right in his eyes. He canna see us."

The going became easier once they reached the far side of the ridge, and the trench deeper where the ground was soft, away from the flints. It had been dug with a zigzag pattern to avoid exposure to enfilading fire, and where it was deeper they ran, crouching, to the point where it joined the firing line. A sandy-haired sergeant led them along the trench to the dugout of Captain Robinson's company headquarters.

Pearson barely recognised the man he had last seen by candlelight at dinner in the barn at what seemed an eternity ago. Two day's growth of beard and streaks of sweat and mud had changed the smooth young face, ageing it with the harrowing malevolence of war.

"I'm so glad you're here," said Robinson in a voice flat with fatigue. "I'll show you our casualties."

Pearson had not been in a firing line before. It had been dug wide enough to walk past men in their firing positions, and deep so that it was no longer necessary to crouch. It's like standing at the bottom of a grave, he thought, where claustrophobia creeps along the crumbling walls. Robinson showed him four bodies lying in a neat row against the wall in a wider section of the trench, covered by a length of sacking to keep away flies attracted by the smell of blood. Pearson examined them briefly to ascertain the cause of death. Deep lacerations scored their heads and shoulders where shards of metal had ripped through flesh and the fabric of uniforms. One side of de Courtney's face had gone, his head sheared in half, almost down the line of his centre parting and his remaining eye stared up in silent accusation. Without warning, death would have come, swift as an unseen axe blow, from a shrapnel shell bursting directly overhead.

He forced himself not to vomit, and looked up from where he knelt and saw the blessed sky, a narrow oblong of light as if it were a ceiling. He replaced the sacking and followed Robinson round the traverses to another dugout roofed with tin sheets and earth. In the dim light men sat on an earth step against the wall, or lay on the cold damp soil, waiting for help with the patience of resignation.

"I'll need some light," said Pearson. "Either that or I'll have to work out in the trench. And a table of some sort." He began to assess wounds, deciding priorities, playing God again while they brought him some carbide lamps, and all the time the diapason of the guns swelled and faded and swelled in a percussive brutality of sound.

An orderly brought him a lamp and held it so that he could see.

"Who did the first aid?" Pearson asked him.

"Mostly me, sir."

"You've done well."

"I read the manuals last week, sir."

"Very wise. A good use of your time. So far I've only seen limb and head wounds. Are there any abdominals?"

"You mean here, in the guts?" The orderly held his free

hand over his belly.

"Yes."

"I don't think so."

"Good. We'll start with the head cases. Where's that table?"

Pearson worked for two hours, doing what he could, wishing he could do more, bitterly frustrated by the limited supplies in his case. All the time he talked to his patients, comforting them, encouraging them, sometimes commanding them to retain the will to survive until they could be taken to safety.

He worked by the light of the carbide lamps, improvising all the time in a departure from the strict rules of medical school. You have to do the best you can with this limited equipment, he told himself, and take it one step at a time. But he knew that beyond the arc of his lamps other men waited, blood seeping through hastily applied dressings, in an atmosphere rank with the smell of fear, and occasionally a round of shrapnel would explode overhead, and they would listen to the deadly metal rattling off the thin tin of their roof.

He came to love the men for their courage, and for the hope that shone from their eyes as they looked to him, patient and uncomplaining, for the relief of their suffering.

"I can't feel my legs any more. Can you help me, please?"

"Will I be all right?"

"I'm cold. So cold."

And frightened, he thought, and so terribly tired. How he wished he could do more. It was a far, far cry from the crisp starch of the Millbank wards and the floodlit sterility of the operating theatre with its ever-present smell of antiseptic. He stood up to ease his aching back and thought again of Agnès in the hospital. It was only a few hours since he left her there, that lovely girl who said she'd marry him, and he had better not think now how she looks with her hair up the way she does it, and the long curve of her neck showing.

He bent again to the man on the rough-sawn planks they had put on trestles for his table. This man is lucky, he thought, realising that it was the case he had prayed for on the train that first morning in France. A nice clean wound in the fleshy part of his upper arm, with no bone damage and the bullet gone straight through. He cleansed the wound and stitched it, talking quietly to the man and thinking there couldn't be many more to do now, but how long would it be before they could get the serious cases away for proper treatment?

"That's the one we've been waiting for," the orderly said.

"No more?"

"Not for the moment, and it's gone quiet outside. In our sector at least."

"I hadn't noticed." Pearson started to sterilise his instruments and packed them into his case. "What do you do apart from this?" he asked the man.

"Bandsman, sir. I play the flute."

" 'And gentle soothing flutes'," Pearson quoted.

"Is that from the carol?"

"Yes, I think it's a carol."

"They say we'll be home for Christmas."

There came a time towards mid afternoon when Pearson rested for a while, knowing he could do no more. The enemy's guns had concentrated their fire away on the right flank and 'B' Company stood to, manning their posts on the fire-step, watching their front through loopholes in the parapet. He borrowed a pair of field glasses from Robinson and crept into a position from where he could safely look out between sheaves of wheat over the slope leading down to the Cambrai road.

The air reeked of cordite and high explosive, and the late August sun blazed from the high dome of the sky. He scanned the cutting, three hundred yards below. That's where they will have put their machine-guns, he thought. That cutting must be full of German infantry lying over the lip with the road running behind them. You could hide a whole battalion in there and from here you wouldn't see a thing. He focused the glasses until he could see individual stems of wheat on the uncut headland of the field. A field-mouse scurried in front of him.

From further along the trench to his left a rifle started cracking away, single shots against the roar of artillery pounding the hill on the right flank. He saw sudden puffs of dust where bullets plucked at the ground at the edge of the cutting, and a brief glimpse of grey cloth and a flash of sunlight reflected from metal.

He swung the glasses round to the right, to the back of the hill where the Suffolks held out. He adjusted the focus to the greater range, turning the knurled eyepieces with his fingers, and studied the ground above the trees where he had found Watson. Cloud shadows drifted across the blue slope but where the the sun lay bright he thought he saw a movement. He rested his hands on a lump of earth and pulled the glasses back into his eyes. In the absolute focus, grey figures crept up the hillside in the cover of corn stooks. He shut his eyes for a moment and looked again. There was no doubt about it. The enemy had turned the right flank, working round to the Suffolks' rear. He swung round in panic, looking for Robinson, but Robinson shook his head sadly.

"I know," he said.

"But they're surrounded. Can't we do something?"

Robinson shook his head again. "It's two thousand yards."

"What about artillery?"

"They've had to stop firing. The target's too close to our infantry."

"Christ, they've had it then."

"Yes, I'm afraid so." He shrank back against the back of the trench, his face numb with defeat.

A man came running towards them, jumping over

ammunition boxes. He saluted Robinson. "The CO wants you, sir. He's on the telephone."

"All right." He took hold of Pearson's arm. "You'd better come too."

Pearson picked up his case and followed Robinson along the trench.

In the dug-out, the Highlander beckoned them over. He held out the telephone receiver. "It's no very clear, sir. We've still some trouble with the connection."

Robinson took the instrument from him and put it to his ear. He looked awfully pale.

"Robinson here," he said.

A tinny voice crackled in the air and Robinson bent forward in concentration. He listened for several minutes, seeming to shrink within himself before saying: "Yes, sir. I understand... Yes, he's here." He looked as if he might faint as he passed the telephone to Pearson.

"That you, Doctor?" Battalion HQ might be only a few dozen yards away but Hartwell's voice sounded disembodied, drifting through the ether.

"Yes, sir."

"We're pulling out. Robinson will give you the details. Anson and Mansell are moving their men now and I want..."

The voice faded away, drowned by the roar of nearby explosions. Pearson felt the ground shake and lumps of earth fell from the dug-out walls.

"Can you repeat that, sir. I'm afraid I lost you." He pressed the receiver to his ear.

"Are you under fire again?"

"Yes."

"Damn. I want you to get back here if you..."

The voice went again as shrapnel clattered onto the tin roof. Pearson thought of the open communication trench. It would be suicidal to try it now.

"There are several casualties here, sir," he said.

"This isn't easy. I can't afford to lose you. If you stay

171

there you will be at great risk of..." The line went dead.

"Hallo....Hallo..." Pearson shouted, but the connection had gone. "There's nothing," he said to the Highlander.

"It'll be the wire oot in the open. It's very vulnerable unless it's buried."

Robinson stood, ashen-faced, working his fingers together in distress. He raised his voice over the thunder of bursting shells, sweating with the effort.

"The battalion's withdrawing. We've got to make a stand to let the others get away. Covering fire he said, but that was before this started." A shell exploded over the entrance to the dug-out, lifting the tin and filling the air with foul yellow smoke. The tin fell back, out of place, and earth cascaded from the roof. "Christ," Robinson shrieked. "We can't give covering fire in this. Hartwell's bloody well sacrificed us." He stared around showing the whites of his eyes. Saliva trickled down his jaw.

Pearson seized his shoulders. He could feel the man shaking in terror, and saw a dark stain spread down the front of his trousers. He led Robinson over to the back of the dug-out and made him sit down. He rummaged in his case.

"I'm going to give you a shot," he said, filling a syringe, and plunged it into Robinson's arm. "It's just to help you think. You're suffering from shock. It's nothing to worry about."

But Pearson knew there was a great deal to worry about. 'B' Company was isolated in the firing line without a commanding officer.

"Who is your senior platoon commander?" he asked Robinson as gently as he could, but the man stared back at him with vacant eyes, slowly shaking his head.

"I'll find someone," the Highlander said.

"Well, for God's sake keep it quiet."

"Aye, it's nae panic that we need."

Pearson thought, let it not be Smith-Fenton or one of the other boy-soldiers. Please God, let it be someone with experience.

The Highlander returned almost immediately with a tall handsome lieutenant, hatless, brushing earth from his hair, whom Pearson recognised but could not name, and the sandy-haired sergeant.

"I'm Hartingdon," the lieutenant said. "I gather we've got problems."

"Robinson's had it," said Pearson without preamble. "He's completely shut down mentally. Someone's got to take over."

"That will be Mr. Hartingdon, sir," said the sergeant. "He's your man."

"All right. We've lost contact with battalion HQ now but we had the CO on a few minutes ago and he's had orders to withdraw. He told Captain Robinson to cover them and..."

"It's derailed him," said Hartingdon looking over to where Robinson crouched like an animal, holding his knees and swaying.

"Yes. I've given him a tranquillizer." A fresh salvo crashed along the trench, making the ground heave. "What the hell's going on out there?"

"The Germans are closing in on the Suffolks," said Hartingdon. "I think this is to keep us out of it. Did the CO say how long we are to hold for?"

"I don't know. He spoke to Robinson."

"All right." He turned to the signaller. "Keep trying to raise HQ will you?"

"Aye, sir, but it's a broken wire for sure. I'll have a look but I'm betting it'll be oot in the shallow part of that trench." He gathered up a spool of wire and disappeared round the corner.

"Come on, Sergeant," said Hartingdon. "We'll go and spread the good news."

He's like Mansell, Pearson thought, wondering what it was that made one man so cheerful in adversity and another like Robinson go to pieces. He walked over to where Robinson sat, curled in the corner, in a deep sleep. Christ, he thought, I may have given him a bit much. But better that he should sleep than spread the virus of fear. 'Hartwell's sacrificed us' was not the sort of message you wanted to send along a trench of already frightened troops.

He tried to put himself in Hartwell's position; a commander with some of his men cut off in an exposed firing line, with orders to retreat. Clearly he would withdraw as many as possible, but what about the others, swept by shell-fire the other side of a ridge with a communication trench that was all but useless? And it was still hours before the safety of darkness. Hartwell had told him to go back but would he still expect him to with shells bursting all around? With a bit of luck the Highlander would be able to fix the telephone link. In the meantime, what could he do but wait?

Earth poured from the roof and he feared it might cave in on him. Hemmed in by a wave of claustrophobia, he staggered out to the sunlight of the open trench. Immediately he understood the effect of heavy shelling with high explosive. In a stupefying concussion of noise, explosions had gouged craters so that the trench wall collapsed wherever a shell burst on the parapet. And yet men stood in close order sending volleys of rifle fire down the slope in front. He peered over the shoulder of a rifleman filling his magazine from an ammunition box and watched in appalled fascination as German infantry below ran from stook to stook, climbing the slope towards them.

"When did this start?" he asked, fighting to keep the fear from his voice.

"Just a moment ago," said the man. He snapped the magazine back into the belly of his rifle, took aim and fired, and down the slope a grey figure slumped forward on its knees, the head bent low to the ground in an attitude of prayer. Four more times the man fired, working the bolt backwards and forwards, snicking it as smooth as clockwork, and other figures spun like toys in a fairground, falling in untidy heaps. Spent brass cartridge cases tinkled to the ground. But men still emerged, running over the lip of the cutting, hiding behind stooks, always climbing higher up the slope, and bullets from their machine-guns, fired from hidden positions down by the road, cracked and whined along the parapet.

A yard from where Pearson stood mesmerised by the awful violence, a man fell back, spinning sideways, clutching at his neck with blood spurting between his fingers while his rifle clattered to the ground. Blood poured from the carotid artery where machine- gun bullets sliced the side of his neck and windpipe, like a circular saw against a log. Pearson held him, comforting him, loving him, knowing he could do nothing but watch a life drain away.

They brought other casualties to him and he worked kneeling on the ground under an inferno of noise with only the cover of the trench wall for protection, dressing wounds and using morphine for the relief of pain and when his supplies ran out all he could do was make crude tourniquets from torn-up shirts and pray for the cover of night.

But with the long shadows of evening, the enemy came for them again. The barrage of artillery shells lifted suddenly, switched off by some distant command, and men in grey rose from the stooks in a wave. They came, crouching low, running and firing, and dying but others still coming on, stepping over their dead, and always firing.

'B' Company manned the loop-holes, returning fire with their Lee Enfields rattling like machine guns. From their advantage of the high ground they forced the enemy attack to a halt. For a few desperate minutes the two sides shot at each other at point blank range before the Germans broke and ran for the thin cover of corn stooks, dragging their wounded behind them. The stubble was littered with dead, some lying flat on the earth, others hunched like grey boulders.

Hartingdon ran round a corner of the traverse. Mud coated his uniform and a trickle of congealing blood mixed with sweat lay like a scar down the side of his face. "Quick," he said. "If Hartwell wants you back, now's your chance."

"What about the signaller?"

"That Highland chappie?"

"Yes."

"Christ knows. Just get the hell out of here. You can't do any more for us now. They'll think twice before attacking us again and we'll give you covering fire for a couple of minutes. Tell Hartwell we'll hold them off, and fall back as soon as it's dark. Oh, and thank you, Doctor. You deserve a medal." He gave a lopsided grin and disappeared round the corner.

Pearson ran up the zigzag network of earthworks, dropping to his belly in the shallow communication trench towards the top of the ridge, panting with the effort. His way was blocked by the Highlander. The man had died, pulped by high explosive, crouched over his spool of precious wire as if protecting a baby.

Pearson waited, indecisive, fighting back nausea. To stand up and run would be suicidal, to crawl over the crushed body unthinkable.

"God forgive me," he said and pulled himself over the Highlander, using his elbows. The still-warm body reeked of blood. In a daze he heard volleys of rifle fire behind him as the men from 'B' Company shot blindly through the wheat sheaves on the slope below the firing line. Sobbing and exhausted, Pearson crawled to the safety of the far side of the ridge and ran, bent double, down into the headquarters dugout.

"Christ," said Anson, his voice thick with disgust. "Where the bloody hell have you been?"

"That's enough," Hartwell barked. He stared at Pearson, visibly shocked. "We thought you'd had it." He pointed at Pearsons blood-soaked uniform. "Have you been hit, or is that from someone else?"

Thursday 27 August 1914

All night, Pearson rode with the battalion as they marched south-west towards Paris, keeping his horse close alongside ambulance wagons carrying wounded men too seriously hurt to walk. He learned that day something else they didn't teach him at Millbank. There had been no lessons in treating casualties on the run. Ambulances were unsprung, and when the wheels fell into potholes, casualties were thrown about like the playthings of some monstrous giant.

He craved sleep but he knew that there were other men who had fought the retreat all the way from Mons. Some had been on the move for a week, kept going by God alone knew what inner strength. Exhausted men, disillusioned from failure, were sorely tempted to lag behind under cover of night. It was so much easier to throw away a rifle and surrender to blessed sleep and an enemy patrol. A German prison camp, even with stale bread and turnip soup, seemed more welcoming than another night of marching under the foul-mouthed bawling of the sergeant major.

A thin rain at dawn brought no relief, merely outlining the endless stretch of the road ahead The relentless tramp of boots rang in an unwanted symphony.

At sunrise, under a sky of stained yellow, the column halted and Pearson examined the most serious casualties, making them as comfortable as possible. Robinson lay curled up, deep in shock. Some had died in the night and lay, stiff-limbed, in the wagons. Men, already drained of energy, were detailed into burial parties, forcing awkward shapes into narrow roadside graves, and when they had fixed rough-sawn crosses they marched on again with heads hanging forward, staggering with fatigue. At dusk, at the end of the second day, they crossed a bare ridge of ground, where low buildings crouched among a clump of stunted pines. Pearson read the sign: Desolation Farm.

The blessed order came to bivouac. Men, too tired to eat a

short ration of biscuit, fell asleep in the shelter of a windblown hedge. Pearson hitched his horse to the cart carrying his medical supplies, and asked the horseman to give it some feed. He found Rowntree there with a billycan on the boil.

"Tea, sir?"

"God, you're a tough nut, Rowntree."

"We had to march a bit, on the veldt." He passed over an enamel mug of hot sweet tea.

"My parcel safe?"

"Safe as houses. I put it in with the medicines as you wanted."

"Thank you. Watson got away I hope?"

"Yes, sir. He was just in time before all this started. He asked me to look after you. Said you would need a new man. I've got all your stuff."

"Bit of a comedown for a corporal, isn't it?"

"Batman? It won't be my first time. And there are advantages."

"Yes, I suppose so." The tea tasted of sugared hay. "Thank you for that," Pearson said. "We had better sleep now."

"Under the cart, sir?"

"Under the cart sounds good."

Rowntree spread a palliasse for him, and Pearson lay down, grateful for the soft straw. "No idea how long we'll be retreating, sir?" Rowntree asked.

"God alone knows."

"It doesn't seem right to keep running. I've heard the French aren't up to much."

"I wouldn't say that. We haven't done any better."

"Fritz can't keep pushing on though. They'll be just as knackered as us."

"Yes, I expect you're right there."

"Well, goodnight, sir."

"Where are you sleeping, Rowntree?"

"Along the hedge a bit. Under one of the ammunition wagons."

"Well, for God's sake don't smoke."

Pearson nestled into the straw. His uniform stank of sweat and the Highlander's blood. There might be a chance to change in the morning, he thought, and have a shave. He listened to the soft slap of harness as his horse shook its head, and wondered if Agnès would still be in the hospital, safe with Gaston? The Germans would surely need her if they had taken in their wounded there. He hoped she would wear her cap. Two long days and a night had passed since he left her. It seemed longer, but everything seemed longer when you had no time to think. She would be finding the same, working day and night on the ward.

He prayed to God that she might be safe, and when he had prayed for her, he prayed for his family at home in Hampshire. It was a long time since he had prayed, and he felt a slight embarrassment that he should ask something of God. He recalled his confirmation classes at school. ACTS, the chaplain had told him. Adoration, confession, thanksgiving, supplication, in that order of importance. He cursed himself for getting it the wrong way round and starting at the easy end, with supplication. Thanksgiving was easy, too. He gave thanks for the love of Agnès; for his time with her; for his own life, safe in the battle; for his training and for his family. And for the tapestry which he would keep by his side as a memento of the woman he loved until he could take it back to the church and marry her. Yes, thanksgiving was easy.

Confession was harder, and more painful. If fornication were a sin then he was doubly guilty. That was a sin of commission. But was it really a sin to sleep with a woman you were in love with? And if he were guilty, what about Agnès? He could not bring himself to think of her as a sinner.

There were sins of omission too. The bandages on the man

179

with gangrene was a sign of his arrogance. He had thought he knew better, and it took a dying man to show him his failure. Perhaps Anson had been right to question his ability. He cursed himself for having allowed Anson to rattle him. He should have turned the other cheek.

He forced his tired brain to think about adoration. It was difficult to do this unless you thought of God as a person. You could not easily adore an unseen spirit, a universal power that had no visible structure. But was it not cheeky to endow God with a face that you could recognise? Would his God be the same as Mansell's? Or Rowntree's, or Agnès's. And might not even Anson have an image of God, too? A roundabout of possible faces began to whirl in his mind; an identity parade with Agnès and Hartwell, Alazard, and poor dead de Courtney with his one eye.

His mind drifted to what daylight would bring, praying that the retreat might stop so that he could do something to relieve the suffering of the casualties.

Two weeks later, Pearson's prayers had been answered as the battalion headed north again. The French had turned the tide on the Marne, defending the last approaches to Paris, and the allied armies began a slow leapfrog with the Germans as both sides tried to outflank each other on the way to the channel ports. He found some hessian and removed the paper covering of the tapestry, thinking to wrap it more securely. The thing was centuries old, Father Albert told him. He unrolled the tapestry and smoothed small creases in the fabric. He stared at it, lost in remembering how he had stood in front of it with Agnès in the church. At the pool she had taught him about colours as clouds drifted through her fingers. The tapestry was so lovely. It was the colour of evening light. With an aching sense of loss he crushed the fabric to his face, to his lips, breathing it in as if it were the skin of his love.

With great care he wrapped it in the hessian and tied the

tapestry under the wagon's roof. It was natural for a medical officer to check his stores each day, and knew he could go there to touch it and feel it firm and dry. It became like a baby to him; something for him to hold and cherish, as if it were his own, and he came to associate it in his mind with Agnès, so that he believed she would be safe so long as he had it with him.

Pearson sat easy in the saddle alongside Mansell as the horses plodded slowly along the grass verge. The fields showed little sign of the ebb and flow of armies, and autumn sunshine cast long shadows from roadside trees.

"I looked at the map this morning," he said to Mansell. "We're level with Le Cateau again. Just a few miles over there to the east."

"Thinking of your woman?" His black eyes twinkled.

"All the time."

"I think of mine too. And my daughter." He looked across at Pearson. "It's her birthday next week."

"She'll be four?"

"Yes. Four."

"And no leave yet."

"No. Six months they said. That takes us to February."

"It's a long time for a Blighty."

Mansell laughed. "Picking up the slang?"

"Rowntree told me. D'you think we've got the *Boche* on the run now?"

"Well, it does look better. Bit early to say though. I suppose it depends what happens when we get up to the coast. We're heading for Flanders, I think."

Pearson looked round. There was no one else in earshot. "I'm going to marry her when this is over," he said.

"Oh, John. How wonderful. That's such good news."

"I want you to come. Will you be my best man?"

"Of course I will. God what fun. In France, presumably?"

"I hope so. But we didn't have much time for planning things."

"No, I suppose not. Are we allowed to celebrate? In the mess, I mean."

"I'd rather not. At least not until my parents know. I want to tell them in person. Not quite sure how my father will take it."

"Oh don't worry about that. Your mother will sort him out. Mothers are good at that."

"I can't wait to get back to Agnès. It's awful knowing she's just over that hill and I can't see her. I hope to God she's all right. There's the tapestry, too. It's become a talisman to me. It was Agnès who first showed it to me, you see. It's part of us both now. The priest let me take it. He said it was the will of God."

"My dear boy, you've got it bad, haven't you?"

"Yes, I'm afraid so."

"Smile for me?"

"Oh yes. Sorry."

"That's better. And don't worry. My lips are sealed."

The horses clattered over a narrow bridge, following a long column of infantry.

"Robinson's in bad shape," Pearson said.

"Yes. He can't go on like that. They'll have to send him home."

"Who'll take over 'B' Company?"

"Hartingdon's acting o/c. They've made him up to captain."

"He was awfully good under fire. Particularly after they lost de Courtney like that."

"You made quite a name for yourself. Nerves of steel, I heard."

"Balls. I was bloody terrified. The noise is so appalling you can't think straight. You know how I got through that?"

"Tell me."

"It was the others," said Pearson. "The ordinary riflemen. I saw them on the fire step, calmly reloading their magazines and shooting. Shooting properly, you know. Not just blazing away at random with their heads down. Amongst that awful din and shrapnel flying around they actually stood up and took aim."

"They're trained to do that."

"Yes, I know. But I saw men falling across the field, two, three hundred yards away at first. Then up close, within a few feet before they turned and ran for cover in the stooks. It was like a bloody shooting range at the fairground. I thought if our chaps could behave like that, be so cool like that under fire, then I could too. It was the most sobering experience of my life and I don't think I would be scared if it happened again. I had a terrible sense of elation."

"Why terrible?"

"I wanted to shout out loud with joy when those Germans ran. But I knew I had failed some of our wounded. I ran out of everything and they needed more. That was the worst part. I didn't take enough stuff in."

"You can't blame yourself for that. I saw what you took in. It would have been enough if that bloody communication trench had been deeper."

"God, that trench."

"Anson says no one could have done better. Hartingdon told him all about you."

"Anson? He thinks I'm a playboy."

"Not any more. He won't tell you, of course. He's too knotted up for that."

"There's another thing, Richard. We killed a lot of people on that slope. Young men like ours, but wearing grey. I could hear them screaming out there where they had been shot. It was after the barrage lifted. You could hear things then, when the shelling stopped. I couldn't help hoping they had a doctor who would come. But he wouldn't have, out in the open like that. They just had to lie there. Some of them lay flattened into the ground as if steamrollered. As if their bones had been sucked out. Others all angular, with a knee stuck up in the air. Some tidy, like a roll of carpet. And the groaning of dying men. It was awful."

"You can't afford to think like that. You have to think of them as enemy."

"Yes, but it might have been you, or Smith-Fenton, or Rowntree or Philips."

"Better not to think."

"I've seen some things. In the hospital at Le Cateau, and out in that trench. If a wounded man is going to live he needs help fast."

"It's not easy."

"You need to get the aid post right up there with the action. Not half a mile back."

"Hartwell won't like it."

"I'm going to persuade him."

"You're either mad or hopelessly brave. He won't let you sacrifice yourself."

"Maybe it won't happen again," Pearson laughed. "Maybe we'll get to Flanders and the *Boche* will give up and go home, and we shan't have to fight any more."

"And pigs might fly."

"Do you like champagne?"

"Love it. Why?"

"Because we're going to drink lots of it at the wedding."

Friday 30 October 1914

The battalion didn't have to fight again until the last days of October, when they joined forces with French and Belgian troops outside the town of Ypres. They dug trenches along a low ridge overlooking a saucer of land with the town at its centre, and prepared their defences while the enemy drove the remains of the Belgian army out of Antwerp.

"This can't last," said Hartwell. "The Belgians don't have the strength. If they collapse, the Germans will have a clear run to the channel ports."

"There's talk of them opening the sluices," said Donaldson. "They could flood all the country north of Ypres."

"Hell of a sacrifice of their precious land."

"It would stop the Germans though. Make a bloody great lake. Miles long they say, and several feet deep."

Pearson took his coffee over to the window where Mansell stood looking through binoculars.

"Could they really flood all that?" he asked.

"Apparently they could. You'd have to time it with the high tides on the coast. Let the sea pour in. Make the hell of an obstacle."

"For us, too, if we wanted to attack through there," said Anson. "And guess what? If the *Boche* can't move in the north, he'll probably have a go at us here." He looked at Pearson. "If I were you, I'd check my kit, Doctor. You may need it again soon." He said it kindly, as if talking to a friend.

Anson was right, and within a week the Germans attacked the British line where it bulged around the Ypres salient. The timber and earth roofs of trenches dug into the sloping ground were no match for high explosives, and Pearson struggled to keep pace with casualties, working in a forward dugout with the help of orderlies. For several days the battle raged, surging backwards and forwards over a mile of countryside, with a mounting death toll and countless wounded. Two savage beasts fighting to the death over the carcass of a town. Winter brought cold too, and rain that turned the trench floors to slime, squelching under the duckboards. At night, wet capes on the sentries shone like black glass in the light of flares and flash of shellfire. You were lucky if you got two hours sleep in twenty-four.

Pearson wept on the evening they brought in Smith-Fenton on a stretcher. The boy lay on his back, his face, drained of colour, turned to one side. It was unmarked, the skin ashen with a haze of blond hair like mist. His eyes focussed on something far away, and no sound came from his lips, parted a little in a way that a girl would love to kiss. The lower part of the boy's tunic was mashed in a seepage of blood. Pearson lifted it carefully and saw the wound, deep and pulsing, a dark gash through the centre of his belly. He railed inwardly at his inability to help. There was no treatment for casualties with their stomachs ripped open. All he could do was minimise the boy's pain and wait for intra-abdominal haemorrhage to do its worst.

He worked late into the night by carbide lamps, thinking of Agnès in the kitchen of the teacher's house, with the summer sun bright at the window. They had talked about young men dying for their countries. Smith-Fenton was not the only one that night. When he had finished, Pearson sterilised his instruments, and prepared his equipment for the morning.

In a blur of fatigue he walked along the trench to 'C' Company's headquarters dugout. Flares popped above him, bright points of light floating on parachutes and drifting downwind with trails of smoke. A squall of rain rattled on the entrance of the dugout, and a twisted sheet of corrugated tin scraped in the wind against a metal stake.

They had made a little home there. A heavy tarpaulin hung from a beam as a door, and someone had found a table where two candles burned. Mansell sat in an old wooden armchair. There was a smell of brandy.

"Cognac for the doctor," said Mansell, and Pollock poured from a bottle.

"Hine," said Mansell, holding his glass to the light. "One of the better brands."

Pearson let the liquid drain slowly down his throat. "Thank you," he said.

"A spot of Dutch courage," said Mansell. "We're going in again tomorrow. You may have heard."

"Yes. I know. I'm coming with you."

"Christ, John. It's not going to be a picnic. We've been ordered to push them off the crossroads south of the town."

"It's part of a big show by the division," said Pollock.

Pearson nodded. "I talked to Hartwell again. I told him I wanted to be up there with you. It's vital, you see, for wounded men to get help fast. We can set up a new aid post down there."

"And he agreed?" said Mansell, astonished.

"Eventually."

"You must have been very persuasive." He took a sip of cognac. "Many casualties today?"

"Too many. Too many young men."

"Smith-Fenton?"

"Yes."

"We heard a rumour," said Pollock.

"The casualty rate's very high. Not just us. It's all down the line."

Mansell stood up. "It's their artillery. The whole bloody salient's open to it."

"There's a lot of men missing, too," said Pearson. "Not accounted for."

"That's HE for you," said Mansell. "If one of those goes off close there's not much left to account for."

"I'm turning in," said Pollock. "Early start tomorrow." He went out and the tarpaulin swung back bringing a gust of cold air.

"He sounds pretty relaxed," Pearson said.

Mansell spoke quietly. "We're all the same. Scared stiff but trying not to show it."

"You too, Major?"

"I'd be a fool not to be."

"I want you to do something for me, Richard."

"If I can."

"It's if anything happens to me."

"Nothing's going to happen to you."

"No. But just in case."

"All right."

"Will you take all my stuff back to Hampshire? And give it to my mother?"

"This is awfully morbid for a boy who's getting married."

"Yes, but will you?"

"Of course, old man. And vice versa if I blow up?"

"It's a deal. There's the tapestry, too. You would have to take that. I promised to keep it safe. It's hung up under the roof of my main supply wagon."

Pearson lay on the bed Rowntree had made up for him in the aid post and drifted into an uneasy sleep. He dreamt he was in a trench, with enemy charging up the hill towards him and when the first of them came over the top, he was caught up in the desperate cut and thrust of men fighting with the bayonet. In a blind fury he tried to draw his revolver as a figure in a *pickelhaube* straddled the parapet, but the revolver was welded to his leg like some monstrous wart. A hammer blow in the side of his chest hurled him backwards to the ground, a broken rag doll sprawling amongst spent cartridge cases and empty ammunition boxes.

He lay while the mêlée raged, unable to move his legs, choking on his blood. He felt no pain, but an awful numbness of shock. He saw the boots of men struggling in hand-to-hand fighting stamp on his legs, but his legs were no longer part of him, and he felt nothing. A dead rifleman fell across him, as if embracing a lover. He wanted to make the rifleman more comfortable but could only move one hand, so he laid it on the man's head and felt the warm stickiness of blood.

This cannot be, he thought, as the fury of conflict slowly burnt itself out. In the quiet that followed he could hear the groans of wounded men crying for help. He heard the choking gurgle of a man suffocating in his own blood. He felt nothing. It was as if he were a spectator, separated from the surrounding carnage, his senses disconnected from his useless body. The gurgling sound came again and he watched in fascinated horror as he saw that it was his own blood that was being coughed over the front of his tunic. This cannot be, he thought again. I am a doctor and I am going to be married.

He tried to shift his legs again but it was no use. He felt a wetness between his shoulder blades and knew that the bullet had gone through, mushrooming when it hit his ribcage, shattering his spine. A wave of revulsion swept through him that he should have been allowed to know hope and strength and delight, and the sweetness of love, only for it to end with his being trampled into the mud of a French ditch.

He saw Agnès bending over him, her hands caressing his face, and those wonderful dark eyes telling him she loved him. He tried to tell her that he would marry her as soon as he was better, but there was too much blood in his throat and he could not speak. Mansell walked past, stepping lightly over dead bodies, laughing and carrying the tapestry under one arm. And somewhere coalescing in the dim light beyond the trench, he thought he could see the Highlander holding up a telephone, dangling from a broken wire. He tried to call out but no sound came, and the dead rifleman was too heavy for him to move. He wanted desperately to ask the Highlander to telephone Gaston and tell him that he must look after Agnès.

He awoke, crying out from the nightmare. A candle flickered beside his bed, a small beacon of hope, and in the winter cold of the dugout his breath hung like crystals in the air. He looked at his watch. The attack would begin in two hours, at dawn.

Part Two

June 1965

David Pearson put down the telephone, shut his eyes tight, and leant his forehead against the cool leather of his desk. His grandmother was dead. Loss and longing seared his soul, the loss irretrievable, the longing like a homesickness, a yearning for something beautiful and inaccessible. He knew the call would come one day, but he had dreaded it, understanding its inevitability, yet refusing to acknowledge it. He rose to his feet, crossed over to the window, and stared down at the traffic crawling along St. James's Street.

His grandmother was dead. There had been no warning. Mrs. Clarkson, the housekeeper, told him that the old lady died quietly in her bed, at home. The news tore at him, blurring people and cars in the street below into a watercolour through his tears.

His grandmother was dead, and he had driven down to see her in Hampshire at the weekend, for her birthday. She had sat upright in her armchair, in a corner of the room with her back to the light, her white hair tidy, and a woollen cardigan around her shoulders. She smelled of a sweet blend of fresh talcum powder and expensive lavender water. She had always been the same. A tall, spare figure in a long tweed skirt, and a cotton blouse with a high frilly collar.

They drank weak Earl Grey tea from fine bone china cups. A silver tea strainer, a sugar bowl with silver tongs, and a saucer containing freshly-sliced lemon crowded a tray beside her. She pressed him to eat a cake that Mrs. Clarkson had made.

"Come on, David. You'll have to do better than one slice. Everyone else is dead. Thank you for your card, by the way. Ninety-five! Am I really as much as that?"

"You don't look it."

"Nonsense. You should have had me put down years ago. Thirty-five years a widow is far too long." She put down her cup, rattling it a little on the saucer, and looked him straight in the eye. "And it's ages since you told me about you."

"What about me, Granny?"

"Oh, don't look so innocent. You know perfectly well what I mean."

"Do I?"

"For heaven's sake! The only thing I've got to look forward to. A grandchild, you chump." She picked up her cup again and looked at him over the rim. " You're an attractive young man, David. The girls must swoon all over you. How old are you ?"

"Granny, you know that. Twenty- five."

"Well, there you are."

"Where?" he laughed.

"Time for babies."

"Am I allowed to marry someone first?"

"I should hope so. But do get on with it."

"All right. I'll see what I can do. But there's really no hurry. You've got years left."

She waved a hand dismissively. "Well, that's as may be. Just don't get into another war, David. They don't do any good, leave a lot of old people very lonely, and boys like you without a father."

"I can't get into a war. I'm not a soldier. "

"That's what they all said. It doesn't work like that. I should know."

"Don't worry, Granny. It's not going to happen."

When he kissed her goodbye later, her cheek felt cool and soft as a powder puff.

"Thank you for coming," she said. "You're all I've got left."

Mrs. Clarkson found a box for the rest of the cake. He put it beside him in the car and drove back to London.

David turned away from the window. He looked in the mirror on his office wall, and felt a sudden weariness as though his grandmother's death had removed some vital ingredient from his soul. She had always been an important part of his life, an anchor holding him against the stream. His mother was there too, of course, but when she remarried and went to live in the Highlands, she became a distant figure in the background. David had come to think of her as an ethereal figure drifting across the hills, partly obscured by mist. It was to his grandmother that he had gone when he needed advice.

He returned to his desk and picked up the telephone. He heard his voice as if it came from outside himself when he called *"The Times"*: "On Thursday 3 June 1965, suddenly, at home. Grace Elisabeth Pearson, aged 95..." The details flowed without his having to think.

"I'm going out for a while," he told his secretary.

She peered up at him. "Are you all right?"

"No." He tried to laugh, shaking his head. He told her about his grandmother.

"Oh, David. I'm so sorry."

"It had to happen some time. I won't be in tomorrow. I need to go and sort things out. There's no one else, you see."

He went down in the lift. It stopped on the second floor, and as the doors shut again, a girl he hadn't seen before, ran in, almost colliding with him.

"I'm late for lunch," she laughed. In the foyer, she smiled at David and hurried away, with her heels tap-tapping on the tiles. She wore a mini skirt, and had her blonde hair up in a beehive. She trailed a fragrance of lily of the valley.

David wandered aimlessly along St. James's Street where the traffic clogged in hopeless congestion. There had been no rain for a month and the air reeked of hot electricity and exhaust fumes, stinging his throat. He bought an Evening Standard from the paper boy at the entrance to Green Park.

American aeroplanes were spraying defoliant on the Vietnamese jungle again.

He couldn't believe he would not see his grandmother again. The thought of her lying dead in her bed made him want to cry. She just looked as if she were asleep, Mrs. Clarkson told him. He had often seen her like that in her chair, her head back and her eyes closed, with just the faintest rise and fall of her chest. She would have wanted to look like that in death, composed and tidy. He drew out a handkerchief from his trouser pocket and blew his nose. He would have to pull himself together.

**** ****

David sat at his grandmother's desk, amazed at the meticulous state of her box files. He sat back, and clasped his fingers behind his head. There would not be much for him to do. She had made it very easy for him.

He looked at the photographs on the desk in their silver frames. His grandmother on her wedding day with his grandfather, a ramrod figure in the dress uniform of a 21st Lancer. Uncle John, a long-legged fair haired young man wearing spectacles, in tweeds, carrying a shotgun, with moorland heather behind him. Freddy Pearson, the father David had never known, leaning against the 1937 MG, with one foot on the running board. David had always loved that photograph. His mother had been given the car for her twenty-first birthday.

Later, he looked in the wardrobe in her bedroom. It smelled of lavender and mothballs. With a strong feeling that he ought not to be invading her privacy, he pushed aside the dresses. What on earth did one do with them, or the shoes lying there neatly on their racks? And why were there so many pairs? She couldn't possibly have worn half of them for years.

He found a large metal box at the back and brought it out

into the light of the room. He swept dust away with his hand. The initials of her maiden name, GES, stood out in gold lettering against the black enamel.

Mrs. Clarkson knocked on the door. "Your grandmother usually had a glass of sherry about now, if you want," she said.

"That's probably what kept her going so long." He held up the metal box for her to see. "I found this in her wardrobe. It's locked. Do you know what's in it?"

"I'm afraid not," she said, examining the initials. "I'll get you a sherry."

"I hope you'll have one?"

"I often used to have a glass with her." She laughed at the memory. "She seemed to like it that way. She said one should never drink on one's own."

"You were fond of her, weren't you?"

"I felt I was lucky to know her. You had to admire her. I've never met anyone with such inner strength. She was utterly uncompromising. Things were either right or wrong. It's not like that any more."

"I hope you'll stay on for a bit? Until we find a buyer?"

"We'll have to see."

Mrs. Clarkson brought the sherry and David rummaged around in the drawers of the desk until he found a key that fitted the box.

"Look," he said. "Some old photographs. This is another one of uncle John." He held it for her to see. It was a young man in uniform with RAMC shoulder badges, and a captain's three pips. He pointed to the silver frame on the desk with the man on a grouse moor. "Same chap, d'you see?" He turned the photograph in his hands. The pencil had faded but the date was clear enough: 'The last one. 1914'. "How all those mothers must have suffered," he said. "Did she ever talk about him – or my father?"

"Hardly ever. Except when I was dusting in there. She used to say: ' Be careful, Mrs. C. They're all I've got left'."

David took a sip of his sherry and delved into the box. He pulled out a framed black and white photograph of a tapestry hanging on a tree in someone's garden, with the corner of a cottage in the background. He switched on the desk lamp to examine the photograph under the light. A figure sat as if writing something, but it was hard to see clearly. The glass hadn't been cleaned for years. He thought he could make out a pattern of flowers. On the back of the frame, his grandmother had written:

'Major Mansell took this tapestry away as a gift, with our blessing. February, 1915.'

He showed the tapestry to Mrs.Clarkson. "Any clues about this?"

She shook her head. "Nothing. I'm afraid I'm not much help. But it was all so long ago. Fifty years."

"It's as if she shut that whole time away in the back of her mind. She used to talk to me about my father occasionally, but she hardly ever mentioned uncle John. And even then it was always as if he were still alive. I don't ever remember her mention him as if he were dead. There was never any finality for her."

"That's the hardest thing for a mother. The not knowing."

He came back to the desk when they had eaten, with a glass of brandy Mrs. Clarkson found for him. She had gone to her rooms and the house was silent in the dusk. Through the open window he could hear a song thrush singing from the garden.

He opened a folded paper from the box. It was a letter dated 19 August 1914. The sense of intruding into his grandmother's privacy swept through him again, pricking at the corners of his mind as he read her son's description of the channel crossing to Boulogne and the train journey through northern France. It read like the letter of a man happy in himself, enjoying an adventure at the beginning of a new career. As David turned the page, he was drawn again to the name Mansell.

..........*I am billeted with Mansell, one of the battalion's company commanders, in a comfortable village house. The men are camped out in a wood bordered by a lovely river. Not quite the Test but it's full of fish and flows peacefully through meadows where brown and white cattle graze. The men train busily during the daytime and I pretend to be busy checking my stores and equipment. We are in the house of a teacher, Monsieur Alazard, and his daughter. She reminds me of you with her calm, patient way of talking, and the gentle, willowy way she walks. It cannot be easy for families like hers to have foreign soldiers billeted on them and I rejoice in the manner in which we are accepted.*

The mess at battalion headquarters is in a rambling farmhouse and we are all quite comfortable there. Please tell Father that the others have all made me feel perfectly at home.

I could do with some more socks like the ones in the drawer in my room. And another stick of shaving soap - the sort Father uses would be fine.

Your loving son, John

He found two other photographs in the box. One, faded and torn at the edges, showed a pretty, dark haired girl looking straight at the camera, her face full of mystery in the grainy light. In the background, a pony's head showed over a stable door. He turned the photograph but the yellowing paper held no clue.

In the other photograph, over exposed in strong light, the same girl stood in front of the baroque façade of a church, shading her eyes with one hand. She wore a full length dress and a hat.

From the bottom of the box he pulled out a card with large handwriting sprawled across both sides:

20 Aug. 1938

Darley,

What horrid news of Freddy.
I am so sorry for you, and just thank God that poor Charles
was spared knowing. I insist you accept these baubles. They
were my mother's and I haven't worn them for years. Please
take them along as well. I quite understand the need for
discretion and you can count on me. I've a beastly cold which
I wouldn't wish on anyone but I'll try to get down to see you
soon. And TALK. London stifles.

With my best love, S.

He assumed that 'Darley' was an affectionate name for his
grandmother, but the 'S' meant nothing to him. Some old
friend of Granny's, he thought. But what on earth could the
crisis have been with his father? He would have to ask his
mother about it the next time they met.

He walked across the room and stepped into the garden.
At the far side of the lawn a copper beech tree rose, massive
against the night sky, blotting out the stars. Moths fluttered at
a street lamp beyond the garden wall, and a car drove slowly
along the village lane in a cocoon of light, the sound of its
engine trailing into silence.

What had happened out there in France, he wondered,
fifty years ago? And what was the significance of the
tapestry? And who was the girl in the photographs? He
wished he had found out more from his grandmother. But
now she had gone and it was too late.

He went back inside, and closed the French windows
against the cool night air. He examined again the photographs
of John Pearson and the dark-haired girl. She was certainly
pretty. He thought suddenly of the lily of the valley girl in the
lift, and wished he had asked her name. He put everything

back into the box, crossed over to the door and turned to face the room, putting a finger on the light switch. Two days after the old lady's death, her presence lingered on in the air, with a light fragrance of lavender.

July 1965

A month later, and trying to show a confidence he did not altogether feel, David strolled into the reception area of the second floor offices that he knew to be occupied by a firm of lawyers.   In his mind he had christened the girl with the beehive hair Otis, from the sign above the doors of the lift where they had met: 'The Otis Elevator Company'. As a boy he used to play a 45 from his mother's record collection, and the words came back to him:

When she woke up and found that her dream of love had gone,
Madam,
She ran to the man who had led her so far astray
And from under her velvet gown
She drew a gun and shot her lover down.
Madam, Miss Otis regrets, she's unable to lunch
today.

Otis would make a nice name, he decided, imagining her swivelling on her typist's chair with her legs crossed, writing on a shorthand pad. And with that skirt there wouldn't be much room for her to hide a pistol in her underwear.

The receptionist appraised him coolly from her desk as she finished a call and replaced the telephone.

"I'm trying to trace a girl who works here," David said. "Blonde, with hair like this." He waved his hands above his head.

The receptionist looked disapproving. "A lot of people work here. What is this in connection with?"

"I'm not sure yet, but I should be awfully grateful if you can help me."

"You're not making it very easy. How can I help without a name?"

"I'm afraid I don't know it."

The receptionist sat back in her chair. She studied David's tie and well-cut suit.

"What do you want me to do?" she said. "I can hardly organise an identity parade."

In the end it was easy because the blonde girl came into the room carrying a file and David said the first thing that came into his head: "Hallo. We met in the lift the other day and you wear a lovely scent. I wonder if you would let me buy you lunch." He steered her away from the reception area as she clutched the file, and he saw colour rush past her ears. "My name's David Pearson," he told her. "I've got an office further up." He pointed through the ceiling.

"Good Heavens," she said. "This is all a bit sudden."

"Yes, I suppose it is."

"You don't even know my name."

"No. I was hoping you might tell me."

She smiled at him from pretty blue eyes. "All right. Cynthia Mesurier."

"That sounds French," he said.

"I'm from Jersey. It's a Jersey name."

He took her to The Stockpot in Old Compton Street and they had *boeuf bourguignon* at seven and sixpence, and a half bottle of Nuits St. George, and afterwards they walked back together to St. James's Street. She told him she had never liked the name Cynthia because it sounded like a shade of puce in an herbaceous border. So he said he would call her Otis as it reminded him of the first time he saw her. She looked very pretty when she thanked him for lunch and, when he asked her, she said she would like to see him again.

They met several times, in the lunch hour, walking in Green Park, or having lunch in pubs around the area. He told her a little about his family and his grandmother and her funeral, and one evening he took her to the cinema to see a film about some bounty hunters with Clint Eastwood. She squeaked a bit at a shoot-out and clung to his arm. He walked her back to her flat off Lupus Street afterwards, and felt her embarrassment at the doorway when they said goodnight. She was tall and beautiful with her blonde hair down as she fumbled in her bag for the key. She had told him the beehive was only for the office. He stood back, sensing that she was someone who would not want to hurry things. She turned to him as she opened the door and waved goodbye with her lovely smile.

"Do you know Stonehenge?" he called.

"Well, I've seen it from the road."

"Will you come with me at the weekend? We can drive out and take a picnic if it's fine."

"All right," she laughed. "That sounds lovely."

The pavement felt softer than usual as he walked back to his flat.

He picked her up from Lupus Street in his Jaguar, with the top down, and she wrapped a scarf round her head while he headed out of London on the A 30. Beyond Basingstoke he turned onto the A303 and took the car up to a hundred on the run down to Amesbury. She sat still and calm with her hands folded in her lap. She wore a long tweed skirt and a cashmere pullover, and her lily of the valley scent eddied round the cockpit. He parked in a lay-by and they scrambled over a cattle fence and walked among the massive stones.

He carried a picnic basket and an old rug and spread it on the grass. They ate cold lobster which David had bought at Fortnums, with potato salad, lush with mayonnaise, and finely chopped chives. Otis gave him a bottle of pink champagne to open which she had kept cool wrapped in newspaper.

"You would have to believe in something very strongly to build all that," she said, waving at the stones and sipping the wine. She leaned back against a fence post with her legs straight out in front.

"It must have taken years. Do you know all they had for tools were picks and shovels made from antlers and bones."

"Jaw bones from asses?"

"That sort of thing."

"Samson, wasn't it?"

"Yes."

"And then he met Delilah and she cut off his hair and they blinded him."

"When I first read that, I really wanted him not to tell her about the hair."

"But then you would never have got the story about the pillars and the Philistines," she said, laughing.

"No. As a child I had a bible with lovely illustrations. There he was with his hair grown long again and the muscles bulging in his shoulders as he seized the pillars. Blind Samson straining every sinew, and the place collapsing and all those Philistines dying in their pointy helmets and thongs wound round their legs."

The air weighed heavy with summer, and the hum of traffic on the A303 came like bees in the distance.

"I want to show you something," he said when they got back to the car. He opened his briefcase and pulled out the photographs from his grandmother's box. He gave them to her to hold. She had lovely hands.

"Was this your father?" she asked.

"Yes. With the MG. The other one's of my uncle John."

"The one you told me went missing?"

"Yes. In 1914."

"There must have been a big gap," she said. "Between the two of them, I mean."

"Yes. John was fourteen years older than my father."

"He looks awfully smooth in that uniform. And who's this pretty girl?"

"I don't know. It might have been taken in France."

Otis looked at the next picture. "It looks like her again," she said. "In front of a church. It's hard to tell in that light."

He leaned over her. "This one of a tapestry's a complete mystery," he said. "I cleaned the glass so you can see it properly."

"Oh, it's beautiful," she said. "Even in black and white." She looked up at David, her eyes dancing. "Who is he? He's rather dashing."

"He looks like a friar. Or a monk?"

She read the writing on the back.

"Written by my grandmother," he told her. "She and uncle John must have been involved in some way. I want to try and find out about it."

" Of course you do," she said. "And Major Mansell? Do you know anything about him?"

"Only what the letter says. That he was in France with my uncle. They were in the same battalion. I may be able to trace him through the old regimental records."

"You're beginning to sound like a detective." She peered at the photograph of the tapestry. "Those flowers. Do you know what they are?"

"Lilies?" he guessed.

"Or iris. Fleurs-de-lys. The heraldic flower of French royalty. That's another French connection for you."

On the way back to London she told him she was going home to Jersey for a few days, and she would love it if he could take a bit of holiday and come to stay. She told him he wouldn't need the car, so he could come over to the island from Southampton on the ferry.

Otis. He had not kissed her properly yet, apart from some light pecks on her cheek. He wanted very much to do so but, unusually for him, something held him back even though everyone talked about free love all the time and that anything went. He had a friend in the office called Rory, who was always going on about sex as if it had only just been invented, and was truly the most wonderful thing, and that you owed it to yourself to indulge as much as possible.

"There's plenty of fanny about," Rory told him. "You need to get your share. London's full of Audrey Hepburn lookalikes waiting to break your heart. Take a walk through the Ritz. Women in swirly dresses, smoking cigarettes and clicking silver Dunhill lighters, laughing with their heads back and necks like swans, seducing you as naturally as saying hello."

David had had the odd skirmish in the back of taxis and on various sofas, and at twenty-three lost his virginity quite unexpectedly on a furry hearthrug in front of a coal fire in a suburban house in Southampton. Joyce was an eager accomplice when they made love on weekends in Hampshire and occasionally in London. David knew she wanted to spend more time with him in London, and she sulked when he began to make excuses. In the end they stopped seeing each other. He was relieved, but felt badly about it, knowing that he had hurt her.

He wanted things to be different with Otis, and it would be fun to go and stay with her in Jersey for a few days. She made the house sound lovely with its big rooms, and gardens with shrubberies, and no doubt there would be opportunities to embrace her amongst the evergreens.

He saw her waving from the end of the harbour wall as the night ferry came in from Southampton. She was on her own, as he hoped she might be, when she met him on the quayside, and kissed him lightly on the cheek.

"Welcome to Jersey," she said. Her blue eyes were full of light.

She led him to the car parked half up on the kerb at the top of the harbour, and he held the door open for her while she got in. She smoothed her skirt over her knees and fiddled with the rear-view mirror. She wore flesh toned lipstick that he hadn't seen before.

"Any news about your tapestry?" she asked him as she

pulled out into the town traffic. Her hands were suntanned, with the knuckles paler where she held the wheel.

"Slow. But I got the address of the regimental records people. I've written, but I gather they're like the mills of God. They grind exceeding slow."

She laughed, and asked him: "Might Mansell still be alive?"

"Maybe. He'd be in his eighties though."

"You must be longing to hear from them," she said, turning to him.

She drove him up to the north coast through a steep wooded valley that seemed almost to cut the island in half. At the top they came out into a countryside of small fields surrounded by banks with coppiced oak and chestnut trees. Dark-faced island cattle grazed on tethers among ancient apple trees, and the narrow road ran between stone walls and houses, their gardens colour washed with hydrangeas. It was a Lilliputian landscape, full of charm and sunshine.

She braked to allow an oncoming JMT bus to pass, and swung the car between granite gateposts into a short driveway that led to the house, a pretty building with two dormer windows on the third floor.

Her father was a retired naval officer who regarded David with a baleful eye, as if to cast an invisible iron ring around his daughter. David expected at any moment to be asked about his intentions towards her, and the prospect of liaisons inthe shrubbery grew increasingly remote. Mrs. Mesurier treated him quite differently, as an equal. She drifted calmly through the days with an Abdulla No. 2 in the end of her long cigarette holder, blue smoke almost concealing an ever present whiff of gin.

They bicycled down to the little harbour at Rozel and jumped off the pier to swim among the fishing boats, and David bought ice cream and lemonade from an old woman in the corner shop. And when a big wind came up the channel from the Atlantic, they drove over to St. Ouen's bay on the west coast and rode surfboards out on the combers. She wore a one-piece swim suit, blue and white like a Nivea advertisement, and she looked lovely, showing the muscles in her calves when she ran over the sand.

The commander took them out to fish for bass in a twenty foot clinker-built longboat with an air-cooled diesel engine thumping in a box toward the stern. He sat with his knees together, the tiller in one hand, wearing a yachting cap and an old tweed coat over grey flannel trousers with turn-ups, erect and alert as if on the bridge of a destroyer.

David sat on a thwart beside Otis, with the boat rising and falling to a gentle swell, where a shingle bank connected two rocks and the flood tide ran strong. The boat smelled of fresh paint warmed by the sun, tar, and sump oil. The commander told him how the bass would lie tucked in out of the tide against a steep shelf in the shingle, and he brought the boat in close, a boat-hook's length from the beach, and held her there, stemming the tide with the engine throttled back, barely moving over the ground.

"Put 'em out," he called over the noise of the engine, and they let out the hand lines, one on each side of the boat, weighted with two pound leads. The spinners ran deep in gin-clear water. The tide sucked at the shingle, sweeping sand eels to the waiting bass, while two miles to the south, the island crouched, carved out of old granite, and a warm summer breeze brought the scent of gorse across the water.

"Fish!" the commander shouted. Otis let out a shriek of excitement and stood up, with the line jerking in her hands. David went over to help her as she braced her legs against the movement of the boat.

"You don't need to maul her about, boy," her father called. "She's quite capable, you know."

Otis pulled the bass over the boat's rail and struck the back of its head with an iron pin. "Look out for the spikes on the dorsal fin," she told David. "They're like needles." The fish measured eighteen inches, and flopped about on the boards.

Mrs. Mesurier sat smoking in the bow, with a pink cotton headscarf tied under her chin, and looked at David with encouragement. They caught another two fish in the next half-hour before the commander told them to get in the lines.

"No point in overdoing it," he said. "Never take more than you need." He turned the boat for home and called to David: "Know how to steer?"

"Yes, sir."

"All right." He handed over the tiller. The boat swung with the tide, and raced back along the shingle. "See the beacon on that rock? The one covered in bird shit?"

"Yes," said David.

"Keep that in line with the gable end of the big house up on the cliff." He stood with his feet apart, facing David, comfortable in the motion of the boat. "Cynthia says you're looking for some piece of old cloth," he said.

"Well, I would like to find it if I can. It might have come from my uncle, you see."

"Yes. She told me. Fifty years ago, I gather? Probably rotted to bits by now."

"It's quite possible, of course. But I want to try."

"No harm in that, I suppose. You're probably wasting your time though."

The commander opened the throttle and the bow came up, the engine roaring with the extra revolutions. He walked up the boat to supervise the tackle and examine the fish. He looked ahead to check their course, and aft, behind David, where the wake of the boat ran white across the water, straight as a ruler. He nodded his approval, sat down on the centre thwart, and put a protective arm around Cynthia's waist.

When it was time to leave the island, her father drove them to the airport, unloaded their cases from the boot, and kissed the top of his daughter's head. He turned to David, squared his shoulders, and held out his hand.

"Good bye, young man. She's very precious to me, you understand?" He opened the door of his car. "She's going to be a lawyer."

"Yes, sir. I know."

The commander made a harrumphing sound as if he had hawked up something unpleasant from the back of his throat, and got back into his car. They watched him drive away, and went through the swing doors of the terminal. An old Jersey Airlines Dakota, painted in BEA livery, waited on the tarmac with its nose up.

October 1965

Autumn leaves floated through the branches of the copper beech tree at the bottom of the Hampshire garden, and lay in a rich carpet on the lawn as David stood on the gravel outside the house, waiting for the estate agent. David had met Mr. Smythe twice, and did not care for him. He had an over familiar manner and wore loud suits. But the solicitor had recommended him and, to be fair to the man, Smythe had acted efficiently, had held out for almost the asking price, and the sale of the house had been concluded within three months of it going on the market.

Now, as he waited in the chill of the late October morning with his hands thrust deep into the pockets of his coat, David thought it really was the end of an era. His grandmother had lived there since the last years of the previous century, and in all the time he had known the place it had hardly changed at all. He went back into the house to find Mrs. Clarkson in the kitchen.

"Don't bother to wait, Mrs. C." he said. "I can make them coffee if you want to get on."

"No," she said. "I'd like to see it through."

"I'm so grateful to you for staying on. A place like this can go downhill quickly if it's left empty."

"Do you know the new people?" she asked.

"No. He's a retired brigadier though, which seems appropriate." A sudden thought occurred to him. "Would you want a job here if they are looking for someone?"

She laughed quietly. "No, I don't think so. It's time I retired. Anyway, I don't think I could work here for another family. Your granny was such a marvellous person to look after that I can't imagine working for anyone else."

They heard the swish of tyres on the gravel, followed by the banging of car doors.

"It sounds like the enemy has arrived," said David. "I'll go to the door and see if I like the look of them."

Two cars had drawn up in the driveway. Smythe got out of one wearing a Prince of Wales check suit. The brigadier and his wife stood by a black Rover, looking up at the roof of the house. Smythe introduced them.

"Freddy Pearson any relation?" said the brigadier.

So Smythe had briefed him, David thought. "Yes," he said. "He was my father."

The brigadier nodded. "Thought so. Same division as me. I knew him slightly. We had a smoke together in the dunes at Dunkirk. The Stukas were dive-bombing the hell out of us. His nerves were all shot to pieces and I didn't think he could take much more of it. I remember him telling me that his wife was having a baby. You look about the right age?"

"Yes. It was me."

"Darling," said the brigadier's wife, "I'm sure Mr. Pearson won't want to talk about all that now."

"Really? Oh. Anyway, I was sorry he didn't make it home. But I wasn't surprised. He had that sort of look about him, like a rabbit in the headlights. As if he knew."

David felt unsure of the best way to end this. "Mr. Smythe tells me everything is settled," he said, stiffly. "And that the survey report is satisfactory."

"What? Oh yes, that's all fine."

"It's really just the furniture to look at," said the brigadier's wife. "Mr. Smythe said you would let us see it before it goes off to auction." She smiled at David, kind grey eyes from a face still showing the tan of summer. Smythe rubbed his hands together as if he were cold, and made shepherding movements towards the front door.

"Please come in," said David. "Mrs. Clarkson has got some coffee for us."

Watching the new owners examine the furniture was a depressing business for David. It reminded him of picking through a salad *niçoise*. All the olives and anchovies went, and you were left with old lettuce leaves. But he had no need or space for the stuff, and Smythe had been adamant that the opportunity to buy what furniture they wanted, in situ, had helped smooth the way to a sale. Contracts had been exchanged, and completion was set for early December.

When they had gone, David took a last look round the grounds, with the brigadier's uncalled for remarks about his father ringing in his ears.

Freddy Pearson died amongst the sand dunes at Dunkirk, leaving a young mother carrying his child. But she brought David up with Freddy's presence strong amongst them. "Your father would want you to do that," she would say. "Your father loved roses. Look: the Albertine there on the barn wall. Daddy planted that." And when he came in for lunch from playing in the fields : "Wash and brush up time, David. If your father could see you like that, he'd have a fit." When David was a boy, she talked with him about his father, not obsessively, but easily and naturally, so that David felt he knew something of the man behind the familiar photographs.

A sudden gust of wind sighed through the branches of the copper beech, scattering leaves across the garden in a kaleidoscope of colour. He looked back at the house, thinking of the memories hidden behind its walls, and of the old lady from Victorian times who had held it all together. They had buried her alongside the general in the graveyard of the village church where she had worshipped for so long. David was moved to tears when half the village turned out for her funeral. He had expected a dozen at most and Mrs. Clarkson had been taken by surprise by the numbers queuing for the tea she laid on afterwards. The vicar made the inevitable joke about loaves and fishes.

Back in the house, he found Mrs. Clarkson tidying the kitchen. She had agreed to stay until the end of November before moving in with her sister a few miles away. He told her that a lot of the furniture and rugs would be staying.

"Oh, I'm so glad," she said. "They do belong here really. I hope you liked the new people?"

"He's a bit stiff upper lip and highly polished shoes, but his wife is sweet and appreciative of how you have kept things looking so nice. They've got grandchildren too, so the old place will get shaken up a bit."

"A house this size needs children. Tell me, did you ever find out about that tapestry?" She put the clean coffee cups away and closed the cupboard.

"Not yet. I'm waiting to hear from the army records people. I'm trying to trace the man whose name was on the back of the photograph." "Well, good luck. I'm sure something will turn up."

He went slowly back to London, saddened that he wouldn't see the house again. When the money from the sale came through he had decided to buy a flat from the proceeds, and give up the tenancy of the place he rented. Everyone said that bricks and mortar were a good investment.

He drove on, thinking again about his father. He had always assumed his father had been as brave as any man under fire. It was painful to think that he might have died cringing in terror like an animal on a fire-swept beach. It seemed so out of character from the man his mother had built up for him. But perhaps there was a flaw in the crystal like that alluded to in the card from his grandmother's box. He had tried to persuade his mother to go to Dunkirk with him in May for the twenty-fifth anniversary of the evacuation, but she was reluctant to leave Scotland. He thought he ought to try again. She always came south for a few days before Christmas, and he would try to persuade her to go over to France with him for a couple of nights and talk about his father.

He looked at his watch. There was time for him to go back to his flat and change his clothes before picking up Otis. She wanted him to take her to see Thunderball, the new Bond film. She said Sean Connery was her heart-throb. It was six weeks since she put her hand in his as she sat beside him on the 'plane. She looked so pretty with sunlight coming in through the window. Outside, above the clouds, the propeller of the port engine had cut a silver disc in the sky.

December 1965

Arm in arm, David and his mother walked slowly along the beach, bent forward into a thin northeaster that carried knives from the Urals, and swirled dry sand eddying like wraiths of mist. A long breakwater stretched out to sea, an accusing finger dividing the beach from a grey winter sky. Waves, driven by the wind, broke there in a fury, surging and sucking at the rocks. It was a place of desolation.

"God, it's cold," she said. "Perhaps we shouldn't have come."

"Nonsense. I'm glad. We should have done it before. It's like closing a book at the end of the last chapter. To sign off unfinished business. Where do you think he might have died? You said it was in the dunes somewhere."

"That's what they told me."

"I've always hoped it was there, and not in one of those dreadful lines of men wading in the water."

"Better in the dunes," she said.

"Yes. I know it sounds ridiculous, but if you have to die on a day in May, the sea would still be awfully cold. It would be better to die in a warmer place, like among the dunes. You could curl up there like an animal. You couldn't do that in the water. What actually did the letter say?"

"From the colonel? It just said how sorry he was to have lost a fine soldier and that he died doing his duty. He must have had to write dozens like that. It's all quite impersonal really."

They splashed through a shallow pool of water stranded by the ebbing tide. Gulls wheeled overhead, pale scraps of wind-blown paper against the darkening sky, and the surf roared out on the tide line beyond the rippling sand.

"Can we go back, darling," she said. "This bloody wind is cutting me in half."

They turned and leaned back against the wind, looking down the run of the beach with the town rising, a low hump, on their left. Ragged smoke from factory chimneys streamed flat over the land. It must have looked like that in 1940, he thought, with smoke from bombs and shellfire as the Germans encircled the town, driving the retreating armies onto the beach. He remembered the photographs he had found in the library. Long ropes of men in extraordinarily disciplined lines, linking the sand with ships where waiting men stood up to their necks in water. A man lying on his back on the sand firing his rifle into the sky at an attacking aeroplane. Tangles of anti-tank obstacles and wire, the sand littered with the hunched corpses of nameless men caught by machine gun fire and shells. The enormous quantity of equipment, guns, and vehicles - all the paraphernalia of a retreating army lost to its pursuers.

Churchill called it a miracle. Three hundred and thirty thousand British and French troops taken off in just over a week by an armada of little boats ferrying them to the destroyers.

He held his mother's arm, feeling her warmth through their coats, and walked with her back across the sand into the town where they could find a café. Street lights flickered into soft amber life, and they went to sit in a café on the corner where condensation misted the windows. A burly man in an apron took their order. She took off her scarf and ran her fingers through her thick greying hair. She always looked so beautiful, he thought, when knocked about a bit by the weather, with the colour of the wind in her cheeks.

The waiter brought them steaming cups of café au lait.

"Can I ask you something, Mum?"

"Of course, darling." She held the coffee in her hands, warming her fingers.

"When I went to meet the buyers of Granny's house, he told me he met Daddy on the beach here."

His mother sat still, her cup half-way to her lips. She seemed to wither from inside with a look of fear he had never seen before.

"What did he say, David?" It came out as a whisper, and in the silence that followed he could hear the café's awning flapping in the wind.

"He said that Daddy was terrified, his nerves all shot to pieces by the Stukas. He said it was as if Daddy had resigned himself to dying. I didn't want to believe him."

"You poor darling."

"I can't imagine my father like that. He has always been my hero. The tough man you showed me, taught me to believe in. A man to be proud of, a man who would have led from the front."

"You poor darling," she said again, and there was something in her voice that made him look up at her and he saw that she was crying.

"It's my fault," she said through her tears. "I wanted you to grow up loving your father even though you never knew him. I wanted you to have the idea of a father as other boys have in reality. I wanted you to know only the best in him."

"Shouldn't I be grateful for that?"

"I don't know." She twisted her hands in distress. "Oh God, I've always dreaded this."

"This? What are you saying, Mum?" The feeling of relief, of something accomplished, that he had experienced on the beach, was turning sour.

"Can we get something to drink?"

"Yes, but what are you trying to tell me?"

"Can I have some brandy?"

"Brandy? It must be awfully serious."

"And ginger ale."

He called to the barman: "Do you have any ginger ale?"

"We 'ave a Canada."

"Canada dry? A small bottle of that and two cognacs, please."

"Is a 'orse's neck, no?"

"Yes," said David. "Two horse's necks."

The barman clattered about, filling two glasses and adding

spirals of lemon peel. "I am reading about this in a magazine," he called from the bar. "An American magazine."

"There was a conspiracy between me and Granny," David's mother said. She took a deep breath. "Your father led a sort of double life that we kept from everyone. We had to, to stop the regiment from finding out. We agreed to keep it from you too. I'm so sorry, darling. For twenty-five years I've lived with this, hoping it would never happen." She held his hand while the barman put their drinks on the table with a slip of paper for the bill.

"Two 'orse's necks, Monsieur."

David felt as if he had been struck by some enormous weight that left him breathless with a rushing noise in his ears.

"Are you going to tell me something about Daddy to destroy everything I have always loved about him?"

"David. Your father was in some ways a wonderful man."

"But?"

"It was money," she said. "He was hopeless with money. It ran through his fingers like sand."

"I know lots of men like that."

"Yes, but it was money he didn't have."

"So he got into debt?"

"Yes. No." She shook her head, distraught. "We wouldn't let him. I bailed him out."

"For the sake of his career? So the regiment didn't know?"

"Yes. And for Grace."

"For Granny? So she could hold her head up with her friends?"

"Yes. You have to remember that John went missing in the first war. Disappeared into thin air. She never got over that. Freddy was her blue-eyed boy. It would have broken her if it had got out."

"So that's why she never spoke much about Daddy. I could understand her not wanting to talk about uncle John.

But Daddy? She knew I loved him, from what I had learned from you. And yet she said nothing about him. In case I questioned her, I suppose, and put her on the spot."

"It was what we agreed, darling. We thought it best."

"So why tell me now? Why not run with the lie?"

"Because you asked me. And because she isn't here any more. I always told her I couldn't go on with it if you asked me."

"I only said that I couldn't believe my father died crouching in terror, like an animal."

"What would you have wanted me to say? That your old brigadier was wrong? Build on the lie? Can't you see that this has been burning a hole in my heart all these years? I need release from it, David."

"And you had to wait until Granny had gone? So you could break your torrid agreement? I loved her you know, as a true friend, while you swanned off to your grouse moor."

"That's not fair, David. You know that's not fair." She shrivelled, as if she might collapse.

"No. I'm sorry. Tell me about the money," he said, quietly.

"Are you sure?"

"I don't know. How bad was it?"

"He lost everything. Gambling in the mess. Backgammon mostly."

"In the mess? But they must have been peanut amounts."

"Don't you believe it. The others were all rich as Crœsus. They bled him dry, and every time he paid up they came back for more. He let them think he could afford it. I had to sell the MG."

"I don't believe this."

"Oh yes. And God knows how much stock. The broker kept asking me if everything was all right. Grace helped too. She popped her lovely diamonds."

David pushed back his chair. "Oh, Christ," he said.

"What is it, darling?"

"Did you know someone, a friend of Granny's, who might

have signed a letter, a card, with an S?"

"Just S? Like that?" She drew in the air with her finger.

"Yes. And called her Darley."

"David. What are you talking about?"

"There's a card. I found it when I went through Granny's desk. It's dated 1938, addressed to 'Darley'. Someone wrote it, sending jewellery to help with a crisis. It referred to Daddy acting out of character and was signed with an S. It meant nothing to me when I read it."

"Oh God. A friend of Grace's helping with Freddy's bills?"

"It would fit."

"I don't know." She emptied her glass and thought. "She had so many friends. I suppose one of them might have helped. But if they did, she kept it quiet from me. There was an exotic old girl called Sophia, a Russian refugee. Her family got out in 1917. She used to go down to Hampshire for house parties before the war and play tennis with Grace. Grace tried to persuade her to leave London when the bombing started, but she refused and was killed later in the blitz. It could have been her."

"So who else might have known?"

"I don't know. Anyone, I suppose. God, gambling's a bugger."

"Why on earth didn't someone stop him?"

"It's a disease, David. You can't control it. Thank God you didn't inherit it."

"Poor Mum." He stroked her cheek. "You should have told me before. Losing money isn't everything."

"No, David," she said in a low voice. "But there's more."

"Do I need to know?"

"Yes. Now you know some of it I couldn't bear to think of you finding out the rest from someone else."

"The rest? How much is there?"

"They were collecting money in the mess to buy a retirement present for the RSM. He was a fine old man who had gone right through the first war in the trenches. They kept a pot in the mess and invented a game with a whole lot of silly rules, and when someone broke a rule he put a pound in the pot. It went missing one day – several hundred pounds. Nothing was ever proved but I knew Freddy took it. He owed a lot of money to a London nightclub and I refused to pay."

"Oh God, no."

"But the worst for me was his other woman."

"Look, you don't have to tell me this."

"Yes, I need to. Darling, I have to get rid of it. Please see that." He could feel her fingers gripping his arm. "I put up with it for a while hoping she would go away. But then he began to rub my nose in it, compare my body with hers and tell me I was letting myself go. He kept on about her bloody waist. And then he blamed me for getting pregnant with you, told me I should have been more careful, that we couldn't afford to have children. And all the time he was busy fucking that bitch."

She began to cry again, letting the tears roll down her cheeks. The barman looked over in concern, but David held up a hand and shook his head. He leaned across the table and took his mother's hands.

"Can you understand," she sobbed, "that I was glad when he went away to France with Gort's army? And, God help me David, I was glad when he didn't come back. I never let Grace know about the missing money, or his woman. I don't have much to be proud of but I am proud to have kept all that from his mother."

"No wonder you didn't want to come here."

"Well, you can see why I never came on my own."

"Did you ever love him?"

"Of course. At the beginning. You always do."

"When did it go wrong?"

"Soon after we married."

"No hints before?"

"There are always hints, but you get good at ignoring them."

223

"And hope."

"Yes, there's always hope. I'm so sorry, darling. I've ruined today for you. You look awfully shocked."

"Yes. It's going to be hard to get used to the idea that my father was a bastard."

"I'm so sorry, darling," she said again.

He drove her back to the hotel. He had booked rooms for them which looked out across the sea, and over dinner he began to tell her about Otis. She asked him how long he had known her.

"Six months."

"And?"

"She's about five ten with long blonde hair which she puts up for the office. Wonderful blue eyes and little hollows here." He held his fingers under his cheekbones. "She's got lovely long legs and looks terrific in old jeans and a shirt."

"I hope you've told her that."

"Mmmm."

"David? You have, haven't you?"

"Maybe not exactly."

"Tell her. Women like to be told that sort of thing."

"Won't that famous female intuition do it?"

"Don't tell me you're a coward."

"'Like father, like son'?"

"Please," she said. "Don't."

"No. That was bad. I'm sorry."

"But you can talk with her? I mean really talk."

"Oh yes, we can talk."

"It's all so much easier nowadays. Your generation seems to have sprung free from all the old conventions."

"I've got a friend in the office who would agree with that."

"And you don't?"

"Free love and stuff? I'm afraid I'm quite conventional really. I think it's still rather nice to put a girl on a pedestal."

"As an object to be admired?"

"Well you said they like that."

"Women prefer to be *told* things, not used as an exhibit. Are you in love with her?"

"Let's put it this way. Granny was always going on at me about finding a nice girl and having babies so she could be a great-grandmother. I wish they could have met. Granny would have loved her."

"That sounds promising, darling."

The waiter brought coffee, and fussed about, arranging their cups.

"There's something else I want you to tell me," said David. "Did you ever hear Granny talk about a tapestry. With some connection to uncle John?"

"She wouldn't talk about him. I used to try and get her to, but it was hopeless. She had a will of iron. I think not knowing how or exactly where he died ate into her soul, and she refused to talk about him. She kept her grief very private. I don't think she ever mentioned a tapestry. What was it?"

He told her about the photographs. "I've found someone who may be able to help," he said. "In 1915, Granny wrote on the back of the photograph saying she gave the tapestry to a Major Mansell."

"And you can find this Mansell?"

"No. He died ten years ago but I got the address of his widow from the regimental records. Mansell was in the same battalion as uncle John. I spoke to the old girl on the telephone, and she's got loads of papers and stuff going back ages. She's invited me to tea next week."

" Oh! I hope she'll know something."

"So do I. This tapestry is turning into an itch I can't stop scratching. It's a long shot, but she's the only clue I've got. I want to find out about John. Even more, now I know my father was a bugger." He looked at her with a lop-sided grin. "You can't have more than one black sheep in a family can you?"

They talked on until the waiters made them feel uncomfortable. Later, in his room, David pulled back the

225

curtain and peered out into the night. The wind had eased a little and broken cloud streamed across the moon. A rising tide flooded the land where they had walked. Waves pulled and broke on the new shore as he listened to the surf, subdued now behind the hotel's windows. He shivered, watching the waves moving under the moonlight where the sea heaved, black in its restlessness. He had to find out about John and the tapestry. Otis's father had written it off as a piece of old cloth, but David knew there was more to it than that. For him, belief in the existence of the tapestry had assumed its own vitality, a belief necessary and absolute. The tapestry was a direct link to John, binding them together after the shocking discovery of his father's empty worthlessness. To fill the vacuum now, he must cling to the memory of a man who, fifty years before, had disappeared into the hell of the Ypres salient.

David never heard that his mother found out at the end of the war, when he was five, that his father shot himself with his service revolver at the foot of the Dunkirk breakwater

David sat squeezed on the sofa beside Mrs. Mansell, with her photograph album on his knees. Her darting eyes and the quick movements of her hands reminded him of a small bird. A coal fire burned in a shallow Victorian fireplace, warming the room, and every piece of furniture was adorned with silver photograph frames and delicate pieces of china, the collection of a long life. It's like a little nest, David thought.

"You seem very cosy here," he said.

"I'm afraid it's rather cramped. I came here after Richard died. It's much smaller than where we were before, and I had a frightful job deciding what to bring. Luckily the children took lots of it. It was really my daughter's idea to move me. I hated it at first, but she was quite right. I can cope much better here on my own. Do you have a family?"

David smiled. "No, not yet."

"Well," she said, "I'll go and make some tea." She pointed to the album. "Have a look in there. The ones from the war start about half-way through."

"Are you sure I'm not intruding?"

"Oh no. You mustn't feel like that. There's one or two of your uncle, I'm sure. See if you can find him." She stood up and walked through to the kitchen with small neat steps.

David turned the pages, pausing to look at photographs of a bride and groom. It's obviously her, he thought. He could tell from the vivacity in her face. The groom had dark, rather rumpled hair and vigorous eyebrows, full of humour. A few pages later, officers in army uniform standing in what looked like the garden of an English country house, looked self-consciously at the camera. The man with eyebrows was laughing at one side. Over the page, a nursemaid pushed a pram from which a baby peered out. A professional portrait showed a serious-looking major with rather long hair and very dark eyes. Underneath, someone had written 'July 1914'. On the deck of a ship, a small group of officers stood leaning on the rail. In the background a coastline merged into mist.

David turned the page again and felt his heart miss a beat. John Pearson grinned out at him, standing alongside the man with bushy eyebrows. There was no doubt about it; the fair hair, spectacles and RAMC insignia. Behind them, the top half of a stable door hung open under what looked like a hayloft.

"I've found him," David said, much louder than he intended. He jumped to his feet to help Mrs. Mansell with the tray. "I've found him for sure," he said, putting the tray on a stool by the fire. "Look. This one here. That's him on the left."

She peered over his shoulder. "Oh yes. With Richard. How lovely. That was taken in France. Soon after they arrived there. I think they shared a billet."

She sat down and poured tea.

"I know it's an awfully long time ago," said David, "But can you remember if your husband said much about John?"

She turned to face him with sparkling eyes. "Oh yes. And I can remember almost everything from Richard's first home leave. I hadn't seen him for over six months and already I knew several girls whose husbands had been killed. I ticked off the days on a calendar on the kitchen wall, trying to make the time go faster. We were so happy together and I couldn't wait for him to see the baby again." She fingered the collar of her blouse. "I'm sorry. I'm rambling on about Richard. He used to talk a lot about your poor uncle. He said he was a wonderful doctor. They became very good friends, you know." She sat back in her chair, with her eyes focussed far away, beyond the room.

"I can remember Richard coming into the cottage we rented as if it were yesterday. He had bought a French doll for the baby - a little milkmaid with blue eyes - and he had a lot of things which belonged to your uncle. After he had gone missing. Some clothes and photographs of his family. Oh, and a box Brownie. It's funny how one recalls things like that.

"He was distraught to have lost John. So many men were killed, of course, but Richard thought the world of your uncle. He said he was the bravest of the brave. He insisted on working right up at the front, with no regard whatsoever for his own safety, and used to make sure the men knew he was there to help them if they got hurt. He told me they loved him for it." She squeezed her eyes shut for a moment.

"Anyway, Richard took everything over to John's parents. They only lived a few miles away. When he came home afterwards, he had a parcel with him which they had given him."

David leaned towards her, holding his breath.

"It was wrapped in hessian and we undid it on the dining room table. It was a lovely tapestry and they had asked Richard to find a home for it. I never quite knew why, but I always assumed it was too painful for them to hold onto it. Some people cope with loss that way. We didn't know what we should do with it. Richard had brought it back from France, you see. He said he and your uncle had a sort of pact to look after each other's things if anything happened to either of them."

"Did it look like this, do you remember?" He showed her the photograph of the tapestry.

She studied it for a long time, holding it up to the light. "That's our old garden," she exclaimed. "That's an apple tree in the garden, and you can see the corner of the house. Richard took this. He must have hung the tapestry up to photograph it in a good light. Where on earth did you find it?"

"It was in my grandmother's papers."

"Richard must have sent it to her."

"Have a look on the back."

"Oh God," she said. "There's his name." She put a hand over her mouth and stared at David. "We took the tapestry to the school."

"Can you remember where?" He tried to keep his voice calm so as not to agitate her.

"It was a catholic school. I'm sure of that. Richard said the tapestry had come from a French church. It was of some saint or other so we thought it ought to go to a catholic place. It was up north. Richard had a friend who had been there."

"Up north?" He tried to think of catholic schools.

"Yes. It was in the middle of winter, 1915 I think it was. Everything was frozen, and as we couldn't do much at home, we left the baby with nanny and got on a train with the tapestry rolled up again in the hessian. Richard was only home for ten days you see, and with time so precious, we wanted to be together. The trains were very good back then and we got there quite easily. We stayed the night with some old friends of mine and came back the following evening on the sleeper. I remember it all being a terrifically exciting little adventure. Will you have some more tea? I'm talking too much."

"Thank you." He held out the cup for her. "Can you tell me which school it was?"

Her fingers twisted together. "Oh dear. I don't remember."

"Can you remember what might have happened at the school?"

She thought for a moment. "I'm afraid I can't. I'm so sorry. I'm not being very helpful and this is important to you, isn't it? But I know we came home without the tapestry so they must have agreed to keep it."

"Can you tell me where your friends lived?"

"Oh, they died years ago," she said with a laugh.

"But it might have been near the school, you see."

"Oh yes, I suppose so. How silly of me not to have thought of that. They were in Yorkshire. I forget the name of the village but it was near Darlington."

David put a hand on her arm. "Do you think the school was quite near Darlington?"

"Well, we went in a hansom so it can't have been far."

"A hansom? Pulled by a horse?"

"Yes. That's how it was then."

"Of course. I wonder if the tapestry is still there."

"I don't see why not. Those places don't change much."

"I want to find it, and try to take it back to France. For John's sake."

David drove back into London, weaving the Jaguar through the Sunday evening traffic. The old lady had been wonderful, recalling her memories of her husband and his friendship with the medical officer of fifty years ago.

Freddy Pearson might have been a gambling addict, a thief, and a womaniser, but uncle John was a hero, working up at the sharp end of the trenches, loved by his men. That was something to be proud of. And Mrs. Mansell knew about the tapestry. He would bloody well find it and get it back to France where it belonged.

He parked the Jaguar in Lupus Street, and rang the bell of Otis's flat. She came to let him in, wearing a pair of jeans and a checked shirt and looking like a cowgirl. But when he kissed her cheek the familiar scent came to him. He followed her into the kitchen.

"What do you know about catholic schools in Yorkshire?" he asked her.

"Not a lot. Why?"

"Because that old lady told me she and her husband took the tapestry to one of them. It might be near Darlington."

"You *have* done well," she said. "What did you do to her?"

"Drank her tea politely and looked at her photograph album."

"This is getting awfully exciting, detective. Should we have a drink?

"Certainly."

"Gin?"

She rummaged in the fridge and found some tonic and ice.

"What about Ampleforth?" she said. "That's up there somewhere. There's an atlas next door. On the bookshelf."

She brought in their drinks and he turned the pages of the atlas.

"It's too far," he said. "They went in a cab from Darlington. A horse cab. Look. It's miles from Ampleforth. Any other ideas?"

"Shall I ring Daddy? He's bound to know."

"He might forget if he knows I'm here."

"Don't be daft. He likes you."

He watched her while she picked up the telephone. "Trunks, please," she said to the operator. "Jersey, Northern 684."

He took his drink to the window and looked out over the dark street. It had begun to rain. The rain slanted over yellow haloes at the street lights, and glistened on the wet road. Otis chatted away happily for a few minutes and he turned to face her when he heard her say : "Thanks, Daddy. You're brilliant."

She came over to David. "Bingo," she said. "St. Benedict's. Just over the border in County Durham."

They looked on the map. "Eight miles to Darlington," he said. "A horse could do that couldn't it? We're closing in."

They walked up to Churton Street and ordered corn on the cob, and duck and orange from the big blackboard with its chalk writing. The waiter brought Beaujolais nouveau. David poured the wine into the restaurant's Duralex tumblers. They sat opposite each other at the simple wooden tables, and in a small silence between them, he picked bits of wax off the stalactites dripping down the bottle that served as a candlestick.

"What is it, David?" she asked.

"Nothing, really."

"You can't just be nothing."

"Thinking is all right?"

"Thinking's good. Much more positive."

"What about sad thoughts?"

"Permissible, but a bit out of character for you."

"I'm sorry." He swigged his wine and poured again from the bottle.

"Tell me how sad," she said.

"Middling sad."

"Out of ten?"

"Say, six. Maybe seven."

"That's much worse than middling. Five is middling."

"I always have difficulty with maths."

"Seven could be serious." She leaned forward, low over the table. "I know. You're going to dump me?"

David burst out with laughter. People at the next table looked up in surprise at his sudden explosion. The waiter brought sweet corn with melting butter, and sprinkled black pepper and salt.

"I love it when you laugh like that," Otis told him as the waiter left.

"No dumping," David said. "But you've got butter on your chin."

She dabbed with a napkin. "Tell me why you're sad. Surely it's good news about the school?"

"Oh yes. That's wonderful."

"But?"

David chewed sweet corn, working from end of end. Otis was going round and round. "You know how some boys worship their fathers?" he asked.

"It's not just girls. Daddy's as square as a paving stone, but he's always been my hero."

David took a long breath. "Last month, at Dunkirk, I found out my father was worthless. Worse than that. He was a thief, a liar, a gambler, and unfaithful."

"No, David. You said...."

"All lies. A bloody great pack of lies." He pushed away his plate and began to tell her, haltingly at first, and then, as her quiet listening encouraged him, with increasing confidence, everything he had learned about his father.

The waiter brought them half a duck each, smothered in

233

orange sauce. It looked pretty enough, with shreds of peel and dark green watercress, but David picked at it without enthusiasm.

"Why didn't you tell me before?" Otis asked him. "I would have understood."

"I should have done. I was embarrassed."

"Silly boy." She stroked his cheek with the back of her hand.

"Can you imagine what it's like for me to be ashamed of my father? Too ashamed to tell you? It's like living with a lie all your life. I wish to God she hadn't told me. It was all right before."

"Don't blame her, David. She's had to live with all this for years."

"It doesn't stop me wanting to scream."

"If you need to scream, rail against your father."

Afterwards, they drank black coffee, and she was happy when he ordered a double brandy. At her doorstep afterwards he kissed her on the lips and she tasted of slightly salted wine.

Late January 1966

The man opposite David in the compartment might have been a gamekeeper. His thick tweeds smelled of wet gun dog. David sat with an attaché case on his knees, reading again his uncle's letter from the Western Front as the train rattled north from King's Cross.

He looked up at the sharp rasp of a match. The gamekeeper was lighting a pipe, puffing blue smoke and tamping the burning tobacco with his finger. A small spark fell into his lap and lay there unnoticed until smothered by the damp tweed. David looked out of the window wondering what a gamekeeper might have been doing in London. Rain, flattened by the wind, streamed sideways across the glass. Small beads of water formed moving patterns, obscuring grey fields and woodland.

At Darlington station, he waited for a taxi to take him to the school. Wind buffeted his umbrella, threatening to turn it inside out. He jumped back onto the pavement as the taxi arrived to avoid a wave of water thrown up from a puddle by the car's wheel. He climbed into the back and wiped condensation from the window with his hand. He looked forward eagerly to his meeting with Brother Thomas, the friar responsible for what St. Benedict's called their antiquities. He had spoken to the man on the telephone and felt a mounting ferment of excitement at the thought of seeing at last the tapestry that Mansell had brought from France.

"Coming up on the right, sir," said the driver, as they followed a high flint wall and swept into a driveway between iron gates. David peered through the windscreen at St Benedict's. He saw a long brick building with a porticoed front door, standing on a low ridge of land, overlooking the school's other buildings, and playing fields laid out with rugby pitches.

"Makes me feel quite at home," he said.

"You know the place then?"

"No, but it's got 'institutional' written all over it. They're all more or less the same. Any local gossip about this one?"

"Nothing special, but they say the friars are pretty tough on the boys." The driver swivelled in his seat to get change from his pocket.

"Comes from wearing hair shirts I suppose," said David.

In appearance Brother Thomas was anything but the epitome of a rubicund prelate with a hearty appetite. It was as if a diet of theology and dusty books had drained him of life, shrivelling his skin into brittle brown paper, and his handshake was a cold reptilian grasp. A few thin wisps of grey hair failed to cover the flaking baldness of his scalp.

"You had better come and see it," he said. His voice was like dry wind over sandpaper. He led the way to the college chapel, his black cloak flapping in his wake.

The tapestry hung on dark oak panelling, a jewel of colour, taller than a man and five feet wide.

"I wasn't expecting it to be like this," said David, after a long pause.

"You're disappointed?"

"No. Surprised."

"What did you expect?"

"Less colour, I suppose."

"Why?"

"I always think of religious tapestries being inclined to be duller. More dowdy." It sounded awfully pompous.

"Is tapestry your speciality?" Brother Thomas looked irritated.

The tapestry reminded David of a modern painting. He was not an expert at painting, and certainly not at embroidery, but he had seen paintings in the Summer Exhibition at the Royal Academy which lifted his spirits, with colours so intense that he wanted to sing. He said at last. "I had no idea it would be so colourful." He pulled the photograph from his attaché case. "Look, this is all I have had until now. I can't believe how lovely it is in real life. Black and white tells you

236

nothing. This was taken in 1915. Look on the back. There's my grandmother's handwriting I told you about."

Back in Brother Thomas's office, the friar regarded him with hooded eyes behind an eagle's beak. "The difficulty we have, as I hoped I had made clear on the telephone, is that our records show that the tapestry was brought to us in the winter of 1915 by a..." he consulted his papers. "Yes, by a Major Richard Mansell. We have nothing to corroborate that your uncle, John Pearson, was involved in any way."

"But surely Mansell must have left some explanation?"

"As I have just said, we have no further information on the matter. If your uncle had brought the tapestry here himself, no doubt things would be easier for us all."

"I've talked with Mansell's widow. She told me that her husband brought home some of John Pearson's possessions from France. The tapestry must have been amongst them. Otherwise, my grandmother would not have been able to give it to Mansell. Anyway, surely the writing on the back of the photograph must help? You can't just ignore it."

"I ignore nothing. You posit that your uncle was involved with the tapestry in some way. But you have given me nothing to support your case. Merely conjecture. You must appreciate that all the evidence shows that the tapestry was given freely to the college by Richard Mansell."

"What evidence? What have you got to suggest it was anything other than a temporary arrangement while the war lasted. A sort of loan, perhaps?"

"As I said, we have nothing to suggest it was not an outright gift."

"But nothing to prove that it was. After all, Mansell was acting purely on the wishes of my grandparents. He was not in a position to decide whether it was a gift or not."

"I grant you that. But it was, nevertheless, an act on Mansell's part with no strings attached of which I am aware." The eagle sat, motionless, displaying the possibility of infinite patience.

Your grammar is awfully good, thought David, and appropriate for a man of learning. "So," he said, "We have moved from a gift to an act. I need hardly tell you that there is a significant difference between the two terms."

"If you have come here to threaten me, I must warn you that I have all the considerable resources of this college behind me."

"And that is not a threat? I have come simply to try and do the right thing. It's fifty years since this tapestry came here either as a gift, which you cannot prove, or as the act of a man who was given it by the parents of his friend when he was on leave from some of the worst fighting mankind has ever seen. Whichever it was, it is difficult not to conclude that the right place for the thing is back in France."

A cough, dry leaves scraping over flagstones. "It is the Lord who makes judgements over what is right."

"And man who has to interpret them." He said it with a smile, trying to lighten an atmosphere that had turned sour like curdling milk.

But Brother Thomas was sculpted of marble, seemingly impervious to argument. His lips parted, trailing a thin thread of mucus over yellow teeth. "If we could accept," he said after an interminable pause, "that we are dealing with a temporal issue, then it might be possible to consult the board of trustees. In any event, they would need to give their approval, which I doubt will be forthcoming. Particularly after fifty years. As you know, we are a Jesuit foundation, and we regard relics such as this tapestry as a valuable part of our heritage." He gave a smile, stretching bloodless lips into a rictus. "We do not divest ourselves lightly of college property."

I bet you don't, thought David, rising from his chair. "Please will you ask them?" he said. "No doubt with their Benedictine background they will be men and women of charity."

"Another frequently misused word."

"Another?"

"Charity. You will have to write. Nothing can be decided without a formal approach." He stood up and wrapped his cloak around his bony shoulders. "I am afraid that is all I have to say on the matter."

So, thought David as he waited outside for his taxi, the scrawny creature was as miserable as his scurfy hair. The rain had stopped, and shouts from the rugby field rang in the northern air.

'A formal approach', Brother Thomas had said. He would waste no time, and write it in the morning. He was not certain as to the exact involvement of his uncle with the tapestry, but having seen it hanging in the school chapel, David was determined to find out. The intransigence of Brother Thomas smouldered in his head. That tapestry is going back to France, he thought, even if I have to shove a formal approach up the backside of that pestilential friar.

He felt a sudden longing to see Otis again. He had wanted her to come with him to see the tapestry but she had promised her parents to go home for her father's sixtieth birthday. It would be lonely in London when he got off the train on a Saturday night in winter. She had come into his life quite slowly. They had not chased each other, but rather drifted along, available and accessible, sharing small pleasures, happy to be together. David felt himself pulled closer to her since talking to her in the restaurant. He knew he would need time to get over the shattering of his father as an idol. She was soothing ointment on that wound, understanding his sense of loss, and he loved her for it.

The breeze brought a vaguely familiar whiff of tobacco smoke and he heard heavy footsteps behind him. He looked round to see the gamekeeper-turned-teacher striding past carrying an armful of textbooks.

"Oh David, you must make them give it back," his mother said on the telephone. "They can't possibly keep it now."

"They're going to try. I've had a letter from them. Frightfully stuffy from the secretary to the Board of Trustees. They couldn't see any point in me going up there again to discuss it unless they had an official request from the priest. In the church the tapestry came from. And even then they wouldn't guarantee anything."

"Miserable buggers," she said. "You'd better have a go at the priest."

"I've got to find him first."

"Any clues where to look?"

"Just my photographs. There's one of a church. It's a bit of a guess, but I've a hunch it must be somewhere near the front line where uncle John was stationed in August 1914."

"Sounds a bit vague."

"Listen to this, though. I've got a list of the places where his battalion fought."

"Clever boy. How?"

"The regimental records people gave it to me. They've got it in amazing detail. I've studied the maps. Apart from a couple of weeks when they were moving up and down the Marne, all their action took place in three dioceses."

"Which are?"

"Stop yawning."

"Sorry. How did you know?"

"You can always tell. Lille, Arras and Cambrai. I'm going over on Sunday night. Whiz round the diocesan offices with my photographs on Monday, and back that evening."

"Is Otis going with you?" She sounded alert again.

"She's got to work."

"Oh. That's a pity. Well, good luck, darling."

It had meant more time away from the office, and a difficult conversation with the senior partner, but David put the car on a Sunday evening ferry and drove down to the hotel he had booked.

At half past eight the next morning, the clerk in the diocesan office at Lille had been sleepy but helpful, and assured him within forty minutes that there was no church in the diocese that matched his photograph. David thanked the man, checked his map and roared out of Lille on the hour long drive to Arras. The clerk there, a frail old man with a stammer, consulted his colleagues, interminably spreading files all over a table. Eventually he came back to David, shaking his head, and David began to wonder if he had embarked on a wild goose chase. He was beginning to run out of options.

It was nearly one o'clock by the time he had found his address in Cambrai, and the offices were closed for lunch until two. But within five minutes of the doors opening, he had what he wanted. There was no doubt about it, the man said. The photograph was unquestionably of the church of Saint Martin in Le Cateau-Cambrésis, and the *curé's* name was Father Augustin.

"I'll call him for you," the man said. "To make an appointment."

David stood, drumming his fingers on the counter while he waited for the connection.

"Engaged," the man said.

David looked as his watch. "Will you try again, please?"

"Monsieur is in a hurry?"

"I need to catch the ferry."

"A ferry?"

"Yes. To England."

"Ah. One moment."

The man dialled again and made ticking noises with a pencil against his teeth before talking rapidly into the telephone. "It seems Father Augustin is ill," he said to David, holding his hand over the mouthpiece. "Will you see Monsieur Blessier? He is the verger. An old man, perhaps a little deaf."

David drove up into the middle of Le Cateau at three o'clock
in the afternoon. He recognised the church immediately from
his photograph, parked outside, and ran through some iron
railings up to the door. He drew his coat around him in the
biting cold. Thin winter sunlight shone through clear
windows that might once have held stained glass. He heard
footsteps and saw an elderly figure in a cassock cross the
transept.

"Excusez-moi. Monsieur Blessier? My name is David
Pearson." His voice sounded unusually loud.

"Good afternoon, Monsieur," said Blessier. "I am sorry
Father Augustin cannot be here."

"I hope it's not serious," David boomed.

Blessier looked gloomy and placed a hand on his chest.
"His heart. But he will recover soon. It is not the first time.
Incidentally, there is no necessity for shouting. My hearing is
excellent. Now, I understand you wish to talk about a
tapestry?"

"Yes, please." David lowered his voice. "I have this
photograph of it. I believe it may have come from here."

Blessier peered at the photograph through the thick lenses
of his spectacles while David waited, with the winter cold of
the floor seeping into his feet. He wished the old man would
hurry. The muted sound of traffic filtered into the building,
and a sparrow flew across the nave.

"St. John the Divine," said Blessier, at last. He raised his
face to the roof as if seeking inspiration. "When I was a boy, I
took my confirmation classes here. Father Albert was the
priest. There was a tapestry just like this. It used to hang on
the wall, over there I think. Or sometimes in the vestry.
Father Albert used it to impress on us the virtue of humility.
The tapestry was a beautiful thing. It must have been
destroyed when the Germans came. The whole church was

243

wrecked by shell-fire. I was just a boy but I remember the damage. And the dust. It covered everything."

"The tapestry is safe," David told him. "I've found it. In a school in England. I think my uncle took it from here in 1914."

Blessier looked up at the ceiling again. "That would be a miracle."

"I want to return it to you," said David, aware he was shouting again. "But I am going to need your help. The school want to keep it, but if Father Augustin makes a formal request, I don't think they can refuse him. Would he know anything about the tapestry?"

Blessier shook his head. "He has not been here long and knows little of our past. But he will be most interested when I tell him all of this. He loves beautiful things."

"I hope he gets better soon." David pulled a card from his wallet. "Please give him this so he can contact me." He wrote the address of St. Benedict's on the back. "And when he feels strong enough, he can write to the school."

"And we can all pray," said Blessier. "It might help, and can do no harm." He tapped the back of his ear. "Another miracle for you." He pulled out his hearing aid.

Above them the church clock struck four. It had grown dark while they had been talking. David said goodbye to Blessier, and ran out to the Jaguar. He should be able to make the coast in a couple of hours, and catch the evening hovercraft. With the time difference, he could be back in London for a late supper with Otis.

**** ****

The envelope with a French stamp lay on David's doormat on a cold February Monday. It was hand written in blue ink, and on the reverse a printed label read: 'Le Presbytère, Le Cateau'. David put the letter in his pocket, leaving the rest of the mail to be dealt with later. He walked to his office with the collar of his coat turned up against light flurries of snow, revelling in the anticipation of what he would read.

He hoped he might catch sight of Otis but there was no sign of her in the foyer so he took the lift and ran to his office. He sat at his desk with the letter lying unopened in front of him. He looked at the unfamiliar handwriting, and thought of Blessier with his hearing aid, and the priest with a dicky heart. He took a silver paper-knife from a drawer in his desk, slit open the envelope, and began to read:

Dear M. Pearson,

I am so sad I was not able to hear your interesting news about our tapestry myself, but M. Blessier has told me everything. Although I have no knowledge of the tapestry, there is some old people I was speaking with who remember it perfectly from before the Great War. One of them told me that there was some papers removed from the church when it was destroyed in 1914 and taken to the town hall. I have checked in the archives there and am very happy to tell you that I have found a letter dated 25 August 1914, signed by Father Albert Mainil, that he gave a tapestry from the church to a Captain Pearson to save it from destruction in the fighting. Father Albert was shot by the Germans a few days later for hiding a wounded English soldier in his attic, and the papers have lain undisturbed until now.

M. Blessier informs me that he remembers well the tapestry on our wall and that you have said him you wish for it to come back here. That is also my most fervent desire, Monsieur. This church was damaged again in 1945 but now all is restored to its beauty, as you have seen no doubt in your visit.

We offer prayers that the school authorities will find it in their hearts to hear our pleas. I have written to them today also, as you suggested, to tell them of my discovery.

With the blessing of God, and my distinguished sentiments,

Fr. Augustin Baldon, curé.

David sat back in his chair, his fingers linked behind his head, and let out a whoop of joy. The pieces in the jigsaw were falling into place. John Pearson, had taken the tapestry, and the priest had had the sense to record it before the poor man was shot. Blessier had talked about a miracle. It seemed that his prayers had been answered. Nothing, surely, could stand in the way now. The tapestry was going home.

David looked at his watch. She should be there. He picked up his telephone and dialled Otis's office.

"Are you free at lunchtime?" he said.

"Oh yes." She breathed it as if inviting him to something.

"Meet me in the foyer at one?"

"You sound like you're onto something, Detective?"

"A French letter, madam."

"Are you being rude?"

"Strictly factual. One o'clock?"

"On the dot, Inspector."

David called his secretary on the inter office telephone and waited for her, leaning back in his chair.

"Before it gets busy," he said to her, "will you do a letter for me, to France?"

"Hallo?" she said. " Have we a new lover?" She sat at the far side of his desk, a comfortable figure approaching middle age.

"It's a he and he's a priest."

"Ah. In a hassock?"

"In a cassock. Hassock's are for kneeling on."

"I always get that wrong."

He showed her the letter.

"Isn't that wonderful?" she said, handing it back. "What are you going to say?"

"You are going to thank him from the bottom of my heart and say I will let him know *immediatement* when I hear

246

anything from St. Benedict's."

"And then?"

"I'll arrange to go up there to meet them again."

"I hope you'll take Otis this time."

"I'll try. Why do you think I should?"

"How old do you think I am?"

"With the light behind you like that I would say thirty."

"And ten, you fool."

"All right. But why does it matter?"

"It doesn't. But you don't get to forty without knowing a bit about men."

"And?"

"Those trustees. I bet they are all men. Worthy old buffers. They'll feel they have to play hard with you. But with Otis they won't stand a chance. They'll be undressing her in their horny old minds."

"Have you been talking to Rory by any chance?"

"I don't need to talk to him to know what goes on out there."

"Rory's got one agenda. Not everyone shares it."

"Ok, boss. I'll write your letter. Will you let me know how it works out?"

**** ****

At six in the morning on the last day of February, David collected Otis from Cadogan Gardens and drove out of London heading for the Great North Road. She had wrapped herself in fur and sat low on the leather seat of the Jaguar, watching the street lights flick past before dawn came, pink and cold in the east.

"It's a five hundred mile round trip," he said. "It's going to be a long day. Perhaps we should have gone by train."

"It's more fun in the car," she said sleepily. "How big is it?"

"The tapestry? Huge, but we can roll it up. Assuming

they agree to part with it."

"They can hardly refuse with the letter from your priest."

"If they are anything like Brother Thomas they'll be as mean as mouse shit."

"Do you mind if I snooze? It's awfully early."

"You sleep. I'll wake you if anything interesting happens."

As he had hoped, they were clear of London before the traffic built up, and a pale yellow sun rose through a band of light cloud. He joined the A1 at Hendon and the car settled into its stride, clipping over the joints in the tarmac, chasing the road signs to the North. He looked across at Otis. She had put a cushion between her head and the window and lay back, relaxed and beautiful with her hands folded in her lap. Her lips were slightly parted and he noticed a tiny jewel of moisture at the corner of her mouth. A baby, fast asleep. He could see her kneecaps below the dashboard, small pale curves where the bone came close to the surface. He wanted to caress her there but thought she might wake.

He changed down to overtake a line of cars held up behind a lorry. The Jaguar leaped forward, pushing him back in his seat and, as he passed the lorry, he came fast into a roundabout. He took the racing line, ironing out the corners and held his breath, hoping she would sleep through it. He drove on for another hour before pulling into a petrol station with a Little Chef.

"Have I been asleep for long?" she asked him, stretching.

He showed her their position on the map. "This long," he said.

"But that's miles."

"Yes, and now it's breakfast."

A waitress took their order and brought coffee while they waited.

"It's the first time we've had breakfast together," she said.

"Apart from Jersey."

"That doesn't count. I mean just us."

She smiled at him across the table and he thought how

248

pretty she looked. She wore a polo neck in black wool, rolled back high under her chin. He remembered something his mother had said.

"You look lovely in that," he told her.

Her smile grew wider. "Thank you. I'm glad you like it."

"It's good with your blonde hair."

"You're very complimentary this morning."

The waitress brought him an all day breakfast of fried eggs, bacon, sausage, tomato and black pudding. She put a plate in front of Otis with two boiled eggs and some toast. "Four and a half minutes, madam," she said.

Now I know how she likes her eggs, David thought. Fillet steak rare, eggs four and a half minutes. "I'd better get cracking," he said, looking at the pile of food on his plate.

He recognised the railway station where he had taken a taxi, and at five minutes to twelve pulled up at the steps leading into St. Benedict's. A few flakes of snow drifted over the rooftops from a pewter sky. He held the car door for Otis while she stepped out onto the gravel, smoothing her skirt.

"It's very imposing," she said, looking up at the building.

"So are you." He looked up at the sky. "Let's get out of this."

A receptionist led them down an echoing stone-floored passage and knocked at a heavy oak door. Five men, including Brother Thomas, sat at a table that might have come from the boardroom of a prosperous company. The air was redolent with furniture polish.

"Mr. Pearson," the receptionist announced. "And Miss..."

"Miss Mesurier," said David. "My secretary." He avoided Brother Thomas's eye.

"Witherington," said a short grey-faced man in a flannel suit. "Chairman of the trustees." Witherington introduced the others. They sat down, scraping their chairs and shuffling papers.

"Welcome to St. Benedict's," Witherington said to Otis. "Mr. Pearson has been before but this is your first visit?"

"It is," said Otis, smiling directly.

"Good, good. Now, Brother Thomas has filled us in on the background of this case. The tapestry which came here in 1915." He consulted a file. "Mr. Pearson made a formal approach following his first visit; we replied that under the circumstances we could not consider anything without a letter from the curé in France; we received that in due course, and therefore agreed to raise the matter at our next meeting when all the trustees were present. A sub-committee was formed with authority to act on behalf of the board, and here we are." He rattled it off as if it were a clothes list. The other members of the panel nodded in agreement and Brother Thomas stared from hooded eyes.

"Perhaps, Mr. Pearson, you would be kind enough to run through the history as you know it," said Witherington. "Just in case we have missed anything."

David stood up and spoke for ten minutes, pacing slowly across the room as if giving a presentation to a group of clients. When he had finished he smiled at Otis and sat down. A long silence ensued.

Witherington looked at the other trustees. "Thank you. Does that accord with what you know, Brother?"

"It reflects accurately the facts," said Bother Thomas. "The board will want to consider if the facts are relevant."

"Quite so," said Witherington. He blew his nose into a red spotted handkerchief. "The case rests on the implied terms of the receipt here of the tapestry." David imagined the board members knotting themselves up over the differences between a gift, an act, and a receipt. Witherington was beginning to look uncomfortable and the others stared down at their papers. David decided to say nothing. When things get difficult, he had been taught, keep quiet. Let the other man sweat.

"The nub of the matter," said Witherington looking up at the ceiling, "is that you and Father Augustin say that John

Pearson was given authority to take the tapestry to keep it safe from the advancing Germans. But all our records show that someone else, a Major Mansell, brought it here. All our dealings therefore were with this Mansell. We have nothing to connect any of this with John Pearson."

"I have the photograph," said David. "And the writing on the back."

"Which specify that the tapestry was given to Mansell, and Mansell gave it, brought it, left it here, whichever interpretation you want to put on it. I am afraid I have to say that, notwithstanding the letter from the priest in Le Cateau, we have to conclude that we must be guided by that. John Pearson may well have rescued the tapestry from that church but it was brought here by someone else. Major Mansell. With no ifs ands or buts."

You miserable buggers, David thought, recalling his mother.

"May I say something?" It was Otis.

"Please,"said Witherington. He waved a hand invitingly.

She looked quickly at David. "If John Pearson were alive," she said to Witherington, "he would be in his eighties. If he were here now, would you refuse him?"

"Assuming he had brought the tapestry here in the first place, no. We could not refuse him."

"So if Major Mansell were alive, you could not refuse him either?"

"But Mansell is not alive."

"No," she said. "But his widow is."

"That is hardly the same."

"The tapestry was given to Mansell, freely, without strings by Pearson's mother. It therefore became his property. You are not able to claim that he, in his turn, gave it freely to this college. Only that he left it here, perhaps while the war raged on so that the college could be its guardian.

"If, in his will, he left everything to his wife, it follows that, in the absence of any claim the French might make, she is the de facto owner of the tapestry. You would therefore have to return it to her if that is what she wants."

A peacock butterfly, encouraged by the central heating, fluttered against the window, the only sound in the room. It climbed to the top of a pane and spread its wings with their round eye markings, before falling back to the bottom. Beyond the glass, snow blotted out trees at the far side of the car park. David looked at Otis who sat demurely in her chair, her eyes lowered to her hands. You bloody marvel, he thought. You bloody wonderful quick-on-your-feet marvel. You've boxed these buggers in and slammed the lid. The tapestry came from France and now it's bloody well going back to France, and two fingers to Brother Thomas. He looked at Brother Thomas. A purple stain suffused the eagle's face, the eyes shrunken as in a death mask.

"You had better get to the old girl before they do," Otis laughed as they got back into the car.

"They won't know how to find her. Christ, you're priceless."

"I've got a degree in law remember, even if I am only 'your secretary'."

"What if Mansell didn't leave everything to his wife? She told me there's a daughter."

"If she were a beneficiary there's no reason she wouldn't play ball."

"Or it might all have gone to a cat's home."

Snowflakes swirled horizontally, whitening the playing fields and settling on the drive.

"Pity about lunch," he said. "I was looking forward to that. I told you they were mean."

"And I never even got to see the flipping tapestry."

The snow fell more heavily from a leaden sky. David switched on the car's headlights in the premature darkness and the windscreen wipers batted backwards and forwards, piling up the snow. The car slowed, skidding in the corners, and at the junction with the A1, cars queued, wheels spinning in chaos. They had to wait for half an hour where a lorry had spun sideways, blocking the road while the evening closed in and snow formed thick haloes round the street lights. Just before dark they crawled in a line of heavy traffic to Scotch Corner.

"Let's pull in here and get something to eat," he said. "It might ease off later." The bulk of the hotel stood black against the dark sky. He found a space to leave the Jaguar and they ran across the car park. The snow was already four inches deep.

He ordered coffee and smoked salmon with brown bread and butter from the bar and a waiter brought it to them by a coal fire.

"Nasty night," the man said. "Have you far to go?"

"London."

"Oh Lord. I wouldn't want to do that. There's ten inches forecast."

Otis poured coffee from a silver jug and they ate the smoked salmon with lemon juice squeezed over it, and ground black pepper. David went to look outside and saw the snow still falling heavily. The Jaguar was covered in a thick blanket, disguising its pretty lines except where the heat from the engine kept the bonnet clear. A man walked up to the door, stamping snow from his shoes.

"Bloody chaos out there," he said. "I've had to abandon the car. It's drifting right over the road."

"I think we're stuck," David said when he got back to her.

She looked round, wrinkling her nose. "Well, at least it's warm."

"I mean for the night."

"Oh. Do you think they've got any rooms?"

"I'll go and see."

He walked down to the desk where a queue had formed. He could see Otis sitting by the fire. The man with the

253

abandoned car was arguing with the receptionist.

"I'm afraid there's not much left, sir," the clerk said to David when his turn came.

"What is there?"

"There's just one single room and the honeymoon suite."

David looked at Otis. She caught his eye and smiled. He turned back to the clerk. "In the single room, is there a sofa or something?"

"Yes, sir. There should be a sofa. It may be a bit short though for someone tall."

"I'll take it."

"Very good, sir. It's for two?"

"For two, yes. Perhaps you could arrange some spare blankets for the sofa?"

"I'll do that right away, sir." He gave David the key. "Will you be dining, sir? I can book a table if you like. It might pay with the hotel so full."

"Thank you. Shall we say seven-thirty?"

"Seven-thirty it is. Do you need a hand with your cases?"

"We don't have any cases. It's the snow, you see."

The man looked relieved. "The snow. Of course."

David walked back to where she sat by the fireside. She was stroking a marmalade cat, fat from too much time in the kitchen. The cat purred and rubbed its head against her legs, walking high-backed to and fro within reach of her hand. The black polo neck really did suit her, and he could see her kneecaps again, where the material of her stockings stretched tight as she sat with her legs crossed.

"I see you have a new friend," he said.

"He's called Duke."

"He seems to like you."

"Cat's are awfully fickle. It won't last." She indicated the reception desk. "Any good?"

"All the rooms have gone," he said.

"Oh dear."

"Except one single. I've taken it. There's a sofa too,

254

apparently."

"Well, that's all right. I didn't fancy trying to sleep down here in a chair."

"Let's go and see it," he said, waving the key. "It's on the top floor."

Room 382 was over the kitchens and smelt a little of old cabbage, but the sofa was not as small as he had feared, the bathroom was clean, and from the window he could see the Jaguar.

"Look at the snow," he said and she came to stand by him. He felt the current change in the small gap between them while she peered through the window. It was as if they were touching.

"It's beautiful," she said. "I love snow."

"Yes."

"There must be lots of people like us, stuck in it."

"Yes."

"I'll have to let the office know."

"Yes. We can ring them in the morning from downstairs. I've booked a table for dinner at half past seven."

"You can have the bed," she said.

"No. It's for you. I'll be fine on the sofa." There was a knock on the door. "Come in," he said, and a maid brought in two blankets and a pillow and put them on the sofa.

"I've found some wash things and a tube of toothpaste for you," the maid said. "We always keep some for emergencies."

"I wish I had something to change into," said Otis when the maid had gone.

"You look fine like that."

"It seems strange in a hotel room without any luggage."

"There'll be others," he said. "Because of the snow."

They ordered *chateaubriand* steak, cooked rare, with *bearnaise* sauce, and ate it with sauté potatoes and broccoli, and he asked the waiter for a bottle of Volnay. She said she couldn't eat anything else so they drank some coffee and when they had finished he took her to the revolving door and they went to look outside.

The snow had stopped and lay thick over a silent world turned white under a clear sky. A three-quarter moon hung low in the eastern sky. It was bitterly cold. He spun the door for her and led her back in to the lift.

"It's like being in the office," he said as the lift creaked upwards.

"Except we're both on the same floor here."

"You can have the bathroom first," he said when they got to the room. He spread the blankets on the sofa and sat there listening to Otis splashing about.

She came out smiling. "Your turn," she said. She smelled of toothpaste and she had coiled up her hair on top of her head. To keep it dry while she washed, David thought. It made her neck wonderfully long and reminded him of a painting he had seen by Modigliani.

When David came out of the bathroom, she was in bed with the covers pulled up under her chin. She had loosened her hair and it spilled across her pillow, gold in the lamplight. He saw her clothes laid in a neat pile on a chair. Her stockings and a bra dangled from the top. He switched off the ceiling light, stripped to his vest and pants and climbed onto the sofa, wriggling underneath the blankets.

"Good night," he said.

"Shall I turn off my light? There's nothing to read."

"Yes. I'm glad you're a lawyer, clever girl."

She spoke out of the darkness: "David?"

"Yes?"

"Thank you for today. It's been lovely."

"Even getting snowbound?"

"Especially this."

"But you didn't get to see the tapestry. After coming all this way."

"It'll keep until you get it to London."

"I thought I might get Pickfords to bring it down. You're going to love it."

"Let's have a party. A sort of private view. You can ring up the 'Evening Standard'. We'll organise a photographer. A mugshot of you alongside 'The Pearson Tapestry'."

He lay on his back with his knees raised, his feet jammed against the end of the sofa, thinking of the day. And he thought of Rory. Rory, he was certain, would not be quietly lying on the sofa. There was no sound from the road. It must be blocked, with drifting snow burying stranded cars. It was lucky the hotel had a room for them. He wondered who was in the honeymoon suite. Rory would have taken it if he had had the chance. David hadn't seen Otis's panties on the chair, so presumed she was still wearing them. He shivered, wondering if she were warm with no pyjamas.

"David?" she said a little later. "Are you awake?"

"Yes."

"Aren't you cold?"

"Only a bit."

"So am I."

"I'll get in with you."

He took off his vest and felt his way across the room in the darkness. He heard her move to make room for him, and lay down beside her. He pulled the eiderdown over them both and felt her warm in his arms.

April 1966

The nine o'clock hovercraft from Dover swept over wet sand on the beach at Calais hoverport, its propellers beating the air and driving clouds of salt spray across the windows. As the engines died away, the machine sank to the ground, crouching over its deflated skirts. The smell of high octane aviation fuel came into the cabin.

They took the N43 road south from the coast, and at St. Omer, David pulled into a garage for petrol.

"I'll get something for lunch," Otis said.

She wore a knee-length tweed skirt and stockings, with a silk scarf at her throat over a guernsey, and the skirt swung with her walk as David watched her cross the road. He paid the attendant, put down the Jaguar's roof, and checked that the tapestry was secure in its wrapping. When she returned, she carried a loaf of bread and a paper bag, with a box from the patisserie.

"What's in the box?" David asked.

"Lunch."

"What sort?"

"It's a surprise."

"Go on, then." He started to undo the string.

"No!" she laughed. "It's for later."

"How much later?"

"*Later,* later."

Carefully, he put the things she had bought behind the seats, on top of the tapestry, and they drove on through fields of young green corn and roadside verges resonant with birdsong.

At midday he pulled off into a side road that ran down between meadows where cattle grazed, and spread an old waterproof coat on the grass. She opened up their lunch and tore apart the still-warm bread to go with some pâté and ripe camembert cheese and a tomato. Breadcrumbs peppered her sweater, and she brushed them off her breasts with her hand.

She reached for the box and began to open it.

"Now," she said.

"No. I'm full."

"You can't be."

"Full is full. Chokker. Up to the top. I can't eat any more."

She opened the box and took out a *tarte aux fraises,* shiny with glaze. "Sure?"

"No. Come here," he said.

"If you do that there'll be jam everywhere."

"Let me try some." He ate half the tart and gave the rest to her and she tasted of strawberries when he kissed her. "It was a lovely surprise," he said.

He lay flat on the grass with his head in her lap. Her warmth came to him through the texture of her skirt against the skin of his neck. He heard a lark singing and searched until he found the small dark speck hovering overhead high in the blue sky. He closed his eyes and listened to the lark and thought about Otis. She had cried a little when she saw the tapestry for the first time, and felt the smooth roughness of the wool. "I'm so happy for you," she had said. "After all that horrid business with your father." He had put down the tapestry on the sofa, and taken her to his bedroom with their hands frantic amongst her rustling petticoats and the wonderful urgency of their lovemaking.

He stretched out a hand so that he could play with the fine bones of her ankle, and thought how she felt when they were in bed. She had let him touch her breasts for the first time in the narrow confines of the hotel bed. They were slightly conical and lovely to hold. They had not slept much that night.

"Let's go on the minor roads, David," she said. "To avoid the towns. It's such a lovely day." She showed him a route, picking out roads marked yellow on the Michelin map, and they packed up the remains of their meal and walked back to the car.

While she read the map, he drove slowly south-east across Picardy, and stopped on a bridge over a canal. They got out to watch a barge pulling a lighter, deep laden with a cargo of iron ore. Window boxes, bright with flowers, hung from the varnished cabin top at the stern, and washing flapped on a line. The barge came on with a rushing noise from its bow wave and the deep thump of its engine.

"You can rent a barge here," he said, standing close to her as they leaned over the brickwork of the bridge.

"It looks awfully big."

"Oh, something smaller. You can go right through France, down the Rhone, to the Med." He waved to a man on the barge who was tipping something out of a saucepan into the canal.

"I've heard about that," she said. "Daddy's always frightfully rude about it. Says it's for bloody landlubbers."

"Well, it's not quite like driving a destroyer. We ought to do it one day. You can take bikes, and whizz off into towns along the way for shopping."

"I'd like to do that with you, David."

He held her hand and they ran across the road together to look down at the barge. Heat from the exhaust puffed up in their faces, and when the barge had passed, its wake sucked and splashed along the bank, stirring reeds into a dance.

On the road out of Cambrai he ran the car up onto the verge to show her a War Grave Commission cemetery. Within a low wall, between a field of fresh green wheat and another of young sugar beet, they walked in silence along rows of white stone crosses set on greensward crisp as a park in Tunbridge Wells. A regiment of death lined up in perfect symmetry, the named remains of human lives given up for King and Country fifty years before.

He heard her call, and went over to her where she stood looking down at a headstone.

"Look," she said. Someone had laid a granite stone there, smooth on one side, with the writing: 'For Hughie. A little piece of home, for ever.'

"Who is he?" David asked.

She bent to read the inscription carved into the white limestone, and read it for him: "Second Lieutenant H.C. Baird, the Royal Flying Corps, killed 19 August 1914".

"August the 19th? The war had hardly started."

At the gate on the way to the car, she stopped to blow her nose. "Thank you for bringing me here, David," she said, looking back down the rows.

"It's just one of hundreds."

They drove up into Le Cateau, to the hotel where he had reserved a room, and the porter, an old man in an apron, unlocked the garage door and waited while David parked the Jaguar and brought out their bags.

"A fine car, Monsieur. You have come far?"

"No. Not far. Just from the coast."

"Give me your bag, Madame, and I will show you the room."

David followed, hoping Otis would like the room, as they climbed two flights of narrow stairs covered in a fraying carpet.

"Voilà," said the old man, opening the door of a high-ceilinged room with windows overlooking a garden at the back. He moved aside to let them into the room. "The bathroom is at the end of the passage. Dinner will be served from seven-thirty." He put Otis's bag on a low table at the foot of the double bed.

"It was nice of him to call me Madame," said Otis when they were alone. "It makes me feel respectable."

"I don't want you to be too respectable."

"Will they stare at us in the dining room?"

"Probably," he said.

"Well then, let's be respectable until after dinner."

**** ****

A small crowd gathered in the square on the Sunday morning. At one side, buds of pollarded plane trees burst into life where games of boules would be played later in the day, and on the other, the flags of France and Britain hung from poles angled over the war memorial. Stallholders at the market sold vegetables and flowers, and a pretty girl laid out goats cheeses on a wooden trestle table. A smell of coffee and *Gauloise* cigarettes drifted from the tables of a café.

David stood with Otis in the hall of the Mairie with the mayor, a chunky middle aged man with grey hair cut short, *en brosse*, waiting for the clock to strike eleven. With them, two boys from the town held the tapestry suspended between wooden poles, nervously debating the best way to get it out through the open door into the square without it dragging on the ground.

"You must go out together, side by side," said the mayor. "You cannot go one after the other."

"But there will not be room for the tapestry to be spread properly if we are side by side," said the taller of the two boys.

"You must carry the poles between you horizontally, and hold the material with the other hand and as soon as you are outside you will be able to lift it up and move apart so that it spreads out nicely. It will be easy enough. Christian," he said to the tall boy, "You are the elder. You will set the time, and Henri, you will go with him exactly. Go slowly with small steps, and together. It will be very impressive and stately."

At exactly eleven the church bell began to chime. David straightened his tie, held Otis by the hand, and with a final word of encouragement from the mayor, the young men held their poles at the correct angle and walked out of the building. Spontaneous applause broke out amongst the crowd and a lone voice started to sing the Marseillaise, soon joined by others.

"*Merde*," said the mayor under his breath. "They are not supposed to sing until we arrive at the war memorial." But his voiced was drowned by the singing, and the tapestry was carried down the steps into the crowd. People hurried over from the market stalls, eager to get a first glimpse of this piece of their history that was coming back to town.

The mayor held up a hand. "Mesdames, Messieurs," he began, and the crowd fell quiet, expectant. Someone coughed, and a child cried out.

"Merci," said the mayor. "Welcome to you all. This is a most important day for us in Le Cateau. Fifty years ago, Captain John Pearson, a young English doctor, rescued a beautiful tapestry from our church which was under attack from German artillery. Today, this lovely piece of our heritage has come back to the place where it belongs. I would like you to welcome Captain Pearson's nephew, without whose efforts we would not be celebrating here today."

David acknowledged the fresh burst of applause and the mayor continued: "Many of you will remember 1914 and the terrible years that followed. The sacrifice of a generation is written in stone all over France, and in the villages of Great Britain, on memorials like this.

"It is a matter of profound regret that Captain Pearson was lost during the conflict, and we are fortunate that one of his comrades was able to take the tapestry to England for its safety. Our church is now restored after the damage it suffered in the two world wars, and today we come together to celebrate and to place the tapestry once more on the wall. Will you please join me in thanking this man who has made it possible."

"Thank you," said David when the applause had died down. He had known for some time that he would have to make a speech, but panic filled him at the sight of the throng before him standing patiently in the spring sun.

"I will not take up much of your time," he began. "It is market day and you have much to buy and sell." A ripple of appreciation ran through the crowd. "I first heard about the tapestry of St. John a year ago, after the death of my grandmother. I am so pleased to have been able to trace it, and to persuade the school in England, where it had hung since 1915, that it should be returned to Le Cateau. My uncle would have brought it back here a long time ago if he had survived the war.

"I know that he found happiness during the short time that his battalion was stationed in this area before fighting began. I hope to find out a little more about that time and I am very glad to have this opportunity to thank your community for giving such a welcome to a British soldier, far from home. Thank you."

The procession set off to the church, where Father Augustin stood beaming at the top of the steps. For a man reputed to have a weak heart, he exuded a surprising air of permanence. The congregation settled, scraping their wooden chairs on the flagstones of the nave. Shafts of light from the upper windows lit up tall baroque pillars, and a faint hint of incense hung in the air.

You've been lucky to get involved in all of this, David thought. John Pearson might have sat here, too, and walked in the aisles to admire the tapestry before the shooting started. He looked around at the people near him. Many were over sixty. They would have been young boys and girls in 1914, with memories long enough to remember British soldiers here.

"It was Monsieur Blessier's idea to have this case made for it," Father Augustin told David as the service ended. "The glass will protect the cloth and keep off dust. For today it can rest here on these poles but tomorrow the carpenter will come to secure it inside the case and fix the little plaque we have had made."

The mayor was making clicking noises with his tongue. "If you will excuse me, Father," David said, "we are to have lunch with the mayor. I am sorry you are not able to join us."

While the mayor's wife picked small pieces of langoustine from her teeth, a waiter swept away the wreckage of *fruits de mer* and brought whole, lightly-roasted pigeons, into which foie gras had been stuffed. The *sommelier* took a decanter round the table and poured the wine with reverence into large goblets.

"This is the '52, I hope," said the mayor.

"Of course, Monsieur. The Gevrey Chambertin, as you ordered. But there is not much left in the cellar."

"A pity," said the mayor to David. "It is my favourite *bourgogne*." He held his glass to the light, examining the colour. "This is a happy day for us. Thank you for what you have done, Monsieur. We will not forget this. I hope you will come regularly to Le Cateau, where you can be assured of a good welcome. Incidentally, you will find it easier to get at the foie gras with the little spoon."

David probed into the bird's cavity with his spoon, and drank deeply from the excellent Gevrey Chambertin. The mayor's cousin had moved his chair and was sitting close to Otis, leaning over, deep in conversation. "Does the name of Alazard mean anything to you?" David asked the mayor.

"Alazard? It is a familiar name in this area. There is a plaque in the hospital here in honour of a surgeon called Alazard. Why do you ask?"

"My uncle mentioned the name in a letter to his mother."

The mayor shrugged. "If you come to the *Mairie* tomorrow we can look in the registers."

"Or in the telephone directory," said the mayor's wife.

"The registers of the *Mairie* are more certain," said the mayor loftily. "And it is not everyone who has a telephone. Will you stay long in Le Cateau?"

"Just a day or two. I want to see what we can find out about the Alazard family."

"And while you are in France you will visit your uncle's grave?"

David shook his head. "Sadly that is not possible. I am afraid my uncle was one of those whose remains were never found."

"I am so sorry. There are many others like that. Too many."

"The mayor's cousin is a bottom pincher," said Otis, her heels clacking on the pavement as they walked back to the hotel.

"You're supposed to take that as a compliment."

"And they don't slow up much. With the French I mean."

"They never do. You seemed to cope all right?"

"I'm a Jersey girl, remember." She took his arm as they walked past the church railings.

In the hotel lobby the porter handed him a card. "I was asked to give you this, Monsieur. The gentleman left it earlier this afternoon."

"Was there any message ?"

"No, but I believe there is some writing on the back."

David showed the card to Otis as they climbed the stairs to the refuge of their room. He took off his coat, undid his tie and looked again at the card.

'Maitre Alazard, Jean-Pierre, Notaire', it announced, with an address underneath. He turned over the card and read aloud: *"I hope you will excuse me, but I was in the church this morning for the celebrations and would like to speak with you. If you can spare the time this evening, do please call me. It is a matter of importance and Bazuel is only a few kilometres away."*

"Alazard," said Otis. She kicked off her shoes and sat on the bed. "That name again."

"We'll call him later, and make a date," he said. "A matter of importance, he said. A notaire is a sort of lawyer isn't it?"

"Yes. I better come too. You might need your secretary."

David rolled onto the bed with her. "I have a great need for my secretary right now. God, you taste delicious."

"Take off your shoes," she said.

**** ****

It was five-thirty in the afternoon when he awoke. Otis slept beside him, naked under the cover of a sheet, her hair tousled, half concealing her face. He watched the slow rise and fall of her breasts and felt her breath against his cheek. She smelled of afternoon and sex. He lay still, anxious not to wake her, and wondered what the notaire might have to say. It was interesting that the mayor had heard of a doctor called Alazard who had worked at the hospital. He might have known John Pearson, the medical officer. And a notaire would fit with a family of doctors and teachers. This evening, the card said. He would telephone this evening from the hotel lobby, and in the meantime the bed was very comfortable. The curtains stirred in the afternoon breeze and the soft cooing of doves came into the room, a lullaby from the garden trees. He curled his body against Otis and drifted back to sleep. She appeared walking towards him wearing nothing but a thin muslin gown. He wanted to examine her breasts again, but the lift doors opened without warning and a throng of people pushed in as she disappeared into the crowd.

At nine the next morning Otis was still asleep when David left the hotel and walked up the street to the church. The town seemed at rest, as if sleeping off the after-effects of yesterday's lunch. He wondered if the carpenter would turn up, but his misgivings proved groundless for the church door was open and a man in his early sixties stood on a stepladder, working on the tapestry's glass case.

The carpenter put his face close to the glass, breathing on it, and polished it with a soft cloth. When he was satisfied, he came down from the ladder and stood back, giving his work a final scrutiny. A light hidden in the case radiated colour over the tapestry.

"Bonjour," the carpenter said. "I recognise you from the service yesterday." He pointed to the tapestry. "It looks good in the case, don't you think?"

"Magnificent. And the illumination is a good idea."

"It is the idea of Father Augustin. You can put the francs into the slot there and it will light up for a few minutes. It is a small way to provide for the upkeep of the church." He bent down and pulled a brass plaque from his bag. "All I have to do now is fix this to the case, and *voilà,* I have finished. You can see that you are now to be a part of our church."

David read the plaque:

This tapestry was rescued from l'Eglise du St. Martin by a British officer, Capt. John Pearson, RAMC, in August 1914 when the building was damaged by German artillery. It was returned in April 1966 by his nephew, David Pearson.
Deo gratias

"Thank you," said David." I think that's lovely."

"Then if you approve, I will screw it into place."

He put three brass screws between his lips and, with a fourth, began to fix the plaque, giving it a final polish with his cloth when he had finished. He turned to face David.

"My name is Bouclier. François Bouclier. It will interest you to know that I met your uncle when I was a small boy. I took a message from the doctor at the hospital here to Bazuel with orders to hand it to Captain Pearson. I went on my bicycle and remember it well. It was very early on a warm summer day. It had rained in the night and the road was muddy for my bicycle. And there were troops and lorries everywhere." He stroked his chin, reliving a memory from long ago.

David stood as if sculpted in marble. "Go on," he whispered.

"Your uncle was having breakfast with the people of his

269

house, where he was staying. He asked me if I had eaten. I lied a little because of the delicious smell of their bread, and they gave me some with a cup of coffee. There was a beautiful young woman who made it for me. It is funny how one remembers some things like this. I was very impressed to be having breakfast with an officer of the British army. I never saw him again. The British were driven back the next day when the Germans came through. And that was that for four years." He picked up the cloth and wiped his hands as if to erase the past. "It was a terrible time for us. There was so little to eat, and what there was was taken by the Germans. My father died at Verdun. Many of my friends were brought up without a father too, and for most of that time the front line of the two sides was only a few miles to the west from here. You could lie awake at night and listen to the guns."

Outside the church, David looked up at the spire. Swifts, newly arrived from Africa, flew in tight formation round the onion dome, chasing each other with whirring wings. Others, high in the vault of the sky, flew fast and free for the joy of living. He felt like dancing in the street. He had just met a man, a live link with the past, who as a boy had talked with his uncle over the breakfast table.

At a quarter to twelve, David held the door for her as Otis stepped into the Jaguar. She looked young and beautiful as a girl should who is in love, and who has slept well.

"Time to go?" she said.

"Time to go." He kissed her, started the engine and drove out of the town.

"How far to Bazuel?"

"Ten minutes. Under a railway then the first house on the left as we get to the village. Tall house with white shutters."

"Excited?" she asked.

"Very. And slightly nervous."

"That's not like you. What are you going to say?"

"It's up to him."

"Well, yes, but you can't just launch in with 'now look here my man, what's all this about'."

"No," he laughed. "Softly, softly."

They went under the railway line, suddenly cool in the shade from the bridge, and slowed when he saw the sign at Bazuel. At the house with white shutters he turned in through a double gateway, and drove into a courtyard which led to the front of the house. On the left a black Citroen DS crouched in an open-fronted cart lodge alongside stables.

"Otis?" he said.

"Yes?"

"I wish I knew what this is all about."

"We'll know soon."

"Wish me luck?"

"For both of us," she said.

He got out of the car and looked back at the stables. Something about them seemed vaguely familiar.

A girl of seven or eight with long dark hair hanging down over a bright blue cotton dress sat at the bottom of stone steps. She stood up, clutching a handful of wild flowers, and stared at David from huge brown eyes. An older boy, with a golden crew-cut, circled the gravel on a bicycle, staring at the Jaguar.

David smiled at the girl. "Hallo," he said. She stood up, watching them defiantly.

Otis stroked her hair. "What pretty flowers," she told her, and the little girl smiled.

"Monsieur Pearson?" A man wearing a dark suit came down the steps. A tall man of about fifty with a ruddy complexion and fair hair greying a little at the sides. "Jean-Pierre Alazard," the notaire said. "It is good of you to come." The handshake was firm, his eyes blue. "*Enchantée*", he said, bowing over Otis's hand. "Will you come in, please."

He led the way up the steps to a wide covered verandah ablaze with tulips in terracotta pots, and showed them to some wicker chairs overlooking the courtyard. "Sit down, please, and I will get Isabelle and some coffee."

Isabelle Alazard wore her greying hair swept back into a severe bun and her eyes danced from a suntanned face. She poured coffee into small white cups and sat upright in her chair watching David as if sizing him up.

"You spoke well yesterday in the square," she said, looking at him over her cup. "It is interesting that you knew nothing about the tapestry until a year ago. After your grandmother's death, I think you said."

"Yes. I found some papers when I was clearing her desk."

"Did you not think it strange that she never told you about the tapestry?" said Maitre Alazard.

"She never spoke about my uncle. It was as if she had deliberately shut it all away. I think it was her way of dealing with the loss of her sons. When I read the letter he had written to his mother, I learned that John stayed with the family of a teacher with your name. That's why I was excited to receive your card. Is there a connection between you and the teacher? You must be related?"

Maitre Alazard put down his coffee cup, got to his feet and walked over to the edge of the verandah. He stood staring out over the grounds, gripping the oak balustrade. In the silence, David felt a growing tension as if the air might jump with electricity. He looked at Madame Alazard but she sat calm and quiet, and put her finger to her lips, shaking her head. The beginning of tears trembled in her eyes.

"The teacher was my grandfather," said Alazard, turning back to face them. He stood, irresolute, holding out his hands, the palms spread upwards. "Is it all right to talk in front of Mam'selle?"

"Yes, yes," said David.

"Well, then." He took a deep breath. "Grandfather had a daughter, called Agnès. My mother." He coughed into his hand. "And.... your uncle was my father." His face split into a grin. "That is why I am called Jean-Pierre. It is the nearest you can get to John Pearson."

272

David ran across the verandah. "Of course," he said. "Now I see it." He seized the notaire by his shoulders. "There was something familiar about you when you came down the steps." He opened his attaché case and pulled out the photograph of his uncle on a grouse moor. "Look. John Pearson. See, Madame, you can see the resemblance immediately." He looked at Otis before rummaging in his case again until he found his photograph of the girl with dark hair. Surely the stables in the background were those he had seen when he got out of the car? He handed it to Alazard.

The notaire studied the photograph closely, leaning over the coffee table. When he lifted his head, his eyes were full of tears. "My mother," he whispered. "We have some others of her, but none as beautiful as this."

"It was the stables," said David. "When I saw the stables they reminded me of something." He looked at the photograph again. "John must have taken this," he said in wonder. "But they can't have had long together."

"I am afraid it was only for a very short time," said Alazard. "But long enough to fall in love. Just a few days until the Germans swept through here. And then pouf! All gone."

"And Agnès? Is she still alive?" He did a quick calculation, his mind racing through the possibilities. She would be an old lady ...

But the notaire shook his head. "She died when I was three. The Spanish 'flu came here at the end of 1918. Many people died."

"But why are you named after your grandfather, and not John Pearson?"

"When the war ended, my grandfather tried to contact John's family in England. He got the address eventually and wrote to John's mother. I was only about five but I can remember him telling me later that she wrote back immediately, refusing even to consider the possibility that her son could be responsible for me! It was a fierce, uncompromising response and humiliated my grandfather. But he came to accept it. He had recently buried his daughter and he must have understood the trauma John's mother felt about the disappearance of her son.

"There's another thing about my name. This is a quiet country area and in 1915 it was still quite unusual to be born without a father. I think my grandfather believed that things would calm down more easily if the new baby took the family name. My mother christened me Jean-Pierre. She could call me that, and every time it would remind her of John Pearson. And people in the street need not know the little secret."

"Did that work?" Otis asked.

Alazard laughed: "No, of course not. Bazuel is a small community, and you cannot hide things like this from inquisitive people. I was teased a little at school but it settled down all right in the end."

"And there would have been many children without a father. From the war?"

"Yes, Mam'selle. So many. I was not unusual." He put his coffee cup on the table and stood up. "There is something indoors I would like to show you. Excuse me for a moment please."

When he returned, he handed David an envelope. David opened it and drew out a piece of paper, torn from a notebook. It was a poem, written in ink:

Before you, I thought I knew
Something of life
Until you came out of the orchard.

But then what I had known wilted away
To nothingness under a yearning
For everything still to come.
Now as the guns come closer
All I can do is gaze and gaze
Upon the impossibility of your beauty,

Listen to the soft cadence
In your voice, and inhale you
Until the sight and sound and scent of you
Are burned, brand marks
Into my aching soul

August 1914

"My grandfather read it to me as soon as I was old enough to understand the English," Alazard told him. "He was at the bedside when Agnès was dying, and she made him promise to keep it safe for me. I love to think of my father writing that. She is buried in the cemetery here." He blew his nose. "My grandfather told me that when they prepared her for burial, he made sure she wore your uncle's ring."

"His ring?"

"Yes. My father gave her the ring when he was forced to leave her when the fighting started. It was a gift. His signet ring for their engagement. He promised to come back for her."

"Oh God. And then she was stuck on the wrong side of the lines. He couldn't reach her."

"Exactly. But she knew he would come if he could. Every day she waited, and later in the war, when it was possible to receive letters through Holland, she searched the mail each day. But of course nothing came. She never knew what had happened to him, but she convinced herself that he was alive."

"Who brought you up, Jean-Pierre, if your mother died so early?"

"My grandfather. And his second wife. They met at the local *lycée* and married soon after my mother died. They brought me up in this house. I had everything I wanted." He smiled easily at David. "You would probably say that I was very spoilt."

"And this was the house where my uncle lived?"

"Yes, of course." He shrugged expansively. "It is a little

different now, naturally. I built this verandah and it is much changed inside, but *au fond* it is still the same property your uncle knew."

"There was a carpenter in the church this morning," said David. "He said he had met my uncle here, when he was a boy."

The notaire nodded. "There are others."

"He told me about how it was here under the Germans. How hungry they were."

"My grandfather taught me about it. He was determined my generation should learn from it. When the British left, this house was taken over by the Germans for their officers. They made my grandfather stay on as a housekeeper! But he got Agnès away to live in the safety of the hospital. In Le Cateau. When I was born I lived there with her. The Germans made her work as a nurse. At least there was some food."

"Can you remember any of that?" Otis asked.

"No, my dear. I was only three when she died. Spanish 'flu devastated hospital wards. The death rate was appalling. If you go to the café in the village here you will find old men who can tell you about it. They will tell you how bad it was. And about the hunger. There's a retired butcher here. Jean Boulanger. He can tell you if you meet him."

"An odd name for a butcher," Otis laughed.

"He was always teased for being in the wrong shop. When he was a boy of fourteen, his father was shot for attacking a German officer with a meat-axe."

"Why, for God's sake?"

"The man tried to rape his wife. Then they made Jean keep the shop going with only his mother to help him. His two brothers died at Verdun. The Germans needed Jean, you see, to cut their meat. With no waste. They forbade him, on pain of death, to sell meat to the villagers. But Jean had a trick, to fix his scales."

"What did he do?"

" He set them to read light when a whole carcass was

weighed so he could trim bits off and hide them. Then when the joints were all assembled and weighed again he would adjust the setting of the scales so the two weights read the same."

"And they never caught him?"

"No. But he had to be careful what he did with the offcuts. There were people who would betray their own mothers to extract favours from the Germans. If you meet Jean, get him to tell you how your uncle fixed his finger when he dislocated it. It's a nice story. But come with me for a moment. There is something else I want to show you."

He called to Isabelle that they would be back in a minute and led the way down from the verandah, across the gravel courtyard and through an orchard of old, gnarled apple trees, fragrant with the smell of springtime. The children played there on a swing.

"Will you push me higher, Mam'selle?" the boy called.

Otis went over to the swing, swept up the little girl, and sat her on her brother's lap. "Hold her tight," she said to the boy, "and I'll push you both together."

David watched as she swung the children higher and higher in an arc through the dappled light. She seemed so natural, so readily accepted by the children as a friend. He thought of the old house in Hampshire and the swing in the tree by the vegetable garden. How he would have loved it if Otis and his grandmother could have met. He would not have minded if the old girl had dropped heavy hints about the possibility of children.

"Have you told the children about me?" David asked Jean-Pierre.

"Not yet," he said. "We will tell them together in a minute, with Isabelle. But I think they know something. Children have wonderful intuition. Come with me."

Beyond the orchard, in a corner at the edge of the property, a beautiful copper beech tree grew. The new leaves were the colour of smoked salmon.

"Look," said Jean-Pierre. "My mother planted this. It's as close as I can get to my father. See the little sign there."

David stood with Otis, and felt her lean in towards him as they read together the engraved inscription:

In memory of
John Pearson
1914
Chagrin d'amour

A light breeze blew in from the south, whispering through the leaves of the tree. Sunlight quivered among the branches, gossamer in the air, and the children's laughter came like a rumour on the wind.

Epilogue

Maitre Jean-Pierre Alazard, retired from a lifetime's service as a man of law, took his wife by the arm and led her to a bench in the shade.

"Sit with me a moment," he said. "To accustom our eyes to the light."

In front of them the river, swollen from spring rain, tore through the heart of France, pressing against the old stonework of the bridge. Maitre Alazard counted the arches, stretching three hundred yards to the far bank on the Saumur side. Were there eleven, or twelve? Without his spectacles, it was difficult to be sure with the sun glittering over the water. Debris swirled on the current, and in mid stream a tree trunk rotated like an uncontrolled canoe.

"You're very quiet," he said, turning to her.

"Yes."

"Since we drove over from Angers. Since the tapestries."

"They were so beautiful. Why didn't you tell me before? About Le Cateau."

"I wasn't certain you would know," he said. "I thought you might not have noticed it. It's been fifteen years."

She pulled a piece of paper from her handbag. "I wasn't sure until I found this." She passed him the piece of paper. "Read it, Jean- Pierre. Please read it to me. It's in English."

He found some reading glasses in the pocket of his coat, and began to read.

Half way through the Hundred Years War, a period beloved by boys in history books, King Louis 1 of France conceived the idea of commissioning a tapestry. This was no ordinary tapestry, the finished article being seven years in the making and exceeding 100 metres in length. It was quick work for such a piece, and was made entirely of fine wool. The tapestry is a narration of the Apocalypse according to Saint John's Book of Revelation, and is a political comment on the time, portraying the ravaging effect of war.

In 1789, as revolutionary zeal tore France apart, the tapestry was cut up into ninety pieces, some said for its protection, others, more prosaically, for use in keeping frost off the local orange trees.

Nineteenth century attempts to salvage the work were largely successful but sixteen pieces were either damaged beyond hope of repair, or remain unaccounted for.

Many people know about the Bayeaux tapestry. But relatively few have seen the tapestry in the museum at Chateau d'Angers. When your eyes get used to the dim lighting, the wall hangings lie in long rows stretching away round the corner in a magnificent chequerboard pattern of blue and red. You can sit there in the hushed quiet of the gallery and live the legends from the Book of Revelation and marvel at the beauty of 14th century embroidery. It is a humbling experience to witness these things in the carefully controlled half light, before you stumble out into the pellucid clarity of a summer day in the Loire valley. To date, none of the sixteen lost panels of the tapestry has been recovered since the turmoil of the Revolution, but it is easy to imagine that, somewhere, one might have survived in a dusty corner of a French church, dry and sheltered from sunlight.

He laughed, and handed back the paper. "Where on earth did you find this?"

"In the shop at Chateau d'Angers. There was only this one copy. It's charming, and I thought of David Pearson. I'm going to send it to him and Otis, and tell their children about Le Cateau."

"That their tapestry is a bit of the Louis 1 original?"

"Well it is, isn't it?"

"Almost certainly." He looked out over the river. Some ducks chased each other in the shallow water at their feet. "Of course, one can never be sure."

Something in his voice made her stare at him. "But you must find out. Make enquiries."

"Sometimes it is better to let sleeping dogs lie."

"Jean-Pierre. What has got into you. You are a notaire. You have your reputation to think of."

"Yes," he laughed again. "A reputation for discretion."

"You're not suggesting you can just ignore the fact that the Le Cateau tapestry is part of the original?"

"Why not? It's perfectly safe there. My father and David went to a lot of trouble to rescue it."

"Sometimes I think I don't know you at all. You can't keep something like this quiet. It's only a matter of time before the truth comes out." She stood up, looking cross. "I'm going to get the picnic from the car. Perhaps you'll see sense with some food."

He watched her walk away. Short, stiff steps that stabbed at the grass. Across the river, traffic followed the road that led to the bridge.

Of course, he thought, it was only a matter of time. Sooner or later someone else would make the connection. It was surprising it hadn't happened already. But Le Cateau was the better part of three hundred and fifty miles from Angers. Few tourists would ever visit both places, and a local from Le Cateau probably never. True, a wandering cleric might stumble on something, but the two dioceses were miles apart, unconcerned with the niceties of each other's church fabric.

David Pearson had told him about the friars at the school in England, and he laughed at David's description of their dealings with him. If neither the English Jesuits nor the diocesan offices in Cambrai had unearthed anything, then a humble notaire from Bazuel could hardly be expected to know much. There was no need for him to fret. Isabelle would understand when he explained things, and she would soon see that the most important thing was to do nothing that might disturb the work that David Pearson had done for the commune of Le Cateau. He would promise Isabelle to come clean if anyone asked directly about a connection with the tapestries. He looked up at white clouds billowing up over the Loire. After a lifetime as a lawyer, he knew that most questions could be fielded if handled with a little imagination. There was more than one way to skin a cat.

He stood up and stretched his back. Isabelle was on her way back from the car with a hamper and a loaf of bread. There would be, he knew, a bottle of red wine to go with a terrine and some cheese. And what better way was there to enjoy lunch than to sit in the shade of plane trees beside one of the great rivers of France?

Acknowledgements

I am grateful to two old men, both dead, who were my main inspiration in the writing of this novel.

Dr. John Fraser, my grandfather, rescued a beautifully embroidered banner from a bombed out French church in 1918. I discovered it recently, stored amongst some archives in an English school, and hope to return it soon to France.

Hujohn Ripman, a remarkable gynaecologist loved by all, served with the Irish Guards as a doctor in WW 2. Over several whiskies he taught me a great deal about the life of a medical officer on active service.

My thanks, too, to Annabel Sebag-Montefiore for taking such trouble over editing my typescript, and to William Backhouse who read the original on a long flight to Sri Lanka.

The road to writing, like painting, is a lonely one. I hope my wife, Avery, will forgive those times when I needed extra space.

Some 150000 books are published each year in the UK. Books are cheap. You can buy a paperback for the price of a round of drinks. If you have enjoyed this book, please, tell your friends.